ANOTHER MURDER, ANOTHER LIST OF SUSPECTS

Leroy circled her ankles until she scooped him up and carried him toward the living room, where Bruce followed and gently kissed her hello.

"Tell me what you found," he said.

Hayley filled him in—Blodgett's resistance, the students' fervor, the cluttered but undisturbed office. And Peter Baird, the soft-spoken oceanography professor who seemed a little too nondescript for comfort.

"What's his deal?" Bruce asked.

"Too quiet," Hayley said.

Bruce raised an eyebrow. "You think he's involved?"

"I think he's wallpaper. But sometimes the wallpaper's hiding a crack. So many suspects. Blodgett. Baird. Maybe even one of the students. And yet . . . no evidence. No motive."

Outside, the wind picked up, rustling the leaves that hadn't yet turned. Fall was coming—quietly, but with purpose.

And somewhere in Bar Harbor, a killer was still out there . . .

AF895706

Books by Lee Hollis

Hayley Powell Mysteries
DEATH OF A KITCHEN DIVA
DEATH OF A COUNTRY FRIED REDNECK
DEATH OF A COUPON CLIPPER
DEATH OF A CHOCOHOLIC
DEATH OF A CHRISTMAS CATERER
DEATH OF A CUPCAKE QUEEN
DEATH OF A BACON HEIRESS
DEATH OF A PUMPKIN CARVER
DEATH OF A LOBSTER LOVER
DEATH OF A COOKBOOK AUTHOR
DEATH OF A WEDDING CAKE BAKER
DEATH OF A BLUEBERRY TART
DEATH OF A WICKED WITCH
DEATH OF AN ITALIAN CHEF
DEATH OF AN ICE CREAM SCOOPER
DEATH OF A CLAM DIGGER
DEATH OF A GINGERBREAD MAN
DEATH OF A TOM TURKEY

Hayley Powell Collections
EGGNOG MURDER
(with Leslie Meier and Barbara Ross)
YULE LOG MURDER
(with Leslie Meier and Barbara Ross)
HAUNTED HOUSE MURDER
(with Leslie Meier and Barbara Ross)
CHRISTMAS CARD MURDER
(with Leslie Meier and Peggy Ehrhart)
HALLOWEEN PARTY MURDER
(with Leslie Meier and Barbara Ross)
IRISH COFFEE MURDER
(with Leslie Meier and Barbara Ross)
CHRISTMAS MITTENS MURDER
(with Lynn Cahoon and Maddie Day)
EASTER BASKET MURDER
(with Leslie Meier and Barbara Ross)
HALLOWEEN NIGHT MURDER
(with Leslie Meier and Liz Ireland)
EASTER EGG MURDER
(with Leslie Meier and Peggy Ehrhart)

Poppy Harmon Mysteries
POPPY HARMON INVESTIGATES
POPPY HARMON AND THE HUNG JURY
POPPY HARMON AND THE PILLOW TALK KILLER
POPPY HARMON AND THE BACKSTABBING BACHELOR
POPPY HARMON AND THE SHOOTING STAR

Maya & Sandra Mysteries
MURDER AT THE PTA
MURDER AT THE BAKE SALE
MURDER ON THE CLASS TRIP
MURDER AT THE SPELLING BEE
MURDER AT THE HIGH SCHOOL REUNION

Jarrod Jarvis Mysteries
THE ACTOR'S GUIDE TO MURDER
THE ACTOR'S GUIDE TO ADULTERY
THE ACTOR'S GUIDE TO GREED

Downeast Maine Mysteries
THE CHOWDER HOUSE MURDER

Jarrod Jarvis Father-Daughter Mysteries
MY FATHER ALWAYS FINDS CORPSES

Published by Kensington Publishing Corp.

DEATH of a GRILL MASTER

LEE HOLLIS

Kensington Publishing Corp.
kensingtonbooks.com

KENSINGTON BOOKS are published by

Kensington Publishing Corp.
900 Third Avenue
New York, NY 10022

First Printing: October 2026

ISBN: 978-1-4967-4355-8

ISBN: 978-1-4967-4356-5 (ebook)

10 9 8 7 6 5 4 3 2 1

Printed in the United States of America

The authorized representative in the EU for product safety and compliance is eucomply OU, Parnu mnt 139b-14, Apt 123 Tallinn, Berlin 11317, hello@eucompliancepartner.com.

DEATH of a GRILL MASTER

Chapter 1

Hayley Powell was in her element—or at least doing a very convincing impression of someone who had things under control.

From the makeshift cocktail station beside the lilac bushes to the trellises draped in dollar-store fairy lights, her backyard had been transformed into a proper wedding reception venue for the afternoon.

Sort of.

It wasn't Martha Stewart perfection, but it had charm—Maine charm. There were mason jars of wildflowers on every table, the scent of grilled seafood hung thick in the salty air, and a boom box was playing a Bluetooth playlist titled "Betty + Kelton 4EVER" that alternated between sappy love songs and upbeat classics. Currently: "You Make My Dreams," by Hall & Oates.

Somewhere between the champagne toast and the spontaneous limbo contest with a garden rake, Hayley had lost track of how many guests were technically invited versus how many just wandered in from the neighborhood. But she wasn't about to kick anyone out, not today.

Bruce, ever the faithful husband and occasional fire hazard, was manning the grill near the back fence. Hayley watched with a mix of amusement and mild panic as he tried to flip shrimp skewers with the confidence of a man who had never once read the words *flammable* and *cotton blend* on a clothing label.

"Bruce," she called over the hum of conversation and a rogue kazoo, "your shirt!"

Bruce looked down, eyes widening as he spotted a small but determined flame licking at the hem of his vintage Red Sox T-shirt.

"Dammit!" he yelped, batting at the fire with his tongs. Hayley's brother, Randy, raced over with a bucket of cold water left over from chilling white wine and doused him without hesitation.

Steam erupted.

Guests cheered.

"Hey, who ordered the shrimp flambé?" someone yelled.

Hayley sighed and pinched the bridge of her nose. "Only in Bar Harbor."

But despite the literal sparks flying, the afternoon had turned out beautifully. Betty, her beloved hostess at her restaurant, Hayley's Kitchen, looked radiant in her retro lace dress, now speckled with a bit of strawberry glaze from the slightly leaning, lovingly homemade wedding cake. Kelton, Hayley's chef and Betty's new husband, was beaming beside her, sleeves rolled up, eyes misty, as they mingled with friends and family.

Hayley found herself oddly emotional watching them. They were young—well, younger—and in love, and starting out. And despite the chaos, this was their day. It was imperfect, heartfelt, and brimming with joy.

She was reaching for a mini crab roll when she felt a gentle tug on her elbow.

It was Betty.

"Hayley, can I steal you for a second?"

Hayley turned, taking in Betty's flushed cheeks, her eyes wide and brimming with happiness.

"Of course, sweetie. Everything okay?"

Betty nodded, then pulled her aside, down the short flagstone path that led to the herb garden.

"I just wanted to say thank you," Betty said earnestly. "For letting us do this here. For everything. It means so much."

Hayley smiled. "Of course. I love you two. I'd host your vow renewal, too, but I draw the line at theme weddings unless it involves lobsters."

Betty laughed, then her face turned a little more serious. "Actually . . . Kelton and I have been talking about something. A dream, really."

Hayley tilted her head. "Okay . . ."

"We want to open our own place someday," Betty confessed. "A little spot in town. Something casual and fun, maybe a brunch bistro or small plates. You know, still cozy. Still us."

Hayley blinked. "Wow."

"I mean, not tomorrow," Betty said quickly. "We love it at Hayley's Kitchen. We owe you everything. We're just . . . thinking about the future."

Hayley laughed, a little too forcefully. "Don't worry, I'm not about to throw you out of the restaurant in a jealous rage. That's not my style."

Betty looked relieved.

"But if you do steal my chocolate bourbon pecan pie recipe," Hayley added, "I'll burn you in effigy on top of Cadillac Mountain."

"Fair enough," Betty said with a wink, then hugged her. "I knew you'd understand."

As she hurried off to rejoin Kelton for more cake-cutting mayhem from the now-lopsided cake melting under the hot sun, Hayley lingered, staring at her herb garden without really seeing it. The truth was, she did understand. Too well.

She loved her restaurant.

She loved her life.

But lately, she couldn't help feeling like other people's dreams were blossoming all around her while hers were . . . well, wilting slightly around the edges.

A loud cheer erupted from the patio, and Hayley turned to see Liddy Crawford making her entrance.

And what an entrance it was.

She wore a navy-blue polka-dot sundress with a red belt cinched tightly at the waist and oversized sunglasses perched atop her caramel-blond curls (recently dyed she had been yearning for a change). She looked like a pinup poster from the forties had walked off the wall and ordered a martini.

"I'm here!" Liddy declared, hands in the air. "Fashionably late and criminally overdressed."

"Both true," Hayley muttered under her breath, watching as Liddy zeroed in on the bar.

There, standing tall and unmistakably out-of-town in a linen sports coat and suede loafers, was Doug Marsh. Southern accent, devastating smile, and eyes that practically winked on their own. He and Randy had become drinking buddies at Drinks Like A Fish over bingo night and bourbon. Now here he was, sipping a cucumber gin fizz and looking very much like a man who knew he'd be flirted with before dessert.

Liddy glided over, her red lips curving into a grin. "And who do we have here?"

Doug tipped his glass. "Doug Marsh, ma'am. Friend of Randy's."

"Ooh," Liddy purred. "I do love Southern manners. So rare in these parts."

Hayley left them to their banter—there was only so much charm she could witness before needing carbs—and wandered over to the cocktail station, where Chelsea Mahoney was holding court like she'd been tending bar in Bar Harbor for years instead of weeks.

Chelsea's strawberry-blond hair was pulled up into a messy bun, and her I MAKE POUR DECISIONS T-shirt was already stained with lime juice and margarita salt.

"Hey, boss," Chelsea called. "We've got a passed-out man inside. I poked him with a stirrer. No reaction."

Hayley peeked through the window. "That's Reverend Ted. He performed the ceremony and then discovered the mojitos. He'll be fine."

Chelsea arched a brow. "Your town is weird."

"You'll fit right in."

Hayley was about to say more when Randy appeared beside her, looking uncharacteristically nervous.

"Hey," he said, eyes darting toward the crowd.

"Hey yourself. Enjoying the party?"

"Yeah. It's great. You pulled it off."

Hayley eyed him. "You okay?"

He hesitated, then rubbed the back of his neck. "There's something I wanted to talk to you about."

Her ears perked up. "What kind of something?"

He opened his mouth—then clamped it shut.

"I don't know. Forget it. It's not important."

"Oh, no, you don't," Hayley said, crossing her arms. "You don't get to start a conversation like that and then back out. Spill."

"I'm serious, Hayley. It's nothing. We'll talk about it another time."

She narrowed her eyes. "Is it Sergio? Are you two okay?"

Randy looked surprised for a moment—then something flickered in his eyes.

Guilt?

Worry?

"We're fine," he said too quickly. "Don't start sleuthing on me. I just . . . had a thought, and it doesn't matter. I'll catch you later, okay?"

He kissed her cheek and vanished into the crowd before she could press him further.

Hayley stood there for a moment, watching him go.

Something was up.

She hated not knowing what.

By the time she made it back to the grill, Bruce had managed to blacken only half the shrimp. He handed her a skewer and leaned in.

"You talk to Randy?"

"Briefly. He was acting squirrelly."

Bruce nodded, flipping a scallop with the ease of a man who'd learned not to let Hayley near fire.

"I think something might be up between him and Sergio," he said softly. "I overheard a tense phone call earlier. Thought maybe I was imagining it, but . . ."

Hayley's stomach turned slightly. Sergio was not only Bar Harbor's police chief—he was one of her dearest friends. And he and Randy had always seemed solid. The kind of couple who bickered like sitcom characters but always came back stronger.

"You think there's trouble in paradise?" she asked.

Bruce didn't answer.

Hayley looked out over the backyard. Liddy was laughing with Doug; her other BFF, Mona, was holding court near the clam dip; and Betty and Kelton were dancing barefoot under the twinkle lights.

She should have felt content. But something—something she couldn't quite name—was shifting.

And deep down, she knew.

This fall, paradise might not be as perfect as it looked.

Chapter 2

By the time the sun began to sink behind the tree line on their quiet residential street, Hayley Powell's backyard had transformed from festive to borderline unhinged.

The Bluetooth speaker Bruce had dug out of the garage—"state-of-the-art in 2015," he proudly claimed—was blaring dance hits from every decade from the newlywed playlist, culminating in an inexplicably passionate guest rendition of "Uptown Funk" that nearly took out the lemonade cooler.

Hayley, barefoot now and nursing a plastic cup of her signature Jack & Coke, was trying to decide if she had the energy to fish a crab roll out of the cooler or if she should just commit to chips and salsa for the rest of the night.

That's when she heard it—a braying voice loud enough to send three blue jays flapping from a neighbor's maple tree.

"Well, well, well! Looks like the party don't start till I walk in!"

Hayley winced even before she turned.

Strutting up the gravel path from the driveway, cigar clenched in his teeth, gut preceding him like a parade float, was Hank Desmond. His thick white hair was slicked back to an oily shine and he wore a black shirt with red flames curling up from the hem—the closest thing a grill master gets to island wear. Clinging to his arm was Kylie, his much younger wife, who looked like a porcelain figurine placed on the wrong shelf. Hank was the owner of one of the most popular restaurants in town, the Slaughterhouse Smoke Shack. Best barbecue east of the Mississippi. He got even more business than Hayley's place.

Hayley forced a smile and elbowed Bruce. "Wedding crasher at three o'clock."

Bruce sighed. "Of course it's Hank."

They both stepped forward to intercept.

"Hank. Kylie," Hayley said warmly, always the hostess, even if the guest had not exactly been invited. "You made it."

"Wouldn't miss it," Hank boomed, slapping Bruce on the back with such force the tongs flew from Bruce's hand and landed in the bushes. "Heard there was food. I came running. And I needed to talk to Chase before he disappears back to his little millionaire's lair."

Kylie gave a soft wave, then immediately turned her face away, wincing slightly as Hank exhaled a plume of cigar smoke over her shoulder. Up close, Hayley could see she was pale—paler than usual—and her lipstick had smudged at the corners of her mouth, like she'd reapplied in a hurry with shaky hands.

"Didn't mean to crash," Hank added with a grin that suggested he absolutely had. "But I just came from the bottling plant and couldn't wait to share the good news."

He pulled a bottle from the back pocket of his pants—how he had managed to stuff it in there without cracking the glass was a mystery—and held it aloft.

"Desmond's Devil Fire Barbecue Sauce," he announced like he was toasting the Queen. "National distribution. Starting next quarter. We're talking supermarket shelves from Bar Harbor to Boise, baby."

"Oh, boy," Hayley muttered.

"I knew it!" Mona Barnes hollered from across the yard. "I always said this town would produce one world-class condiment!"

Hank laughed, the sound echoing over the fence.

"Where's Chase Wingate?" he bellowed. "I heard that big spender was lurking around here somewhere."

As if on cue, Chase Wingate materialized near the drink station, sipping from a crystal tumbler he'd probably brought from home. Tall, silver-haired, and radiating old money vibes, Chase had the demeanor of someone who owned half the Eastern Seaboard—and the tan to prove it.

He wasn't technically on the guest list, either, but his connection to Kelton's late father—a long-ago college friend and fishing buddy—made his appearance a welcome surprise for the couple.

Hank spotted him, marched over, and clapped him on the back so hard Chase nearly dropped his drink.

"Chase, my man! You're coming aboard my boat this weekend, right? Labor Day fireworks cruise, best view in the bay, booze and brisket guaranteed."

Chase smiled politely, the way rich people do when trying not to make a scene. "Of course, Hank. Wouldn't miss it."

Hayley glanced at Kylie. She was standing just behind them, motionless, eyes trained not on her husband, but on Chase. Her face was blank, except for the forced smile. Her hands clutched the hem of her sundress so tightly the fabric twisted in her fists.

"Excuse me," Kylie murmured, ducking toward the bar.

Hayley watched her go, heart twinging. Something about the look in that woman's eyes—too wide, too glassy, too alert—set off internal alarm bells.

And the way she kept stealing glances at Chase Wingate?

Something was brewing.

And it wasn't just cocktails.

Across the yard, Liddy squealed and flung her arms around Chelsea Mahoney, who was still tending bar.

"He asked me out to dinner!" Liddy cried. "Doug Marsh. Actual Southern gentleman. I've been working on this one for weeks."

Chelsea cocked an eyebrow. "I thought you just met him today."

"Technically. And technically I crashed his cocktail party last week but never managed to get close enough for him to notice me. But today he finally did! I'm going to need an entirely new outfit."

Chelsea snorted. "Good luck finding one in this town. It's fleece vests and fishing boots from where I'm standing."

Hayley joined them, nodding toward the bar. "Doug's got nice taste. Just be careful. He looks like the kind of man who'll talk you into trouble and make it sound like fun."

"I'll gladly let him," Liddy said, dreamily.

Before Hayley could ask if Liddy knew anything about Doug beyond his cocktail preferences, Mona appeared, dragging poor Earl behind her like a kid about to confess to shoplifting.

"Tell her," Mona demanded, gesturing wildly. "Tell Hayley what you told me."

Earl looked like a man on his way to a firing squad. "I really don't like to gossip."

"Oh, give me a break," Mona said. "You already did gossip. Now, be a man and finish the job."

Earl sighed and turned to Hayley. "I overheard something. Sergio. Down at the station. On the phone."

Hayley's stomach did a little flip. "Okay . . ."

"He said something about resigning. From the police department. After almost twenty years. Said he was tired. That maybe it was time."

Hayley's mouth fell open. "*What?*"

"I don't know who he was talking to. Maybe someone at the town office. But he sounded serious."

Hayley's heart was thudding now. Randy hadn't said a word. And she talked to him every day. The idea of

Sergio leaving—of both of them maybe leaving—sent a ripple of something cold and sharp through her.

"Are you sure?" she asked.

Earl nodded solemnly. "I wouldn't have said anything if I wasn't."

Hayley looked across the yard to where Randy was refilling someone's prosecco. He smiled, easy and relaxed.

Why hadn't he told her?

The sun was gone now, and the first stars were flickering into view. The air had taken on that post-sunset chill, the kind that slipped under your skin and reminded you summer didn't last forever, not in Maine.

Hayley stepped behind the bar to grab a blanket from under the table and stopped short.

Kylie was there. Alone. One hand braced against the counter, the other dabbing at her eyes with a cocktail napkin.

"Kylie?" Hayley said gently.

Kylie startled, turning fast and blinking like she'd just been caught stealing.

"Oh—hi. Sorry. Allergies. Ragweed's a killer."

Hayley didn't push. Not yet. "Need a minute?"

"No, I'm fine." Kylie's voice was tight, her smile even tighter. "I just needed some space. Half the town is jammed into your backyard."

She slipped past Hayley and disappeared into the crowd.

Chelsea approached moments later, still drying her hands on a bar rag. "That woman's crying behind the bar and then pretending she's not? Please. I may be new in town, but I've bartended my way through enough Philly weddings to spot a ticking marriage time bomb."

Hayley watched Kylie rejoin Hank, who was now holding court with Chase and a few others, still brandishing that bottle of Devil Fire like it was holy water.

"Yeah," Hayley murmured. "Something's definitely off."

As the crowd thinned and the music faded into softer ballads, Hayley found her way back to Bruce, who was sitting beside the smoldering grill, sipping a beer, his mind elsewhere.

"You okay?" she asked, sitting beside him.

He nodded. "Just taking a moment before we have to scrape grease off everything we own."

They sat in silence awhile before Bruce added, "You notice anything strange with Randy and Sergio today?"

Hayley stiffened slightly. "Why?"

Bruce shrugged. "Randy seemed . . . distant tonight. And I saw Sergio leave the station early this afternoon, looking stressed. I don't know. Could be nothing."

Hayley felt a sudden, unwelcome chill.

"No," she said softly. "I don't think it's nothing."

Chapter 3

Labor Day dawned hot and clear in Bar Harbor, the sky bright and the ocean sparkling.

By 9 a.m., Hayley could already hear the hum of anticipation buzzing through the residential streets—neighbors hauling beach bags and lawn chairs out to the curb, tourists lingering over breakfast sandwiches from Morning Glory Bakery, shopkeepers stringing red, white, and blue pennants along awnings. Someone down the block was already blasting Bruce Springsteen at a volume that suggested patriotic zeal or unresolved personal drama. Possibly both.

It was the day of the "Big Bang on Frenchman's Bay," Bar Harbor's most elaborate fireworks display to date, funded by an unexpected surplus from one of the town's most successful tourism seasons in years. The town council, often gridlocked on decisions involving zoning permits and sidewalk repairs, had unanimously voted to blow the whole thing on fireworks.

Bruce stood by the front door loading their collapsible beach chairs into the trunk while Hayley finished assembling their picnic cooler in the kitchen. She tossed in a container of potato salad, two bags of kettle chips, her roast beef sandwiches with horseradish mayo and extra pickles (Bruce's request), and—wrapped in a dish towel to discourage questions—their metal thermoses filled with "lemonade." Spiked, naturally.

It wasn't that she hated crowds. Okay, she did. But the real reason Hayley had no intention of jockeying for a spot along the jam-packed pier was because she and Bruce had a secret.

About a quarter mile past Agamont Park, beyond the bend where the Shore Path narrowed into a thin dirt trail clinging to the edge of a rocky bluff, there was a flat shelf of granite halfway down the cliff. Big enough for two chairs and a cooler. Surrounded by stunted pines. Invisible unless you knew where to look. It was their spot.

Bruce called it their "cove of solitude."

By dusk, they'd made the short hike out and were settled into their favorite chairs. The cooler sat between them, squat and sun-bleached, its sticker-covered lid keeping everything inside perfectly chilled.

The breeze coming off the water ruffled Bruce's hair as he flipped open his spiral notebook and began scribbling, tongue pressed lightly to the corner of his mouth in concentration.

Hayley sipped her lemonade and smirked. "You're working on your book again."

"I'm outlining," he replied without looking up.

"You better not be killing me off in chapter one."

"I'm not saying anything."

"Oh my God, I am the body in the library, aren't I?"

Still no answer.

Which was as good as a guilty plea.

Hayley leaned back in her chair, closed her eyes, and let the sunlight soak into her skin. In the distance, music from the town pier carried faintly on the breeze—a cover band murdering "Sweet Caroline" with gusto. Boats bobbed along the bay, angling for the best view of the sky come nightfall.

She reached for her thermos again, took a long sip, and exhaled slowly. The lemonade was kicking in. A rare moment of stillness surrounded them.

"I invited Randy and Sergio," she said, opening her eyes.

Bruce looked up. "I figured."

"He said they had other plans. But he was vague. Like . . . evasive."

Bruce nodded, his expression unreadable.

"Do you think it's true?" Hayley asked. "What Earl said? That Sergio's resigning?"

Bruce shrugged and set his notebook on his lap. "Maybe. But Sergio's not impulsive. If he's stepping down, it's not just burnout. It's something deeper."

Hayley stared out over the bay, troubled. "He hasn't said a word to me. And Randy . . . he's my brother. My younger brother. He used to tell me everything. Now I'm getting these tight little texts and half smiles."

"Maybe they're not ready to talk yet," Bruce said gently.

Hayley frowned. "I just hate being kept in the dark."

Bruce chuckled. "You? No . . ."

She swatted his arm.

"Seriously," he said. "It's because you always want to fix everything."

"Is that a bad thing?"

"No. It's one of the things I love about you. But sometimes people don't want to be fixed. They just want space. Even from their very competent, nosy big sister."

Hayley rolled her eyes and took another sip. "Great. Now you sound like Liddy's therapist. Or her stylist. Actually, I think they might be the same person."

They lapsed into silence again, listening to the soft slap of water against the rocks below. Hayley watched as a small fleet of sailboats drifted into the harbor, sails glowing in the moonlight.

Watching them made Hayley think of her daughter, Gemma—who'd once begged for sailing lessons every summer but now lived in New York producing shows at the Flavor Network. She had her own apartment in Manhattan, a staff, interns who ran out for espresso, a demanding filming schedule. Jet-setting between tastings and network meetings and rubbing elbows with celebrity chefs who probably had their own knife lines at Williams Sonoma. Her little girl—who used to stage cooking competitions in their kitchen using Cheez-Its and gummy bears—now flew first class and called her "Mom" in a tone that made Hayley feel both proud and slightly ancient.

Her youngest, Dustin, was in Los Angeles, married, living in his own house with a lemon tree, with a young son named Eli who was already a whirlwind with a toothy grin. Dustin had landed a job at a major animation studio and was climbing the ladder fast. Every time Hayley got a video message of Eli babbling into the camera or drawing something vaguely animal-shaped, she got a tug in her chest—pride, yes. But also longing.

They were both thriving. Which meant they didn't need her anymore. At least not in the way they once did.

She didn't feel sad, exactly. Just . . . displaced. Like the center of her world had shifted while she was still standing in the same spot.

Her attention returned to her husband scribbling furiously in his notebook.

"You're really not going to tell me if I'm the victim in your book?" she asked, nudging Bruce's foot with hers.

He grinned without looking up. "You'll have to wait and see."

She raised an eyebrow. "The sassiest ghost in Maine, huh?"

Bruce finally looked up, startled. "What?"

"That's what you said. If you decide to kill me off, I'd be the sassiest ghost in Maine."

He grinned sheepishly. "I meant sexiest. Definitely sexiest."

Hayley mock-scowled. "Too late now. You said what you said."

He leaned over and kissed her cheek. "You'd be both."

Boat horns echoed softly in the bay as vessels began

to anchor in place. Somewhere behind the bluff, a cheer went up—someone lighting sparklers early, probably. The temperature dropped just enough to make Hayley glad for her zip-up hoodie.

Bruce put away his notebook and thermos, capped the pens, and slid it all neatly into his canvas tote.

Hayley stretched her legs out and looked up.

It was almost time.

The sky was darkening. The first stars blinked to life above them.

The Big Bang on Frenchman's Bay was about to begin.

Chapter 4

The first firework shrieked into the night sky and exploded in a cascade of red stars over Frenchman's Bay. Cheers erupted from the crowd gathered on the grassy hill above the town pier, echoing out across the water. Horns honked from boats in the harbor, their white running lights bobbing like fireflies on the dark tide. Bar Harbor's first-ever "Big Bang on the Bay" had officially begun.

Hayley took a long sip from her insulated thermos, which Bruce had just refilled. The drink inside—a dangerously stiff mix of lemonade and Jack Daniels—warmed her from the inside out. She passed Bruce his matching thermos.

"You know what I like best about Labor Day?" she asked.

Bruce twisted the lid and took a swig. "The opportunity to reflect on organized labor's contributions to the American economy?"

"No," she said, settling back. "The opportunity to eat three kinds of potato salad without judgment."

Bruce chuckled and slung an arm across her shoulder. "They should erect a statue of you in the town square. One hand holding a Jack and Coke, the other flipping a burger, wearing a T-shirt that says, LET ME TELL YOU WHAT YOU'RE DOING WRONG."

"And you'd leave flowers at its feet every Labor Day."

"I'd leave extra pickles."

The sky lit up again—silver sparklers burst into cascading strands, then a green starburst thundered, the boom vibrating in their chests.

Kids dashed barefoot across the grassy bluff in the distance, spinning in circles with glow sticks, shrieking with laughter and blasting whipped cream straight into their mouths from cans of Reddi-wip. Teenagers snapped selfies.

Bruce's eyes drifted left. "I thought Randy said he might stay in tonight."

Hayley followed his gaze.

There, off to the side on a quilt, half in shadow, sat Randy and Sergio.

Quiet.

Holding hands.

Watching the fireworks.

"He was vague," she said, her tone tight.

"And yet . . . there they are."

"Not with us," she said. "Just—off by themselves."

Hayley didn't like it. Something in her gut tensed. Randy didn't avoid her unless he had something to hide—and that was rare.

Still, she didn't want to push.

Not tonight.

Not yet.

Another firework exploded above them, showering the sky in purple and gold.

"There's Mona and Earl," Bruce said, nodding toward the edge of the bluff. Sure enough, they were locked in a passionate kiss by the railing, completely ignoring the explosions above them.

"Oh, I have to get a photo of that," Hayley muttered. "I'll use it to blackmail Mona into donating free lobsters for my feed next weekend."

Bruce winced. "Don't provoke her. Have you seen the violent way Mona tears apart a lobster when she's eating it? It's not a big leap to a human she's annoyed with."

Another whistle split the air. A firework shot skyward—and just as it burst into a dazzling umbrella of white light, something caught Hayley's eye.

A shape.

Moving at the edge of the rocks.

"Do you see that?" she asked, sitting up straighter.

Bruce squinted. "That a dinghy?"

"Looks like it's being pulled up on the rocks," she said.

As the firework's light flickered out, it illuminated a woman—slim, dripping wet, dressed in tight shorts and a dark tank top. She heaved the small boat halfway onto the shore, stumbled slightly, then darted up the rocks and disappeared into the trees without looking back.

Bruce raised an eyebrow. "Who takes a dinghy out during fireworks?"

"Someone who doesn't want to be seen," Hayley said.

"Or a college kid on a drunken dare. Or a really bad first date escape," Bruce added.

Hayley kept staring at the spot where the woman had vanished. "Weird timing."

"Very weird," Bruce agreed.

A final rocket burst above them, glittering gold over the bay, and the crowd erupted into cheers. People began packing up—folding chairs, bundling blankets, tossing half-eaten bags of kettle corn. The spell of summer had officially broken.

Bruce stood and stretched. "Let's go find some overpriced ice cream and celebrate the workers of America by forcing a teenager to serve us for minimum wage."

The air had cooled, and as they began to gather their belongings, they could see the path was lit by soft overhead lights from the marina and the glow of storefronts now closing for the night.

A familiar voice called out to them from behind.

"Hayley! Bruce!"

They turned to see Liddy jogging toward them, slightly breathless and adorably flustered in a floral sundress and denim jacket.

"Have you seen Doug?" she asked. "We were watching the fireworks, and he said he needed to make a quick phone call before the finale. He walked off and never came back."

Bruce tilted his head. "Maybe he found a signal and fell into a TikTok hole."

Liddy blinked. "That . . . is unfortunately plausible."

Hayley placed a comforting hand on her arm. "Reception's a mess down here. He's probably still out by the parking lot waving his phone around over his head like he's catching butterflies. He'll turn up."

Liddy sighed. "If he doesn't, I'm officially swearing off men and adopting a cat."

"Now, that's the spirit of Labor Day," Bruce said.

They waved her off, as Bruce emptied the melted ice from the cooler. Most of the crowd had already thinned, and Hayley bent down to start packing up their thermoses and chairs—

And froze.

Floating in the shallows between two jagged rocks was something dark.

Heavy.

Unmoving.

Her body tensed.

"Bruce," she said quietly. "Hold my thermos."

"What?" he asked, confused.

But she was already stepping out of her sandals, scaling down the bluff, and walking across the rocky beach into the freezing surf. The tide surged around her ankles as she waded closer. The object bobbed in the water, tangled in seaweed and foam.

She reached out—her fingers touched damp cloth.

Grease-streaked.

She gasped and reached again—then screamed.

The man floated face-up, a dark wound in his chest,

soaked apron clinging to him like seaweed. His white hair floated around his head like a ghostly halo.

Bruce sprinted to the edge of the rocks as Hayley stumbled back.

"Hayley?! What is it?"

"It's Hank," she cried. "It's Hank Desmond. He's been shot!"

A scream pierced the night from above.

They looked up to the bluff—and saw Kylie, Hank's young wife, clutching the railing. Her mouth open in a silent shriek, her eyes locked on the body below.

Bruce waded in and grabbed Hayley's arm, helping her back to shore as the waves rocked the large body gently behind them.

"Oh my God," she whispered, teeth chattering. "He's really dead."

Bruce pulled out his phone. "I'm calling Sergio."

Hayley nodded, barely hearing him. She looked out at the water, at the man who had once ruled every Labor Day cookout in town, now floating in the bay and sporting the apron he wore every year like a badge of honor.

Labor Day was supposed to mark the end of summer.

Instead, it marked the beginning of a murder investigation.

Chapter 5

The sirens cut through the late-summer air, their approach slicing through the stunned silence that had settled over the shore. Hayley sat on a rock, wrapped in her hoodie, still damp from the knees down and shivering despite the warm night. Her sandals lay forgotten at her feet. The sounds of laughter and fireworks had long since vanished, replaced by murmurs, radio crackle, and the crunch of boots on gravel.

The flashing lights of the new Bar Harbor Police SUV painted the rocks in blue and red. Police Chief Sergio Alvarez was first on the scene. He jogged down from the bluff, his square jaw tight with purpose, dark eyes scanning the crowd that had started to form at the top of the hill, kept at bay by a single strip of yellow tape.

"Don't let anyone cross this line," he ordered a uniformed officer who had just arrived. "No pictures, no live streaming. Let's do this right."

Sergio's gaze dropped to the body lying in the surf, the blood from the gunshot wound leaching into the seawater, creating a faint halo around Hank Desmond's broad torso. The grease-streaked apron clung to him like a final insult, soaked and stiff with brine.

Hayley watched as Sergio crouched beside the body, brow furrowed, hands on his hips.

He didn't touch anything yet.

Just looked.

Bruce moved closer to her, his voice low. "You okay?"

"I'm not the one floating in the water," Hayley said, her throat tight.

"Fair," Bruce said. "Still. You found him."

Hayley didn't answer. She couldn't stop thinking about the moment her fingers touched Hank's apron—familiar, heavy, grotesque in its lifelessness. Her stomach lurched.

Footsteps pounded behind them.

"Hayley!" Mona called, breathless.

She and Earl jogged down the incline from the bluff, both of them dressed in their end-of-summer best—Mona in a navy linen shirt and jeans, Earl still in his off-duty Bar Harbor PD T-shirt.

Hayley stared at the body, the reality finally sinking in. "I always thought Hank would go out flipping a steak," she murmured, her voice barely above a whisper. "Not like this."

Mona folded her arms, eyes fixed on the scene. "Guess the Grill Master finally burned out."

Earl approached Sergio and tipped his chin. "Need help keeping the crowd back, Chief? I'm off duty, but I can clear the line if you want."

Sergio nodded without looking up. "Appreciate it."

"Happy to help." Earl jogged off, calling up to a few teenagers who had started filming on their phones.

Sergio stood and turned to Mona. "I need to get out there," he said, gesturing toward the harbor.

Hayley followed his gaze. Out in the bay, barely visible in the moonlight, was a midsized boat anchored off the pier.

The *Slaughterhouse*.

Hank's pride and joy.

A grilling shrine on the water, complete with smoker, minibar, custom stainless-steel grill, and surround-sound Bluetooth speakers that usually played Southern rock at punishing decibels.

"That where he was grilling tonight?" Bruce asked quietly.

Sergio nodded. "Probably. But how did he end up here?"

"Drifted in with the tide?" Hayley offered.

"Maybe," Sergio muttered. "I need to see what's on that boat."

"I can take you," Mona said.

Sergio turned. "You sure?"

"She's fueled and ready. Let's go."

Hayley opened her mouth to volunteer, but Bruce grabbed her hand first. "We're coming, too," he said.

Sergio gave them a look.

Not angry.

Just tired.

Surprisingly, he didn't object.

A growing crowd had formed along the pier—

neighbors, tourists, and local restaurant workers who'd wrapped up their shifts and caught wind of the drama. Voices rose: "Who is it?" "Was it a drowning?" "No, I heard a gunshot." "It's Hank Desmond, I swear. The Grill Master."

Gasps spread like ripples in a pond.

Someone sobbed.

At the dock, Mona climbed aboard her lobster boat and started the engine. Hayley and Bruce stepped aboard and helped Sergio as he untied the lines. The motor rumbled to life, a deep, steady thrum that cut through the night.

Before they could push off, Earl appeared with someone wrapped in a shock blanket.

Kylie.

Her hair clung to her cheeks, and the blanket hung low on her bare shoulders. She looked pale. Shaky. Her mascara had run and her flip-flops slapped on the deck with every slow step.

"She fainted and hit her head after seeing Hank," Earl said. "EMTs checked her out. No concussion. Just shock."

Sergio stepped forward. "Kylie. I'm so sorry for your loss."

She nodded slowly, blinking rapidly. "I can't believe it."

"Can you tell me what happened?"

She looked down, her voice barely above a whisper. "I don't know. We were on the boat earlier. Barbecuing.

Drinking. Just hanging out, waiting for the fireworks to start. Hank and I got into a spat."

"What about?"

She hesitated. "Nothing serious. Just . . . dumb stuff. I had too much to drink. I got emotional. We argued. I said something dramatic and got in the dinghy to make my point."

"Did Hank try to stop you?"

She nodded. "He yelled after me. But I just said—" She stopped. Her voice cracked. "I told him to get away from me."

Hayley's eyes softened.

Tears pooled in her eyes. "I can't believe those were the last words I said to him."

"And then you came ashore?" Sergio asked gently.

Kylie nodded again. "I went up the path. Wandered a little. I didn't think—when I saw him—" She began to cry.

Earl guided her back toward the EMTs.

Sergio boarded Mona's boat, and they pushed off.

They cut across the dark bay, the *Slaughterhouse* growing larger with every rumbling yard. The water slapped at the hull, and a breeze picked up, salty and cool. The only sound was the low throb of the motor and Mona muttering to herself about idiots who hosted BBQs on boats.

Accidents waiting to happen.

Hayley stayed near the bow, peering toward the anchored vessel.

As they pulled alongside, Sergio reached for the rope

ladder and climbed aboard first. Bruce followed. Then Mona. Then Hayley.

The deck of the *Slaughterhouse* reeked of BBQ smoke, salt water, and something worse—something metallic and sour. Blood and meat and alcohol. A plate of ribs had been abandoned on the prep counter. A beer can lay crushed beside it. Red Solo cups were scattered everywhere.

But no people.

Sergio called out. "Anyone here?"

Silence.

Bruce motioned to the galley door. It stood ajar. Hayley slipped through it while the others remained on deck.

Down the narrow stairs, below deck, the small cabin reeked of booze and sweat. The light was dim. She turned a corner and gasped.

Chase Wingate was passed out across the bed, one arm dangling off the edge, an open bottle of bourbon at his feet.

"Chase?" she said, stepping closer.

He groaned, barely stirring.

"Chase!"

She shook his shoulder. He flinched, groaned again, then slowly rolled over. His eyes fluttered open.

"Hayley?" he slurred. "What's goin' on?"

She took a step back, then pulled her phone from her back pocket and called Sergio. "You need to come below deck."

Within seconds, Sergio appeared behind her. "Step back, Hayley."

She did as she was told.

Sergio crouched by the bed. "Chase. You know where you are?"

Chase blinked at him. "We were drinkin'. Me and Hank. I don't remember . . . I don't remember anything after that."

Hayley left Sergio to it and made her way back up the stairs, uneasy. There were sauce splatters on the deck. Overturned cups. A stained rag was strewn on top of the grill station. The deck was sticky from spilled beer. No one had bothered to clean up after dinner. Or maybe they never got the chance.

She turned toward the cooler near the prep station. Its lid sat slightly ajar.

Curious, Hayley nudged it open with her shoe.

Inside were ribs, half-submerged in melted ice, their bones poking up like fingers.

And next to them—black metal.

A gun.

She let out a sharp breath, slammed the lid shut, and turned back toward the hatch.

"Earl," she whispered as soon as she saw him climbing aboard from a Coast Guard cruiser that had just arrived on the scene. "I found the gun. In the cooler. But be sure to tell Sergio you found it."

Earl blinked. "What?"

"Just trust me. I think it's better if he doesn't think I'm sticking my nose in things."

Earl grinned. "Happy to take the credit."

He turned and called out, "Sergio! Got something here!"

Hayley stepped aside as Sergio rushed up from below deck. Earl flipped open the cooler, and Sergio's eyes darkened.

Bruce appeared beside her. "What is it?"

"Most likely the murder weapon," Sergio answered solemnly.

Hayley stared out across the water, the town lights twinkling onshore, the sounds of the crowd now replaced by the slap of waves and the creak of the boat in its moorings.

Hank Desmond had been shot.

His body dumped—or dragged—or dropped.

Someone had made a real mess out here.

Chapter 6

Rain threatened but never came.

Instead, Bar Harbor was blanketed in the kind of heavy, late-summer humidity that made your skin feel like it had been brushed with chowder steam. Hayley dabbed at her forehead with a cocktail napkin and took a long sip of her Jack & Coke as she sat with Bruce at a corner table inside Drinks Like A Fish.

They were early for their double date—Liddy was bringing Doug Marsh, a man Hayley already knew from Kelton and Betty's wedding reception a few days ago. He'd been charming, flirty, and had definitely caught Liddy's attention.

Hayley had liked him.

Still did.

But tonight was about gathering a little more data.

The bar was buzzing for a Monday night. String lights twinkled above mismatched tables, and the usual décor—a rusty ship bell, a mounted swordfish in Mardi Gras beads—gave the place its signature blend of cozy and kitschy. A salty breeze drifted in through the open windows.

Behind the bar, Randy moved with his usual efficiency, cracking jokes, pouring pints, but Hayley could tell something was off. He looked preoccupied, distracted. Each time Chelsea approached him, his smile faded a fraction too quickly. He kept glancing toward the office, then back to the taps like something heavy was pressing on him.

She made a mental note to check in.

Liddy arrived with her usual fanfare, her cherry-red wrap dress fluttering dramatically as she burst through the door. Doug followed close behind, tanned and sharply dressed in a white linen shirt. He smiled when he spotted Hayley and Bruce.

"Hey, you two," Liddy said brightly, guiding Doug to the table.

"Hey, Doug," Hayley said with a nod, remembering how he'd danced with every woman over forty at the wedding and still found time to charm the bride's grandmother. "Nice to see you again."

"Pleasure's mine," he said with an easy grin.

Bruce raised his glass. "You've got one shot tonight. Don't blow it."

They all laughed as Doug and Liddy sat down. Chelsea stopped by to take their drink orders, and Hayley noticed again how Randy and Chelsea seemed to be having a lot of hushed sidebar conversations.

It didn't look casual.

It looked . . . loaded.

"I've been trying to talk him into staying a little longer," Liddy said once Chelsea left. "But he's stubborn."

Doug shook his head with a smile. "I have to get back. I've been off the grid too long. Clients are starting to think I'm dodging them."

"But you promised you'd come back," Liddy said, mock-wounded.

"I will. I meant that. And you know, if by January you get tired of scraping ice off your windshield . . ."

"You want me to visit you in Florida," Liddy said, lips quirking.

He shrugged. "Not the worst idea."

Their moment was interrupted by a loud exchange at the bar.

"I'm telling you, it was Chase Wingate," one man said.

"Drunk off his ass," the other added. "They fought, he pulled the trigger, dumped the body, passed out. Case closed."

Hayley's ears perked up. The two men were locals she vaguely recognized—one worked for public works, the other used to ref basketball games at the Y. Both nursed schooners and didn't seem to care who overheard them.

"Chase is a hothead," one said. "And rich enough to think he can get away with anything. Investor money. Real estate. He's got properties up and down the coast."

"And Hank? Who knows what kind of deal they had going?"

Hayley turned back to the table, eyebrows raised. "I don't buy it."

Liddy blinked. "You don't think Chase did it?"

"It's too neat," Hayley said. "If it was a drunken fight, why hide the gun in a cooler full of ribs? Why not just toss it overboard?"

"Or wipe it down," Bruce added. "He had the whole ocean to work with."

Doug leaned in. "Unless someone else put it there."

"Exactly," Hayley said. "Feels staged. Like someone wanted it found—but not right away."

Her eyes drifted toward the bar again. Randy and Chelsea were talking in low tones. Chelsea had her hand on the bar and her chin tilted up like she was making a point. Randy looked . . . resigned. He glanced at Hayley, then quickly looked away before disappearing into the kitchen.

Hayley got up and intercepted Chelsea near the register.

"What's going on with Randy?"

Chelsea blinked. "What?"

"You two look like you're planning a coup."

Chelsea gave her a tight-lipped smile. "We're just working out some business stuff."

"Looks intense."

"It's nothing," Chelsea said. "Anyway, Liddy seems smitten. Should we be expecting an elopement?"

"Nice dodge."

"I do my best," she said, vanishing toward the other end of the bar.

Before Hayley could process that, the front door opened and in stepped Police Chief Sergio Alvares, in full uniform, with Lieutenant Donnie behind him. Both had their duty faces on, and Sergio's eyes scanned the room like he was hunting ghosts.

Randy emerged from the kitchen. He stopped short when he saw them.

Sergio made a direct line for Hayley's table.

"Hayley. Bruce."

"Evening, Sergio," Bruce said with a smile.

Sergio focused his attention on Doug. "Mr. Marsh."

Doug looked up, puzzled. "Yes?"

Sergio's tone was neutral. "The gun recovered aboard the *Slaughterhouse* was registered to you."

Doug's face dropped. "That's not possible."

Sergio's eyes narrowed. "Are you saying you don't own a gun?"

"I'm saying I haven't touched it. As far as I know, it's still locked in the safe at my rental."

"Where were you the night Hank Desmond was killed?"

Doug looked at Liddy. "We were together. Right, Liddy?"

Liddy stared at him, then glanced away. "Yes, that's right. We were together . . . most of the time."

Sergio narrowed his eyes. “You were separated part of the time?”

She hesitated longer this time, her eyes full of worry. “I . . . he went to make a phone call before the fireworks. I don’t know exactly how long he was gone.”

Hayley watched Doug’s expression shift. His eyes pleaded silently: *Please. Just say we were together.*

“I didn’t think anything of it,” Liddy added weakly. “It was only twenty minutes, maybe.”

Sergio’s voice was calm. “Could he have taken a boat out to the *Slaughterhouse*, shot Hank, dumped the body, and gotten back in time?”

Liddy’s face crumpled. “No! That’s insane. He was just making a call.”

Sergio nodded to Donnie.

“Wait, you’re not seriously—” Doug started.

“We have enough to take you in for questioning,” Sergio said.

“What? No! I’m not going anywhere. We’re enjoying a pleasant night out.”

Sergio sighed. “We can do this the easy way, or the hard way.”

Donnie pulled out a pair of cuffs.

“This is insane,” Doug snapped. “I didn’t kill anyone!”

Liddy stood. “Don’t do this. He didn’t—he couldn’t—”

Doug turned to her, panicked. “Liddy, please . . .”

Donnie dangled the duffs in front of him. “You can explain everything at the station. Please don’t make me use these.”

The bar fell into stunned silence as the two officers led Doug out the front door.

Liddy scrambled after them, yelling his name.

Hayley stood up, but Bruce caught her hand. "Don't."

"But—"

"Don't."

The door slammed shut behind them.

A beat passed. The room remained still.

Hayley moved toward the bar again. Randy was wiping down the same spot with increasing aggression.

"Hey," she said.

"Can't talk right now, Hayley."

"I just—"

"I said I'm busy."

He disappeared into the back again.

The door banged open.

In walked Earl, beaming, with Mona trailing behind, arms crossed.

"Holy hell," Earl said, seeing the looks on everyone's faces. "We miss something?"

"You just missed Doug Marsh getting arrested for murder," Bruce said.

Mona's eyes widened. "*What?*"

"They're not arresting him—they're just taking him in for questioning," Hayley said.

Earl whistled. "Well, damn."

He recovered quickly, his grin returning. "We just came from the Reading Room. Best dinner of my life. Candlelight. Soft-shell lobster. White wine. Mona wore earrings. It was like a Nicholas Sparks novel, but with real butter."

Mona rolled her eyes. "Earl. Don't embarrass me."

"I'm just saying it was special."

She poked him. "Focus."

He hesitated.

"Earl. Tell them what you told me at dinner."

He sighed. "Fine. Look, they've got both Chase and Doug on their radar. But they won't be able to hold them for long. Chase's DNA was on the bullets. But a different set of prints were found on the gun. Probably Doug's. They're going to need more to charge them, and Chase already has his lawyer on the case, working to get him released. I'm sure Doug's won't be far behind."

Hayley blinked. "Wait—Chase's DNA? On the bullets?"

Earl nodded. "From when he loaded the magazine, probably."

"And the other prints?"

"On the grip," Mona said, leaning in. "They're pretty certain Doug's prints will be a match. So . . . two men. One weapon."

Hayley's brain kicked into high gear.

"Which means either they were both involved—or someone's being framed," she murmured. "But who held it last? Who pulled the trigger? And why the hell would they both have contact with the same gun?"

Bruce leaned forward. "What if they didn't know they both touched it?"

"Of course Doug's prints are on it. It's his gun, right? Chase could have somehow stolen it to set him up!" Liddy cried.

Hayley looked down into her drink. "But why? And why murder Hank?"

The case was getting murkier by the minute.

And she was starting to feel the pull—deeper into the mystery.

Whatever had gone down on that boat hadn't been simple.

It had been layered.

And deadly.

Chapter 7

The waves lapped gently against the rocky shoreline as dusk settled over Bar Harbor, casting a lavender hue across the water and gilding the windows of the sprawling seaside home just off the Shore Path. Lanterns flickered along the wooden deck, their glow softening the crisp edges of the end-of-summer air. Jazz filtered out of hidden speakers, blending with the rhythmic hiss of the tide. Hayley held a glass of prosecco in one hand and tried not to think about goodbyes.

Sergio and Randy's end-of-season bash was always one of the highlights of the year—casual, intimate, with enough food and booze to sink a whale-watching boat.

But this year, it was different.

Bittersweet.

Everyone felt it.

The party was still lively—Bruce and Earl were arguing about who made the best burger in town, Mona was perched near the drinks table chatting up an out-of-towner with too-perfect teeth, and Chelsea Mahoney was laughing a little too loudly at something no one else had heard.

But the mood had a current running under it.

A quiet hum of finality.

Hayley spotted Liddy standing near the bluff's edge, staring out at the sea.

Alone.

Hayley walked over, gently bumping her arm. "You okay?"

Liddy offered a tight smile. "Define 'okay'."

"You could say you're vertical and holding a drink. That usually passes in this town."

Liddy sipped her cosmo. "Everyone's looking at me like I should be in mourning or handcuffs. One minute Doug's making me laugh about how he once mistook a bidet for a foot bath, and the next he's public enemy number one."

"He's not been found guilty yet."

"Maybe not," she said quietly. "But he's definitely not innocent."

Hayley opened her mouth to reply, but a soft chime clinked through the air. Sergio stood on the deck, wine-glass in hand, Randy beside him with a hand resting lightly on his back. The partygoers quieted.

"Friends," Sergio began, his voice steady but a touch thick, "thank you for being here tonight. I know it's been a hard week for this town. But for Randy and me, it's also been a week of charity."

"Clarity," Randy whispered, correcting him.

English was Brazilian native Sergio's second language.

"Clarity!" Sergio said.

He looked down for a moment.

Randy gave his hand a squeeze.

"My mother's health is declining," Sergio continued. "And after much thought, we've decided to move back to São Paulo indefinitely to be with her."

Gasps rippled through the group.

Hayley felt Bruce's hand brush hers.

She couldn't move.

Randy stepped forward. "As you all know, I grew up here. But I left this town the first chance I got. I never really thought I would ever move back to Maine. But then I met Sergio, and we decided to make this place our home. And honestly, I've loved every minute of it. Owning Drinks Like A Fish. And being part of this community. But with Sergio stepping down, I realized maybe it's time for me to take a step back, too."

Hayley blinked.

"I'll be selling the bar," Randy said. "And I'm seriously considering Chelsea as a buyer."

Now the gasps were audible.

Hayley's heart dropped into her stomach.

Bruce leaned over. "Did you know about this?"

She shook her head. "Not a clue."

Randy smiled, but his eyes flicked toward Hayley and then darted away.

The crowd buzzed with quiet conversation, no one wanting to interrupt the moment, but everyone processing the sudden gut punch of the announcement.

Chelsea stood off to the side, frozen in place, as if even she hadn't expected to be named aloud.

Hayley caught her eye.

Chelsea quickly looked away.

Hayley waited until the crowd had started to disperse toward the buffet before cornering her brother near the grill.

"You were going to let me find out like that?"

Randy turned, already looking guilty. "Hayley . . ."

"I'm your sister. And your best friend. And your unpaid therapist, bar back, and occasional designated driver."

"I know. I wanted to tell you," he said, voice cracking slightly. "But I also knew if I did . . . I might change my mind."

Hayley stared at him.

"I've never done anything like this without you," he admitted. "Moving back to Bar Harbor? That was your doing. Buying the bar? You pushed me. Sergio's always gone along with it—he moved here for me, Hayley. Became police chief when he never even wanted to carry a gun."

"He's been great at it," Hayley said softly.

"He has. But he misses his family. His culture. The food. And I think maybe it's my turn to make a sacrifice. For him."

Hayley felt her chest tighten.

"I'm tired, too," Randy added. "Running a bar takes everything out of you. You know what I mean."

"I do," she said. "Running a whole restaurant doesn't leave you with much, either."

He looked at her, eyes damp. "I'm going to miss you."

"I tell most people you're the older sibling," she said, blinking fast. "Even though I've got you beat by two and a half years."

Randy smiled, pulling her into a hug. "You always were bossy."

She clung to him for a long moment.

As the sun finally dipped below the horizon and the moon began to rise in its place, casting silver on the water, Hayley wandered back toward the drinks table, where Mona had materialized.

Mona leaned in. "There's a rumor going around."

Hayley raised an eyebrow. "What kind of rumor?"

"The juicy kind. Someone at the station told Earl that the police found some . . . interesting photos tucked away in a drawer in Hank's office."

Hayley's heart skipped. "What kind of photos?"

"Compromising ones."

Mona's expression made it clear she wouldn't be getting anything more specific from her—not yet.

Hayley scanned the crowd. Sergio stood near the firepit, chatting with a few of the guests, but his eyes looked distant.

Focused elsewhere.

She walked over.

"You're not really going to leave us, are you?" she asked.

He smiled at her. "You heard the speech."

"I've heard lots of speeches. I've given some. Doesn't mean I always follow through."

Sergio looked at her for a long moment. "I meant it."

There was a pause.

"Can I ask you something—off the record?" Hayley said.

"Hayley . . ."

She gave him a look. The one that always wore him down.

He sighed. "What?"

"Photos. In Hank's office. People are talking."

His expression didn't change, but his eyes flared slightly.

"You know I can't comment—"

"But you will. Because I'm charming and persistent and you're tired of pretending you don't like telling me things."

He hesitated. Then drained his glass and leaned closer.

"We found a manila envelope in a drawer at Desmond's Slaughterhouse. Inside were half a dozen photos. High-resolution. Someone snapped Kylie and Chase together. The kind of photos best left out of the family album. Different times. Different places."

Hayley blinked. "They were having an affair?"

"Clearly. And someone wanted Hank to find out."

"Did he know?"

"Not until those photos showed up. They were sent autonomously."

Hayley paused.

"Oh, you mean anonymously."

Sergio frowned. "Isn't that what I said?"

"Sure."

She thought it best to just let it go.

"Anonymously. No note. No fingerprints."

"Why invite Chase to the boat?"

"I think Hank was planning to confront him."

Hayley frowned. "Was it blackmail?"

"We don't know. But Hank was close to a big distribution deal for that new barbecue sauce line of his. Image was everything. If word got out that his wife was sleeping with a drunk investor, it could've ruined the whole deal."

Hayley muttered, "Someone was stirring the pot."

Sergio nodded grimly. "And Hank Desmond definitely got burned."

Island Food & Spirits
By
Hayley Powell

Shocked. Stunned. Gobsmacked. There aren't enough adjectives in the English language to describe my reaction when Randy and Sergio—at their annual end-of-summer BBQ, no less—dropped the bombshell: They're moving to Brazil. To Brazil. Like, "Carnival, rainforest, soccer, and caipirinhas" Brazil.

After the initial wave of "I'll chain myself to your porch" panic subsided, I sat down with them and heard the whole story. And you know what? It makes sense. They need this. They'll thrive there. And yes, I'll be supportive and happy for them—while also ugly-crying into a pint of Ben & Jerry's every other night. Bruce and I are already plotting a future trip to visit them, which is my silver lining. (That and the fact that Randy will now be surrounded by fruit so fresh it could get its own Instagram account.)

Now, Randy and I have always been close . . . except for the brief period when I tried to sell him.

I was three years old, an only child, the sun around which my parents orbited, when they broke the news that I was getting a baby brother or sister. I looked them dead in the eye, said, "No, thank you," and toddled off.

They tried every sales pitch in the book:

"You'll have a playmate!" (No thanks.)

"You can dress the baby up like a doll!" (I'd rather have a puppy.)

When the big day arrived, I was safely stashed at my preschool best friend Mona's house while my parents went to the hospital. That evening, my dad burst through the door like a man who'd just discovered scallops on sale, scooped me up, and declared, "It's a boy, Hayley! You have a new baby brother!" He handed cigars to Mona's father, Bubba, and they went outside to smoke, leaving me on the couch . . . crying.

Within twenty-four hours, I was on the sidewalk, proudly holding a sign I'd illustrated (I couldn't write yet, so it was mostly stick figures and scribbles) that read BABY FOR SALE $1! The neighbors laughed, cars honked, and my mother—trying to get colicky Randy to sleep—dragged me back inside before I could close a deal.

My next strategy was to bargain with my dad. "Trade Randy for a puppy," I suggested sweetly. Dad laughed so hard I knew negotiations were over.

I held out hope for weeks. Randy wailed through the night. My parents muttered about exhaustion.

Surely they'd take him back to the hospital for an exchange? Nope. The "broken one" stayed.

Then one night, I padded into his room, ready to shush him so I could get back to sleep. I reached into the crib, patted his tummy, and whispered, "Don't cry, Randy." He stopped. Grabbed my finger. Smiled. And just like that, my tiny, stubborn heart melted. From that moment, I became his protector, coconspirator, and very opinionated big sister.

We've had our share of sibling squabbles, but we've always come back to each other. And no matter how far away Brazil is, I know that won't change.

So today, I'm sharing two recipes that are pure "Hayley and Randy" staples—one strong enough to toast a big move, and one cozy enough to soothe the ache of missing someone you love.

First up: The Twisted Sister.

Yes, it's named after the band, but also after the fact that after two of these, you'll be singing "We're Not Gonna Take It" at the top of your lungs on your deck—and your neighbors will be taking it, whether they like it or not.

Twisted Sister

Ingredients

3 fresh jalapeño slices
2 ounces vodka
3 ounces lemonade
1 ounce mango purée
1 lemon wedge, for garnish

Muddle the jalapeño slices in a cocktail shaker. Add the vodka, lemonade, mango purée, and ice. Shake, then strain into a glass filled with fresh ice. Garnish with the lemon wedge if you're feeling classy—or skip it if you're already halfway to karaoke hour.

And now, Randy's all-time favorite comfort food: grilled turkey burgers. He swears by them because they're juicy, flavorful, and just healthy enough that you can justify a second Twisted Sister.

GRILLED TURKEY BURGERS

INGREDIENTS

1 pound ground turkey
⅓ cup seasoned breadcrumbs (plain are fine, but where's the fun in that?)
1 large egg
1 tablespoon Worcestershire sauce
1 tablespoon Dijon mustard
2 cloves garlic, minced
2 teaspoons onion powder
1 teaspoon smoked paprika
½ teaspoon salt
½ teaspoon pepper
4 hamburger buns

In a large bowl, combine the turkey meat, breadcrumbs, egg, Worcestershire sauce, Dijon mustard, minced garlic, onion powder, paprika, salt, and pepper. Mix until combined but do not overwork the meat.

Divide the meat mixture into four equal-sized patties, and with your thumb, make an indention on the top of each patty. This helps to keep the patty from shrinking.

Preheat the grill to medium-high heat and oil your grates to help prevent sticking.

Grill the burgers for 5 to 6 minutes on each side. You want the internal temperature to be 165°F for doneness.

When the burgers are almost done, add the buns to the grill and toast until golden brown.

Assemble with your favorite toppings—lettuce, tomato, pickles, more pickles, maybe a slice of cheddar—and serve with a Twisted Sister in hand. Comfort food never tasted so rebellious.

Chapter 8

"Out of onions," Kelton announced, pushing through the swinging door from the kitchen like he was delivering the news of a death in the family. "And we're down to half a container of paprika."

Hayley looked up from the clipboard where she was finalizing prep notes for the dinner shift. "You're kidding."

"I wish. And we've got three tables with preorders for the Hungarian meat-loaf special, so . . ."

"Okay, okay," Hayley said, already stripping off her apron. "I'll run to the Shop 'n Save. Try not to let Betty over-season anything while I'm gone."

"No promises," Kelton called after her.

Hayley's Kitchen was already buzzing with prep work and the scent of baked bread, garlic, and something caramelizing on a hot skillet. She dashed out the back, purse over her shoulder, hair barely tamed in a headband, and keys jangling as she jumped into her battered Subaru.

Ten minutes later, she was pulling into the jam-packed parking lot of the Shop 'n Save, cursing herself for not sending Kelton instead. She circled twice, looking for anything remotely resembling a space, until finally—like a beacon—she spotted Doris Crimmons, in her butter-yellow Buick, easing out of a prime spot by the front entrance.

Or trying to.

Very, very slowly.

Hayley put on her turn signal and waited. Doris's reverse lights blinked on.

Then off.

Then on again.

A line of cars began to build behind Hayley. The driver directly behind her honked once. Hayley held up a hand in apology but didn't move. This was her space. Doris was finally almost clear—just a little more to go—and then, like a snake slithering through tall grass, a shiny black SUV slid in from the other direction and stole the spot.

"What the—?" Hayley slammed her hand against the steering wheel.

The SUV door opened, and out stepped a man in his thirties, tall, athletic, dark hair, designer sunglasses perched on his nose like he'd just stepped out of a *GQ* photo shoot. He straightened his tie, looked around with supreme confidence, and headed for the store.

"Oh, no, you don't."

Hayley threw her car into park and jumped out, slamming the door behind her.

"Excuse me!" she called. "That was my space!"

The man turned. His Boston accent hit like a slap. "Didn't see your name on it."

"I was waiting," she snapped. "Doris Crimmons nearly died getting out of that spot. You just swooped in like—like—"

"A guy trying to buy groceries?"

"Like a Masshole," Hayley muttered.

His eyebrow twitched. "Wow. Charming. You must be a riot at parties."

Hayley crossed her arms. "This is Maine. We wait our turn here. We don't just cut people off because we're wearing expensive shoes and think the rules don't apply."

The man looked her up and down. "And you are?"

"Someone who doesn't appreciate being disrespected."

He exhaled slowly, then glanced at her car, then back at her. Finally—finally—he sighed and walked back to his vehicle. "You're lucky I'm in a generous mood."

"See how easy that was?" she said sweetly as he climbed back in. "Civility. It's contagious."

He reversed out and disappeared down the aisle. Hayley slid triumphantly into the space and muttered, "Massachusetts plates. Figures."

She grabbed her bag and headed inside.

Back at Hayley's Kitchen, Hayley had barely returned from the store, ingredients in hand, when the dinner crowd started arriving. Betty was adjusting silverware with military precision. Kelton was manning the kitchen like a caffeinated octopus. Hayley was about to unlock the front door for the rush when her phone buzzed.

It was a text from Earl.

The chief wants to see you. Now.

Hayley's heart jumped.

Sergio.

Maybe they had a break in the Desmond case.

She turned to Betty. "Can you cover the front for a bit?"

"Absolutely not," Betty said, then saw Hayley's face. "Fine. Go. I'll survive. Barely. But hurry back!"

Hayley gave her a grateful pat on the arm and hurried out.

The police station was unusually quiet when she stepped inside, the fluorescent lights buzzing above her head. She passed by the front desk just as she heard a sound—sniffling. Loud, wet sniffling. She turned.

Lieutenant Donnie was at his desk, phone cradled to his ear, tears streaming down his face as he blubbered into the receiver.

"I—I just—I gave this place over ten years, Tilly! What am I supposed to do now?"

Nurse Tilly was Donnie's girlfriend.

It sounded as if Donnie had just been fired.

"Donnie?" Hayley said softly.

He looked up, startled, then immediately got up and rushed into the men's room without a word.

Hayley blinked.

Something was wrong.

She moved down the hall and knocked once on the open door of the police chief's office—Sergio's office. "Sergio? I just saw Donnie and—"

She stepped inside—and stopped dead.

It wasn't Sergio.

It was him.

The Masshole.

Sitting at the desk.

Sergio's desk.

In a crisp navy suit with a pocket square. No sunglasses now, just sharp eyes and sharper posture.

"What are you doing here?" Hayley asked.

The man rose. "I'm Caleb Maddox. The new chief of police."

Hayley stared. "*You're what?*"

"Surprised?" he asked, Boston accent cutting through every syllable.

"Uh, yes. Sergio just announced his resignation yesterday. You don't just swap police chiefs like light bulbs."

"The town council's known for months," he said, moving to close the office door behind her. "I was recruited a while ago. Sergio stayed on to ease the transition."

"But he just threw a going-away party!"

"Timing's a funny thing."

Hayley narrowed her eyes. "You texted Earl. You're the 'chief' who wanted to see me?"

"That's right."

She folded her arms. "Why?"

He walked back behind the desk, sat down again, and steepled his fingers. "I've heard about you."

"Oh?"

"Hayley Powell. Food columnist, part-time restaurateur, full-time busybody."

Her mouth fell open. "Excuse me?"

"I'm here to make one thing very clear: your habit of interfering in police investigations? That ends now."

She gaped. "What are you even talking about?"

"You like to dig. Gossip. Harass officers for inside info. It stops. Now. Like, right now."

"I'm trying to help!" she said.

"You're not police. You're not press. You're a civilian. And you're in my way."

Hayley took a step forward. "Do you have any idea what this town has been through? What I've helped solve over the years?"

He met her gaze, unmoved. "This isn't your case."

"I found Hank Desmond's body."

"You're not on the report."

"That's because I—never mind. Look, I have thoughts—real theories about what happened."

"I'm not interested in your theories."

Hayley's hands balled into fists. "This isn't Boston, Chief. You don't just bark orders here and expect everyone to salute."

"No," he said smoothly. "But I do expect people to respect boundaries."

"And if I don't?"

His eyes darkened. "Then we'll have a problem."

The air between them vibrated with tension.

Hayley opened her mouth, ready to unleash a scathing rebuttal, when a knock sounded. The door opened, and Earl stepped in, looking hesitant.

"You needed me?"

"Yes. Please escort Ms. Powell out," Maddox said without looking away from her.

Earl blinked. "Seriously?"

"As you know, Earl, I've been streamlining, making the department more efficient, which means I've had to let a few people go . . ."

Like Donnie, for instance, Hayley thought.

"But I've decided to retain your position," Maddox added. "Just don't forget who you report to now."

Hayley stared at Earl, stunned.

Earl gently gestured to the hallway. "C'mon, Hayley. You should go."

Hayley turned on her heel and stalked out, fire burning under her skin.

The second they were outside, she rounded on Earl. "He's a menace."

"I didn't vote for him," Earl said.

"He's smug, arrogant, dismissive—"

"He's also in charge. My new boss. In case that wasn't clear."

Hayley crossed her arms, heart pounding. "This is going to be a problem."

Earl gave her a sympathetic look. "I know."

She stared back at the building.

Sergio had been her ally. Caleb Maddox was going to be something else entirely.

An obstacle.

And Hayley Powell had never let an obstacle stop her before.

Chapter 9

At 8:03 a.m. on a bright, crisp morning, Jordan's Restaurant was already packed with post–Labor Day tourists elbow-deep in syrup and locals clutching mugs of black coffee like life preservers. Servers darted between tables, hollering greetings over the low hum of conversation and the clatter of cutlery. A little girl at the next booth kept shaking her tiny bottle of maple syrup like it was a maraca. A pair of hungover tourists in matching "Bar Harbor Is My Happy Place" hoodies were passing around aspirin like candy.

And at the corner booth by the window, Hayley was buttering toast and trying to look innocent.

"You're using me for information," Earl grumbled, sliding stiffly into the seat across from her. He was still in uniform—pressed navy shirt, badge gleaming, and a fresh coffee stain already blooming on one sleeve.

"Of course I am," Hayley said cheerfully. "But I'm also buying you breakfast."

"I'm on my way to the station. I shouldn't even be here."

Hayley gestured to the laminated menu. "And yet you are. Because Mona told you to be."

As if summoned, Mona appeared beside their table, removing her sunglasses and planting herself firmly at the edge of the booth like a stern school principal.

"Don't give me that look, Earl. Hayley's my best friend. If this is ever going to work between us, you need to charm the people I love."

Earl sighed. "I'm charming."

Hayley grinned. "You're . . . housebroken."

"You ordered me pancakes, didn't you?"

Hayley didn't answer, just gave a sly smile as a waitress slid a heaping plate of double-stack blueberry pancakes in front of him, syrup already pooled around the edges like a moat.

Just the way he liked them.

Earl stared down at them, visibly wavering. "Damn it."

Hayley leaned forward. "They're fresh. Bursting with wild Maine blueberries. Fluffy, golden brown, buttery edges . . ."

"I get it," Earl said, already picking up his fork.

Mona leaned in, kissed the top of his head. "I've gotta go unload the boat. You behave."

And with that, she was gone.

Hayley sipped her coffee. "So. You miss Sergio yet?"

Earl wiped his mouth and gave her a sidelong glance. "We all do. But it's not our choice."

Hayley rolled her eyes. "That new guy—Caleb Maddox? He's a robot in designer shoes."

"Yeah, I gotta admit, he's . . . a tough nut to crack."

"Is that what we're calling arrogant and insufferable now?"

"He runs a tight ship," Earl said. "Not the warm and fuzzy kind Sergio ran. You showing up with homemade muffins for gossip hour? Those days are done."

Hayley muttered, "He had you escort me out of the building like I was a door-to-door scam artist trying to sell reverse mortgages."

Earl chuckled into his coffee.

"I'm serious," she said. "The guy's got a stick so far up his—"

"Hayley . . ." Earl warned, still chewing.

She dropped her voice. "Come on, you have to admit he's off to a rocky start. No wonder Donnie was bawling."

Earl's expression sobered. "Poor guy. Donnie and I go way back. We joined the force together. It's been ten years—he's like a brother to me."

"Have you seen him?"

"Every day. He's not sleeping. Tilly says he's barely eating. Guy gave everything he had to that job and just got tossed like an empty Dunkin' cup on Route Three."

Hayley's heart softened. "Poor Donnie."

"He doesn't know what he's gonna do next. No plan. No savings. He's floundering."

A moment of silence passed between them, broken

only by the clink of forks and the laughter of the syrup-drunk girl two tables over.

"So," Hayley said, stirring her coffee. "What can you tell me about the Desmond investigation?"

Earl leaned back in the booth. "Not much. Sergio passed the case to Maddox before he left, and Maddox's keeping it locked down."

"Any theories floating around?"

"Just what's already public. Kylie says she and Hank got into it on the boat, she took the dinghy, and she swears when she left for shore he was still alive. Chase says they argued, too—over those photos."

Hayley leaned in. "The ones of him and Kylie?"

Earl nodded. "According to Chase, Hank found out they were fooling around and was furious. But Chase was drunk. Doesn't remember how the argument ended."

Hayley shook her head. "Convenient."

"The new chief thinks it ended with Chase pulling the trigger."

"But it was Doug Marsh's gun."

"Exactly. Found in a cooler full of ribs and melted ice. No one's clear how it got there."

Hayley frowned. "And Kylie? Does Maddox believe she's telling the truth?"

Earl took another bite, swallowed. "I don't know about the new chief, but she kinda gave me the creeps. She came in voluntarily for more questioning. Sat there cool as a cucumber. Like she was glad Hank was gone.

No tears, no regret. Honestly, it was like she'd already moved on, ready to plan her next Tinder date."

Hayley stared into her mug. "So let's say she's lying. Or Chase is. Or Doug is."

Earl looked up.

"But then again, let's say they're not. What if they're all telling the truth?" Hayley asked. "What if they're all innocent? What if Doug's gun was stolen? What if Chase passed out before the shooting? What if Kylie did actually leave before it happened?"

Earl narrowed his eyes. "You're suggesting a fourth person."

"Someone we're not looking at. Someone no one saw. What if someone else was on—or near—that boat? Someone who waited for the right moment?"

Earl leaned in, dropping his voice. "You got a theory?"

Hayley shrugged. "Not yet. Just instincts."

He smirked. "You and your instincts."

"They're usually right."

He leaned back with a sigh. "Don't let the new chief hear you say that."

"I'm not planning on telling that man anything," Hayley muttered. "Not until I can prove him wrong."

Earl pushed his empty plate away. "You know this is exactly the kind of thing he warned you about."

"Too bad," Hayley said brightly, reaching for her own fork. "Because it's exactly the kind of thing I do best."

Chapter 10

Hayley pulled into the cracked-shell driveway in front of the Desmond house and killed the engine. The house sat back from the road, neat behind a row of clipped hedges and a broad, well-kept lawn. Hank Desmond had been the big man in Bar Harbor—his restaurant packed year-round, his barbecue sauce lining grocery store shelves across the state. The place wasn't ostentatious, but it had that polished, new-money shine, the kind that said success without needing to shout.

Hayley climbed the front steps and was just about to knock when she heard faint movement inside—quick footsteps, a *thump* of something being set down. The kind of scramble you made when you weren't expecting company. She knocked twice and waited.

The door creaked open slowly.

Kylie Desmond stood barefoot in the doorway in a loose gray cardigan and faded yoga pants. Her hair was pulled into a haphazard ponytail, and her eyes were puffy, rimmed red, but dry.

"Oh," Kylie said, blinking. "Hi, Hayley."

Hayley offered a soft smile. "Hi. Thought I'd check in on you."

Kylie nodded and opened the door wider. "Come in."

The living room was dim, all the blinds drawn. The only light came from a single lamp in the corner and the flickering screen of a muted TV playing a true crime docuseries. A half-empty mug of coffee sat on the edge of the coffee table, beside a box of tissues and a TV remote.

"Sorry about the mess," Kylie mumbled, gathering a blanket off the couch. "I haven't really been . . . motivated."

"No need to explain," Hayley said, perching on the armchair across from her. "You've been through a lot."

Kylie dropped onto the couch and wrapped her arms around a throw pillow, clutching it like a life preserver. "I can't stop seeing it. His body in the water. Just . . . floating. That apron . . ."

Hayley didn't say anything, just let the silence settle around them. She wasn't acting at all how Earl had described her cool, detached demeanor down at the station.

"One minute he's on deck, grilling pork butt, joking around, passing out beers . . . the next, he's gone." Kylie shook her head. "How does that happen?"

Hayley studied her. The red eyes were there, yes. But the voice was steady. The posture calculated. Her performance had a polish to it—less like a grieving widow, more like a woman who'd watched enough *Dateline* to know the part she needed to play.

"Have you been able to sleep?" Hayley asked gently.

Kylie shrugged. "Not really. Mostly I just stare at the ceiling all night and guzzle coffee all day." She gave a brittle laugh and sipped from her mug. "Cold again. I never seem to finish a cup lately."

Hayley let a few beats pass. "Do you want to go over what happened again? I know you told the police, but sometimes saying it out loud helps."

Kylie gave her a look. "You mean for your husband's column?"

"I mean for you," Hayley said. "I may not write the crime stuff, but I do like to get to the bottom of things."

She hesitated, then looked down into her mug. "We'd been drinking. Well, Hank had been drinking more. We grilled all afternoon. The ribs were practically falling off the bone. He was in a good mood. Loud. Happy. He was talking about that big distributor deal for the sauce. Huge potential. Big money, big future." She swallowed hard. "Then, later that night, right before the fireworks started . . . he went below to get more beer, and when he came back up . . . everything suddenly changed. He said someone had sent photos of me and Chase to his office."

Hayley waited. "And he confronted you?"

"Yes, it was like he had been setting us up all day. Waiting for the right moment to attack. He exploded. Screaming. Called me a slut. Said he was going to bury me and Chase, ruin us both. He said Chase would lose everything and I'd be out on the street." She shook her head. "But he didn't mean it. He was just blowing off steam. That was Hank. Big threats. Bigger bark than bite."

"But you left."

"Yeah. I needed space. I took the dinghy to shore." She looked up. "But he was alive when I left. I swear. I'd never seen him so angry. If I'd known that would be the last time I saw him, I never would have left in such a huff."

She wiped her eyes with a tissue, not a single tear actually falling. Hayley wondered how she had so quickly gotten her eyes to appear so red and puffy before answering the door.

"I made mistakes," she continued. "Chase being one of them. But I loved Hank. That big lug. He was my world. Life with him was never boring."

There was a beat of silence, and then Kylie's phone buzzed on the coffee table.

She reached for it. "Sorry, one sec." She stood and stepped just out of the room, still visible through the doorway. "Hello? Yes. This is she."

Her voice changed. The softness disappeared. Her tone sharpened like a knife.

"What do you mean we can't liquidate for at least sixty days? No, the restaurant's closed this week. But if we could start getting numbers on the retail side, the bottled sauce, projected Q-four revenue . . . Look, I need this to move faster. There's no point letting things sit—he would've wanted me to be practical."

She glanced into the living room and caught Hayley

watching her, then quickly turned away and lowered her voice.

When she reentered, her face was flushed, and her voice trembled again. "Ugh. Just . . . paperwork. Lawyers. So much to deal with. I don't even know where to start." She flopped back onto the couch, the overwhelmed widow persona fully reengaged.

Hayley said nothing. She just nodded slowly.

"I don't even know what's next for me," Kylie murmured. "Everything we built . . . it was all Hank's dream. I was just along for the ride."

"But you had your own life before him."

She smiled faintly. "Not much of one. He swept me off my feet. Took care of everything. I just . . . existed."

Hayley paused. "Why Chase?"

Kylie blinked. "What?"

"If you loved Hank, then why cheat on him with Chase?"

Kylie ran a hand through her hair. "I don't know. Maybe I was lonely. Hank was always busy—ambitious, always on to the next thing. I felt like a toy on a shelf. Something he could ignore when he didn't feel like playing."

"And Chase made you feel seen?"

"Chase was attentive. Flirty. There was chemistry. But that's all it was. Chemistry. Not love."

Hayley nodded. "And the photos? Any idea who sent them?"

Kylie's lips twisted. "No. But someone clearly wanted to blow up my marriage. There were a couple women in town—single or divorced—who hated that I was with Hank. Thirty years younger, blond, loud. I get it. But one of them remarried last year, the other moved to Michigan, so . . ."

"So probably not them."

"Probably not."

Hayley watched her. "Do you think Chase killed Hank?"

"No. I know he didn't. He couldn't. He loved Hank, too—in his own weird way. And he was blackout drunk. He doesn't remember anything. But that's not the same as guilt."

"You're worried about the new chief."

"I'm terrified," she said. "I think he's building a case against Chase just so he can wrap this up with a bow. Look like the big, strapping hero coming in to save the day for the small-town yokels."

Hayley's brows knit. "Was there anyone else . . . who might've had a reason to hurt Hank? Someone jealous of your marriage?"

Kylie hesitated.

"There was someone," she said softly. "Zane. He owns that scuba dive shop near the wharf."

Hayley's ears perked. "The one who takes tourists out diving past Bar Island?"

"We dated. Briefly. Before Hank. When I first came to Bar Harbor."

"What happened?"

"He got . . . possessive. Controlling. Would show up at my work. Follow me. He didn't take it well when

I ended things. I thought I spotted his boat in the harbor the night of the fireworks, but I'm not sure." She glanced out the window. "I wouldn't put anything past him." But her voice trembled—not with anger. With something closer to fear.

Hayley sat back, letting it all sink in. Zane. A dive shop. A man with access to the water . . . and the kind of experience that could make him invisible in it.

"Thanks for talking to me, Kylie."

Kylie gave a slight smile. "Better you than the walls."

Hayley nodded slowly, heading toward the door. She wanted to believe Kylie. She really did. But something about her—maybe all of it—just didn't sit right.

Not yet, anyway.

Chapter 11

Zane's Coastal Dives occupied a squat, shingled building that jutted out over the water. The sign above the door was shaped like a scuba tank, though the paint was faded and chipped from too many salty summers. A plastic skeleton in flippers lounged in a beach chair out front, sunglasses askew, holding a LESSONS AVAILABLE! sign.

Hayley pushed open the screen door, which let out a dramatic squeak, and immediately heard the slosh of water and someone singing—badly—to "Under the Sea" from *The Little Mermaid*.

How perfect.

A moment later, Zane himself emerged from a side room, dragging a dripping wet suit and flashing his trademark toothy grin.

"Well, if it isn't Bar Harbor's own Jessica Fletcher," he said, wiping his hands on his board shorts. "Come to learn the art of underwater espionage?"

Hayley gave him a bright smile, only slightly forced.

"Not today. Just thought I'd pop in and see how business was going."

"Booming," he said without hesitation. "Tourists eat this stuff up. I had an awesome season. Speaking of which—have you and your husband ever thought about getting your scuba certification together? We've got a couples package. Weekends. Includes gear rental, two tank dives, and I throw in a free underwater GoPro session. Memories for a lifetime."

"I'll run it by Bruce," Hayley said sweetly. "But actually, I was hoping to ask you a few questions."

Zane's posture shifted. Not defensive. Just . . . bracing.

"About what?"

"Hank Desmond."

He snorted. "Of course. Figured that was coming."

Hayley leaned casually on a display of waterproof phone cases. "You were in the harbor near Hank's boat the night of the fireworks, weren't you?"

Zane narrowed his eyes. "Who told you that?"

Hayley hesitated. "Kylie thought she saw you in the area."

Zane laughed—short, but not amused. "Yeah? Well, she's full of it. I was on my own boat, watching the fireworks, smoking a little weed. Minding my own business. Didn't go anywhere near the *Slaughterhouse*."

"But you were close," Hayley said smoothly. "Close enough to enjoy the view. Maybe hear something."

He eyed her, then relented. "Fine. I was in the general

vicinity. Doesn't mean I had anything to do with Hank's murder."

"No, but it does mean you were nearby when it happened."

He crossed his arms. "Look, I know people think I had some beef with Hank because of Kylie, but let me set the record straight—I was the one who broke it off with her. She was drama from day one. Hank could have her as far as I was concerned."

"Interesting," Hayley said. "Because she told me you got obsessive. Showed up at her job. Followed her around."

"She threw a rock through my shop window," Zane countered. "Cost me a fortune to replace. She's been playing the victim since the minute she moved here."

"Do you have proof?"

"No. Just instinct. And maybe the security camera was broken that week," he added, with an unconvincing shrug. "But trust me—I know it was her."

He studied Hayley's suspicious expression.

"Come on, Hayley, how long have you known me? I had nothing to do with that nasty business. I'm a pretty chill guy. Besides, everybody in town already knows it was probably Chase Wingate who plugged ol' Hank."

Hayley nodded. She wasn't buying it wholesale, but Zane didn't seem like someone capable of subtlety or stealth. Blunt force, maybe. But not subterfuge.

"If you're looking for more suspects," Zane added, leaning in, "you should talk to Roger and Nancy Larkin."

Hayley tilted her head. "Why them?"

"Because I saw them at the town office last week. I was paying off some parking tickets—my little protest against the greedy meter system. Anyway, they were fighting with a town council member. Real heated. Something about Hank trying to open a second Slaughterhouse next to their diner. They were pissed. Council guy said it was approved. Nothing he could do. Roger looked like he was about to blow a gasket. Said something about 'more direct methods' to stop Hank from taking over the town."

Hayley frowned. "That's awfully specific."

"I've got good ears."

"Zane, are you sure you didn't just overhear something and spin it into a grudge?"

"You can think what you want," he said, pulling out a laminated form. "But if you and Bruce want that scuba package, I can give you twenty percent off if you book today. Deposit's just fifty bucks."

"Tempting," Hayley said, turning for the door. "But I'll pass for now. I've got other fish to fry."

Zane groaned. "Leave the seafood puns to the pros."

Bruce was already seated at a corner booth in Fryer Side Chat when Hayley walked in, a steaming mug of coffee in front of him and his laptop bag perched like a silent third guest.

"Been here ten minutes and already insulted by a server," he said as she slid into the booth. "Apparently I look like the kind of guy who puts ketchup on eggs."

"You are."

"Not the point," he muttered.

Hayley noted he had already ordered. "Tight deadline?"

"Yeah. Column's due tonight. Writing about the new police chief and his very warm Bar Harbor welcome."

"Well, I'm glad you made time for lunch."

Bruce gave her a sideways glance. "I know you, babe. This isn't lunch. This is an ambush."

Hayley didn't bother denying it.

At that moment, Roger Larkin appeared with a plastic pitcher of water.

"Hayley! Bruce! What a nice surprise. Welcome!"

"We wanted to check out the new local gem," Hayley said smoothly. "You're getting rave reviews."

Roger beamed. "Wait till you try the bacon biscuit. Nancy's personal masterpiece."

Hayley glanced at her watch. "Getting close to noon . . . I think I'll go full lunch. That fried green tomato BLT I saw on the specials board when I came in sounds criminal."

"Breakfast for me," Bruce said, scanning the menu again. "You know I can't resist a stack of pancakes."

A crash from the kitchen made the counter guy flinch. Nancy Larkin stormed out a moment later, apron streaked with flour and gravy, and sized Hayley up with a look that could curdle cream.

"You here to eat or interrogate?" Nancy growled with a voice that sounded as if she'd been smoking since kindergarten.

"Can't it be both?"

Nancy squinted. "Your reputation precedes you."

"That's what they keep telling me."

Roger chuckled awkwardly and poured their water. "You want pie with that? Coconut cream just came out of the fridge."

"Let's see how lunch goes first," Hayley said.

Nancy crossed her arms. "We didn't kill Hank Desmond."

Bruce choked slightly on his coffee.

Hayley raised an eyebrow. "Funny. I didn't ask."

"Yet," Nancy said.

"We were on our boat, radio blaring, didn't hear a thing," Roger offered. "*The Daily Catch*."

"You didn't hear a gunshot?"

"I didn't hear my own husband when he said we were out of beer."

Roger nodded. "Fireworks were pretty loud."

Hayley sat back in the booth. "You were anchored pretty close to the *Slaughterhouse*."

"Half the harbor was," Nancy shot back. "You know how busy Frenchman's Bay gets on fireworks night."

"You had reason to be mad," Hayley said gently. "Hank's plans for a second Slaughterhouse . . ."

Roger and Nancy exchanged a quick glance, both caught off guard by how much Hayley already knew about their feud with Hank.

"He was going to run us into the ground," Nancy muttered. "Said it wasn't personal. That's always what people say when they're being personal."

"But you didn't act on it," Hayley prompted.

"If I'd killed Hank Desmond," Nancy said flatly, "I'd have done it with a spatula."

Roger laughed and gave Hayley a wink. "We're too tired to commit murder. Pie-making's enough of a killer."

Hayley smiled, but her mind ticked forward.

"See anything odd that night?"

Nancy paused. "Saw a kayak. Blue and white. Real sleek. The kind people like us can't afford."

Hayley's heart skipped. "Are you sure?"

"Positive."

Hayley exchanged a look with Bruce. "That sounds like Hannah Holloway's kayak."

Bruce rubbed his chin. "You think she just took it out to watch the fireworks?"

"Maybe," Hayley said, already forming her next move. "And maybe she saw something."

They finished their meal—Bruce humming over his pancakes, Hayley poking thoughtfully at her sandwich. When they rose to leave, Nancy waved them off with a grunt, and Roger handed them each a foil-wrapped slice of coconut cream pie "for the road."

As they stepped onto the sidewalk, Bruce turned to her.

"You going to talk to Hannah next?"

"Oh, absolutely."

"You're relentless."

Hayley adjusted her bag on her shoulder. "You love that about me."

Bruce smiled. "That—and your terrifying interrogation skills."

Chapter 12

Hayley wasn't much of a kayaker, but she was excellent at pretending to be one. Dressed in Bruce's old windbreaker and a pair of leggings she'd once bought for a "yoga phase" that lasted all of two classes, she marched into Tide and Trail Adventures with faux confidence and a reusable water bottle clipped to her belt loop for extra authenticity.

The shop was small but efficiently arranged, with waterproof maps pinned on corkboards and stacks of glossy brochures promising eco-excursions and "mindful paddling." A bamboo diffuser in the corner emitted the gentle scent of eucalyptus.

Behind the counter stood Hannah Holloway, dark-blond hair tucked into a braid, wearing a kayak club tank top that revealed deltoids capable of cracking walnuts.

"Let me guess," Hannah said, not even looking up from the clipboard she was marking. "You're here to reconnect with nature."

"Isn't that what we're all doing these days?" Hayley replied breezily. "Disconnecting from phones, reconnecting with ponds."

"Eagle Lake's not a pond."

"Close enough."

Now Hannah did look up. One eyebrow cocked so high it nearly vanished under the brim of her weather-beaten Acadia ball cap.

"You don't look like a kayaker."

"Well, I used to be one," Hayley said, tossing her hair. "Back when I was a teenager. I was practically a pro."

Hannah leaned against the counter. "And then?"

"Life got in the way."

"Right. And now you're here, trying to cram serenity into one afternoon."

"Exactly," Hayley said with a nod, ignoring the sarcasm. "While the weather's still cooperating."

Hannah narrowed her eyes. "You're here to ask about the fireworks night."

Hayley blinked. "Excuse me?"

"I know Zane sent you to the Larkins, who probably told you they saw me out in the harbor that night," Hannah said. "He called me as soon as you left his shop. Told me I should expect a visit from Bar Harbor's resident crime-fighting recipe writer or whatever."

"Island Food and Spirits columnist," Hayley corrected automatically. "There's a difference."

"Right. My bad."

Hayley sighed, busted. "If you knew why I was coming, why play along?"

"Because I wanted to see how you'd spin it. The fake nature quest was a bold move. Didn't think you'd go that far."

"You don't know what I'm capable of," Hayley muttered, but she smiled despite herself.

Hannah scratched her name on a release form and shoved it across the counter. "Let's go, then."

"What—now?"

"You signed up for a guided paddle, didn't you?" Hannah said, already reaching for her keys. "Time to reconnect with nature, Chief."

They loaded two kayaks into Hannah's beat-up pickup, the inside of which smelled faintly like sunscreen.

Hayley had just settled into the passenger seat when Hannah pulled out of the lot and headed west toward Eagle Lake.

"Why Eagle Lake?" Hayley asked.

"Calmer water. Less boat traffic. Lower risk of you flipping over and embarrassing us both."

"Comforting."

"Don't say I never did anything for you."

By the time they reached the lake, the late summer sun had reached that soft golden hour when everything looked warmer, more inviting. The water was smooth as glass, broken only by the occasional ripple of a duck or distant paddleboarder.

Hannah guided Hayley through a basic safety talk,

ignoring Hayley's repeated claims that she'd totally done this before.

Once in the kayak, Hayley discovered just how little she remembered. Her paddle dipped too deep, throwing off her rhythm, and within ten minutes she was drenched from the elbows down and moving in a wide, clumsy zigzag.

Hannah, paddling effortlessly beside her, watched with an arched brow and finally chuckled.

"You gonna make it back to shore on your own, or should I call the Coast Guard—assuming they even bother with lakes?"

"I'm just . . . acclimating," Hayley said through gritted teeth. She splashed her paddle again and overcorrected, tilting so violently to one side she let out a yelp and dropped an oar entirely.

Hannah doubled over laughing. The sound was sudden and unguarded—rare, Hayley could tell.

When she retrieved the paddle and finally found her balance, she let the kayak drift for a moment. Hannah gestured toward a clump of trees.

"Blue heron," she said, pointing. "Pretty common, but tourists lose their minds over 'em."

"They are majestic," Hayley offered.

"So is a good parking spot at the Shop 'n Save, but I don't burst into tears over it."

They drifted a little farther, the lake hushed around them.

When Hayley was sure Hannah had relaxed her

guard, she said, "So . . . you were watching the fireworks that night?"

"Yep."

"From where?"

"Up near the bluff," Hannah said. "I like to be alone. The harbor gets too crowded, and I don't like listening to people scream every time something goes boom."

Hayley nodded, pretending to accept that. "Funny thing, though—someone mentioned seeing a kayak out in the harbor that looked a lot like yours." She watched Hannah carefully. "Makes me wonder if you'd been around more than you let on."

Hannah's jaw tightened. "And I suppose you've heard about the dustup between me and Hank last year."

"My husband writes the police blotter. I hear things."

"Then you already know what you came here to find out."

"Humor me."

Hannah exhaled through her nose, clearly not thrilled. "Fine. Yeah. I showed up at his restaurant last spring. Yes, I had a gun. No, it wasn't loaded. I just wanted to scare the hell out of him."

"That's not usually considered a therapeutic strategy."

Hannah ignored that. "He ruined my summer. I started a BBQ cart. Not even that ambitious. Just a side hustle. I was trying to save for this kayaking expedition in Croatia. I've always wanted to paddle the Dalmatian Coast."

"That's ambitious."

"Yeah, well, dreams cost money. I found a good spot near the Village Green, did everything by the book, but Hank went and reported me to the health department. Said I was storing meat incorrectly. It wasn't true. Just a technicality, a refrigeration permit thing. But he had friends on the town council. One phone call and *boom*—permit revoked."

Hayley frowned. "So, that was it? He shut you down?"

"I lost my cart. My spot. My whole summer." Hannah dug her oar into the water sharply. "He didn't even try to hide what he was doing. Said he couldn't have amateurs clogging up his turf."

"Seems like he had a knack for making enemies."

"Yeah. And he always landed on his feet."

They paddled in silence for a moment. The sounds of the forest crept in—chickadees in the branches, the flutter of leaves in the breeze.

"So you were in position," Hayley said finally. "You know the harbor currents better than anyone. A kayak would've made a pretty undetectable approach."

"You think I shot him?"

"I think you wanted to."

Hannah turned to face her, eyes flat. "If I'd done it, I wouldn't have made it so sloppy."

Hayley didn't respond. Just let the words sit.

"Look," Hannah said, softer now. "I hated the guy. I wished he'd disappear. But I didn't kill him. I watched the fireworks alone, same as I always do."

"No one can confirm that."

"Nope. But I don't have a history of murder."

Hayley eyed her closely. "Why tell me all this?"

"Because I figured you'd find out eventually. And I'm not hiding anything."

"You think Chase did it?"

"Maybe. He had reason. I also heard the police are looking at that guy from Florida, Doug Marsh. But honestly? I wouldn't put it past Kylie."

"Why?"

"She's colder than people think. Everything's calculated. Even the crying."

Hayley filed that away. "Anyone else come to mind?"

Hannah hesitated. "No. But I hope you find whoever did it."

"Even if it wasn't you."

"Especially if it wasn't me."

They turned their kayaks back toward shore, the light fading into gold and then the first blush of pink across the lake. As Hayley struggled with her oar again, Hannah reached out to steady her boat.

"You're better at sleuthing than paddling," she said.

Hayley smiled. "And you're blunter than a butter knife."

They reached the truck, loaded the kayaks in silence. As Hannah tied down the last strap, she looked at Hayley squarely.

"I didn't kill Hank Desmond," she said. "But I'm not gonna pretend I'm sorry someone did."

Hayley nodded slowly, climbing into the passenger seat.

She wanted to believe her. Part of her even did. But she wasn't crossing Hannah Holloway off the suspect list just yet.

Chapter 13

Hayley's house on Glenmary Road looked deceptively calm from the outside. The white clapboard siding gleamed in the slanted late-morning light, the hydrangeas along the front walk had begun to fade to a dusty green, and a blue jay squawked from somewhere deep in the birch trees. But inside, it looked more like a conspiracy theorist's lair.

The dining room table had vanished under an avalanche of papers. Nautical charts, police reports (the public kind Bruce had passed to her), menus from Hank's restaurant, a printout of the tide schedule, a dog-eared copy of the Maine boating safety manual, and a bag of Goldfish crackers she was absent-mindedly crunching through while muttering to herself. She had a highlighter in one hand, a pen in the other, and a pink Post-it stuck to her cheek.

She hadn't slept much. She didn't even remember going to bed. Her last memory was tracing a red line from the cove near Agamont Park all the way to where the *Slaughterhouse* had been anchored the night Hank

Desmond was murdered, a theoretical kayak route someone could have used to slip in and out unnoticed during the fireworks show.

The doorbell rang.

Hayley startled, knocking over a pile of maps. Leroy barked from the living room. She stumbled to the front door, barefoot, wearing an old fleece over her pajamas.

Mona stood on the porch, holding a manila folder and a smug expression.

"Why do I have the feeling you haven't showered?"

Hayley stepped aside. "Because I haven't. Get in here. I need caffeine."

Mona followed her into the kitchen, flinching at the state of the place. A crusted-over coffee mug in the sink, two empty Diet Coke cans on the counter, and the faint hum of Hayley's overworked laptop still running on the dining room table.

"What is all this?" Mona asked, placing the folder carefully on the only clear corner of the table.

"I'm mapping water routes," Hayley said, pointing to a chart with several red and blue lines. "There are at least four possible approaches by kayak that most likely wouldn't have been noticed with all the chaos during the fireworks. If someone timed it right . . ."

"Jesus, Hayley."

"You think I'm kidding? I even factored in currents."

"Do you have a corkboard somewhere with string and thumbtacks?"

"Don't tempt me."

"Well, don't keep me in suspense. What do you got?"

Hayley circled a cove in thick red marker.

"If you launch from the cove at the base of Schooner Head, and the tide's pulling west—which it was that night—someone could've let the current carry them most of the way to the *Slaughterhouse* without even paddling. With the fireworks going off overhead and all eyes on the sky, no one would've noticed a kayak slipping silently through the shadows."

She paused, tapping her marker against the map.

"Of course, the best-laid plans . . . someone *did* notice. Zane. He said he spotted a kayak that night—thought it was Hannah's. That's how I even got on her trail. So maybe whoever paddled out didn't count on being seen. Or maybe they just didn't care."

Mona nodded. "Sounds plausible . . . or insane. I can't decide which."

Hayley nudged Mona playfully in the ribs. "So, did you drop by just to make fun of me or what?"

"Is it too early for a beer?"

"Yes."

"Okay, then." Mona sighed, opening the folder and sliding a few pages across the table. "I stopped in at the town office today and bribed Clara Rogers with fresh lobsters."

Hayley raised an eyebrow.

"Don't get all high and mighty. I didn't need to. Turns out the complaint was public record. Clara printed it out for me with a smile and a quote about transparency in local government."

Hayley picked up the report. The pages were thick with underlines and handwritten notes in aggressive block letters.

"Uncovered meat stored improperly." "No certified temperature monitor visible." "Improvised canopy potentially a fire hazard." "Unlabeled condiments."

"This is vicious," Hayley said.

"Legal overkill," Mona agreed. "Hank got his lawyer to help draft it. Look at the wording: 'flagrant disregard for municipal code.' No one talks like that except lawyers and town managers with superiority complexes."

Hayley scanned the list again. "She never stood a chance."

"Nope."

Hayley looked up. "She told me he got her shut down with a single complaint. I figured it was just a meat thermometer thing."

Mona shook her head. "Nope. He turned on a fire hose."

Hayley sighed, flopping back into her chair. "I don't know. Maybe she did it. Maybe she just snapped."

"What about Doug's gun? How does that fit?"

"It doesn't. That's the problem. Nothing fits. There's Chase, passed out drunk below deck. Doug, who supposedly had his gun stolen. Zane, with his own vendetta. Kylie with the dinghy. Hannah with a motive and the physical ability to paddle in and out. Not to mention the Larkins. And this whole thing is still a tangled mess."

Mona gently sat down across from her. "You're

chasing ghosts. Maybe it's time to let the new chief handle it."

Hayley didn't even respond. She just stared at her friend.

Mona threw her hands up. "Okay, okay. Stupid idea. What was I thinking?"

Hayley grinned grimly. "You've known me how long?"

"Too long."

They both laughed.

Mona stood and stretched. "I've got deliveries to make. Think you'll leave the house today?"

"Eventually. When Bruce gets home, I might put on pants."

"Progress." Mona chuckled. "I'm outta here. I'm gonna steal a beer from your fridge as payment for all my hard work." She ambled into the kitchen as Hayley shot her a look.

"I can see the face you're making behind my back! It's for later!"

She could hear the refrigerator door open and shut before Mona hustled out the back to her truck in the driveway, just as Hayley circled another area on her chart.

It was almost noon when Bruce finally came in, carrying a bag of groceries and looking slightly windblown.

"Hey, babe, what—" He stopped in his tracks, taking in the war zone that used to be their dining room. "Sweetheart, are we plotting a murder or the next season of *Survivor*?"

"Bit of both," she muttered.

He set down the groceries and walked over to examine the map.

"Are those tide calculations?"

"Yes. And current speeds. Also distance markers."

"Okay, that's alarming."

Hayley looked up at him. "I can't let this go, Bruce. I know I'm driving myself crazy. But it's like every time I scratch the surface, something new comes up. Zane saw the Larkins argue with the town council. Nancy admitted they were livid with Hank. Hannah had a motive the size of Acadia and the arms to match. Kylie's trying to act the part of a grieving wife, but it's clear that Hank's death is just a minor inconvenience to her, and Chase is still half-drunk and mumbling and lawyered up."

Bruce pulled out a chair and sat beside her. "So, what's your next move?"

"I don't know. But I'm starting to think there's someone else. Someone we're not even considering yet. And I'm going to find them."

He leaned over and kissed the top of her head. "Just try to eat something that isn't crackers."

"You're lucky I didn't start drawing crime-scene diagrams on the kitchen chalkboard."

Bruce grinned. "Let me know when you switch to dry-erase markers. I'll bring wine."

Hayley stared down at her map, the red line she had drawn curling like a fuse.

She wasn't going to stop until she reached the spark.

Chapter 14

Hayley could tell it was going to be a busy night the second she walked into the restaurant and was greeted by the sound of clattering silverware, the soft murmur of conversation, and the unmistakable *bang* of Kelton's elbow against a pan as he pivoted in the kitchen. Hayley's Kitchen was packed for a post–Labor Day Thursday evening, which surprised her. Maybe it was the warm breeze still lingering in the air, or maybe everyone was clinging to that last taste of summer before September truly set in. Either way, the dining room was full.

Betty, cheerful and efficient as ever, was running the floor like a seasoned cruise director, chatting up tables and gliding around the room like she had wheels instead of feet. In the kitchen, Kelton was barking out orders with his usual mix of charm and chaos, shouting, "Table five, fire the haddock!" one second, then apologizing to a sous chef for nearly elbowing them into a fryer the next.

And Hayley? She just stood there, holding her

oversized canvas bag, wondering what, exactly, she was supposed to be doing. This was her restaurant—her name was literally on the sign outside—but tonight, it was running just fine without her.

"Need anything?" she called toward the kitchen door.

Kelton poked his head out, a smear of something creamy on his cheek. "Nope. We're good!"

"You sure?"

"Positive. Go sit down, relax. You're making us all nervous just hovering."

Well, that was clear enough.

Hayley headed toward the small bar but paused when she saw Betty enthusiastically waving her over from one of the corner tables.

"Guess who's here for date night?" Betty stage-whispered.

Seated at the most romantic table in the house—set slightly apart from the others with a small hurricane lamp flickering between them—were Liddy and Doug Marsh.

Doug looked polished in a crisp white linen shirt, his tan sharp against the fabric. Liddy had on a navy-blue halter dress, her hair swept up in an easy twist that still managed to look deliberately stylish. She'd clearly made an effort.

Hayley smiled and gave a polite wave. "Don't let me interrupt."

"You're not," Liddy said, gesturing toward the empty chair. "Sit."

"I don't want to crash your—"

"He needs to talk to you," Liddy interrupted. "About something he told the police. Something you should know, too."

Doug looked mildly uncomfortable, the type of discomfort that made Hayley's curiosity spike. She slid into the open seat.

"We've got a great waiter for you tonight," Betty chimed in. "Brand new. He's nervous but sweet. He's been practicing his specials in the kitchen mirror for half an hour."

Doug smiled tightly. "Great."

Hayley waited for Betty to leave, smiled at Liddy, then turned to Doug. "All right. Let's hear it."

Doug glanced around, clearly waiting for the right moment. He leaned forward.

But before he could speak, a tall, wiry young man with an earnest expression and a black apron knotted unevenly around his waist appeared at the table with a notebook.

"Good evening, I'm Evan, I'll be your server. Tonight's specials include a lobster risotto with tarragon cream and grilled swordfish with a pineapple chutney—"

Doug blinked. "Actually, we were just—"

"And for cocktails," Evan continued, voice trembling, "we have a blueberry basil mojito that's been really popular, and a house-made peach bellini."

Liddy raised an eyebrow. "That sounds lovely. I'll take the bellini."

Doug sighed. "Martini. Gin. Dry."

Evan scribbled furiously. "And for you . . . ?"

Hayley smiled kindly. "Nothing for me, thanks."

Evan's eyes widened. "You're Ms. Powell . . . I mean—Mrs. Linney, or, I mean—uh—should I call you Ms. Powell?"

She chuckled. "Powell was my ex-husband's name. I kept it after the divorce so I'd have the same surname as my kids. Made everything a little easier."

Evan nodded quickly. "Right. Got it. Sorry, Ms. Powell."

"Just call me Hayley."

"Right, Ms. Powell."

Hayley suppressed another laugh as Evan cleared his throat and launched again into the specials.

But she held up a hand. "Evan. Breathe."

He froze.

"You forgot to write down our drink orders."

His face went pale. "Oh my God, you're right. I—uh—peach bellini and . . ."

"Martini. Gin. Dry," Hayley said, with a kind smile.

"Right! Okay. I'll go put those in. And . . . come back in a few minutes for your food order?"

"Exactly. Take your time."

Evan nodded, relieved, and disappeared so fast he nearly tripped on his own shoes.

"Poor kid," Hayley murmured.

"He's adorable," Liddy said.

Doug took a breath. "Okay. So. What I told the police is this: Years ago, at a barbecue expo in Florida, I was working as a sous chef. I created a dry rub—perfect balance of smoke and heat. It got a lot of attention. Hank was there, too, working a different tent."

Hayley nodded. She could already see where this was going.

"Somehow," Doug said, voice tightening, "Hank ends up entering the contest with my rub. Slaps his name on it, wins a damn award, and does a whole press thing about his signature spice mix. I confronted him; he laughed it off. Called it 'business.' Said I should be flattered."

Liddy made a face.

"I was so demoralized I left the industry. Went into accounting. I was humiliated."

Hayley winced. "So you're telling me Hank Desmond stole your recipe?"

"Yes. And the glory. And then parlayed that into his brand, his sauce line, the whole damn empire."

Hayley leaned back. "That's quite a motive."

Doug shrugged. "The man made enemies like he made ribs. Slow and messy."

Just then, Evan returned with the drinks. His hands were shaking as he set the martini down in front of Doug. A splash sloshed over the rim. Hayley quickly reached over, steadying the glass and setting it safely on the table.

"Thanks, Evan. We're good for now," she said softly.

He nodded, beet red, and backed away like he was leaving a crime scene.

Doug took a long sip. "Listen, I know how this looks. I had a reason to hate Hank. I had the means. But I swear, I didn't do it. I had no idea my gun was even missing. I keep it locked up in a safe at the rental I'm staying in—an Airbnb on Strawberry Hill Road."

Hayley tilted her head. "So, you didn't report it stolen?"

Doug shifted uncomfortably. "I didn't even notice it was gone until the police told me they found it on Hank's boat."

"Doug," Liddy said gently, "you need to be honest. If you're lying now—"

"I'm not," he said, eyes steady. "I swear."

Hayley studied him. His posture was open. His expression calm. A little too calm? Maybe. But his story rang with that odd little bell of truth, even if it came with warning chimes.

Doug excused himself to use the restroom, and once he was gone, Hayley leaned in.

"So. Thoughts?"

Liddy stared into her coffee. "Either he's telling the truth . . . or I'm about to end up in one of those Netflix documentaries. You know the ones. *The Tinder Swindler*, *The BBQ Grifter* . . ."

Hayley chuckled, but then grew serious. "Do you trust him?"

Liddy didn't answer right away. "I don't know. I want to."

They both watched as Doug crossed the room, waving politely at Betty, who gave him a thumbs-up.

Hayley sighed. "Well, for what it's worth, I believe

he's not lying. But I also believe there's a lot more to this story."

Liddy swirled her bellini, lost in thought. "If someone really did steal his gun and use it to frame him . . ."

Hayley nodded. "Then we're dealing with someone smart. And calculating. And close enough to know exactly where that gun was kept."

As the restaurant buzzed around them—silverware clinking, laughter bubbling from the corner booths, the kitchen doors swinging open and closed like a heartbeat—Hayley felt the familiar itch return.

It was always like this when she was knee-deep in one of her amateur sleuthing adventures. A tingling along the back of her neck, a low hum in her blood. There were more secrets to uncover.

She could feel it.

She always could.

This wasn't over.

Not even close.

Island Food & Spirits
By
Hayley Powell

Have I ever told you about the first time I met Sergio—the husband of my brother, Randy, and, oh, yes, our beloved chief of police? Let's just say I didn't exactly make the most graceful first impression.

It was one of Mona's legendary August BBQs, the kind that started years ago because we were all too busy in summer to see each other unless someone forced us to. Leave it to Mona to solve the problem by organizing an annual gathering where the only requirement was showing up hungry. It worked. Everyone came. And it was at one of these BBQs that I met Sergio.

Now, I knew Randy was dating someone. What I didn't know was who. And that was driving me absolutely nuts. Randy usually spilled his romantic secrets faster than I spill sangria on a white blouse. But this time? Nothing. Crickets. After some expert-level pestering, I finally wrangled a promise out of him that he might—*might*—bring his mystery date to Mona's.

So there I was, happily stuffing my plate with

garlic shrimp kabobs, grilled corn, and one of Max Bennett's famous blue cheese burgers (I wasn't about to risk those running out). I found a prime seat at a picnic table with a perfect view of the entrance, just in case Randy arrived with Mr. Mysterious.

And that's when it happened. Mouth full of burger, juice dripping down my chin, I looked up—and nearly choked. Walking in was none other than Chief Sergio Alvarez himself. Our new, devastatingly handsome chief of police. The man who had every single woman in Bar Harbor plotting ways to "accidentally" bump into him at the Shop 'n Save. Including, I'll admit, me.

Panicked but determined, I swiped at my chin, shoved the burger aside, and leapt up, waving both arms like I was signaling a rescue helicopter. "Yoo-hoo, Chief Alvarez!" I yelled, dignity be damned. Every woman within a hundred feet had the same idea, and I was not about to lose.

And then—he waved back. At me. My heart did cartwheels. I was so focused on Sergio's smile that I didn't notice Jon Hall's Labrador, Duke, sprawled out right in front of me. One second I was power-walking toward romance, the next I was airborne, arms flailing, before hitting the ground with a *thud* that rattled my teeth. The dog never moved. Didn't even react to me tripping over him.

Mortified, I squeezed my eyes shut, silently

begging the earth to open and swallow me whole. Instead, I heard a deep, commanding voice. "Everyone step back, give her some air!" A shadow fell over me. I opened one eye, and there he was: Sergio, kneeling beside me, asking if I was okay. He offered me his hand. I was seconds from swooning when—

"Hayley! Oh my God, are you hurt?"

My brother, Randy, appeared, shoving Sergio aside like a jealous bodyguard. He grabbed my hands, dusted me off, and launched into a full play-by-play of my epic pratfall, complete with hand gestures. Mortification complete.

But then I saw it. The smile Randy gave Sergio. The way Sergio smiled back. And suddenly the mystery was solved. Sergio wasn't waving at me because he thought I was cute—he was waving at me because I was Randy's sister.

Instead of being disappointed, I was thrilled. My brother had found someone wonderful. And even if I'd had to break my tailbone to discover it, I wouldn't have changed a thing. (Okay, maybe I'd change the part where I tripped over Duke.)

So, in honor of that fateful BBQ, I'm sharing two of my favorite summer recipes. One's a cocktail that soothes both bruised pride and bruised knees, and the other is for those shrimp skewers that nearly distracted me into face-planting in front of half the town.

Easy Lemonade Margaritas

(Summer in a glass)

Ingredients

3 tablespoons frozen lemonade concentrate
½ cup white tequila
2 tablespoons triple sec
1 cup water

Combine the concentrate, tequila, triple sec, and water. Stir until smooth. Pour over ice in two glasses and clink with your favorite gossip partner.

HAYLEY'S GRILLED SHRIMP SKEWERS

INGREDIENTS

1 pound large shrimp, peeled and deveined
2 tablespoons olive oil
3 cloves garlic, minced
1 teaspoon paprika
Salt and pepper, to taste
Juice of 1 lemon
2 tablespoons parsley (or cilantro, if you're feeling fancy)
Skewers as needed

Pat the shrimp dry. Mix together the olive oil, garlic, paprika, salt, pepper, and lemon juice. Toss the shrimp into the marinade and let sit 30 minutes. Thread into skewers. Grill over medium-high heat 2–3 minutes per side until pink with a little char. Sprinkle the parsley or cilantro on top and serve hot.

Best enjoyed with friends, sunshine, and maybe a reminder to always watch where you're walking—especially if there's a handsome chief of police in your line of sight.

Chapter 15

Drinks Like A Fish was unusually quiet for a Friday mid-afternoon. A couple of older locals sat nursing Bud Lights in the corner, engaged in a heated but hushed debate over the best clam shack in Hancock County. Hayley slid onto her favorite stool at the far end of the bar, where she could pretend not to eavesdrop while scanning the room for her brother.

Chelsea Mahoney emerged from the back with a clipboard in one hand and a frosty daiquiri in the other. Her ponytail was fraying at the edges, and a pencil was stuck behind one ear.

"I'm testing my daiquiri skills," she announced. "You're my guinea pig."

She slid the glass toward Hayley, who took a sip, nodded with approval, and gave her a thumbs-up. "Perfectly tart. And dangerously drinkable."

Chelsea grinned. "I'm calling that a win."

Hayley set the glass down. "Is Randy around?"

"Off today," she said, slapping the clipboard on the

bar. "He's knee-deep in cardboard boxes and travel-sized toothpaste. Brazil prep."

Hayley's throat tightened. "Right," she said, trying to smile. "Of course."

Chelsea paused, catching the flicker in Hayley's expression. "You okay?"

Hayley nodded, but her eyes stung. "I'm just being sentimental. I always thought we'd grow old and cranky together in Bar Harbor. Now he's flying off to start a new life in São Paulo. It's just a lot."

Chelsea softened. "I get it. You two are super close."

Hayley sniffed and took a sip of her drink. "He's my older brother, you know."

Chelsea blinked. "Wait—I thought he was younger. Like, two and a half years?"

Hayley gave a small smile.. "That's what the birth certificate says, but I've always insisted I'm the younger one for vanity reasons. Randy doesn't mind."

Chelsea laughed. "You're my new hero. I want to be your best friend."

"I have a long waiting list," Hayley deadpanned. "But I'll pencil you in."

Just then, a wiry man with a sunburned nose and a lobster trap tattoo staggered up to the bar, waving a ten-dollar bill like it was on fire.

"Raspberry schnapps!" he declared.

Chelsea didn't blink. "We're out."

"You were out yesterday."

"And somehow, we're still out."

He slumped onto a stool, muttering something about tourists ruining everything, then lapsed into a nap with his forehead on the bar. Chelsea turned to Hayley with a flourish and wiped her hands on a dish towel.

"Now that we've handled our most loyal regular," she said, "what's the word, Ms. Powell? Solved the case yet?"

Hayley sighed. "Hardly. But I've got a list of suspects long enough to fill a cocktail menu."

"Spill."

Hayley filled her in on last night's dinner with Doug Marsh. "He said Hank stole his dry-rub recipe, took credit at a barbecue competition in Florida, and ran off with the trophy. Not to mention all future profits."

Chelsea raised a brow. "And he just casually told you this? The guy whose gun ended up in the cooler on Hank's boat?"

"I know. Seems counterintuitive."

"Or really calculated," Chelsea said. "Maybe he thinks honesty makes him look innocent. Or maybe he's trying to throw you off his scent."

Hayley traced a finger through the condensation on her daiquiri glass. "He didn't strike me as the killer type, but that's the problem. I keep saying that about everyone, and someone did kill Hank."

Chelsea leaned forward. "Look, it sounds like Hank had a gift for making enemies. Wouldn't surprise me if one of them pushed back—hard."

Hayley frowned. "Why do you say that?"

"Let's just say I once went on a date with someone with a similar talent for ticking people off. He's lucky I only ghosted him."

Hayley perked up. "Who?"

Chelsea wrinkled her nose. "You're not gonna like it."

"Try me."

"Zane."

Hayley nearly choked on her drink. "Zane? Dive instructor Zane?"

Chelsea nodded. "He asked me out when I first moved to town. I thought, 'Okay, local, kinda rugged, not my type, but maybe he's sweet.'"

"And?"

"He spent the entire dinner ranting about some opportunity with Hank that went belly-up. Apparently, he pitched him a smoked seafood line, and Hank laughed him out of the restaurant."

"Is there anyone in this town who hasn't tried to launch their very own barbecue empire? Doug. Hannah. Now Zane."

"With me, he wouldn't shut up about it. He never let me get a word in. He was too busy fuming about how he was gonna be stuck giving tours to seasick tourists forever. I finally made an excuse and left halfway through dessert."

Hayley shook her head. "That's wild. And that was before you found out about Zane's thing with Kylie?"

"Oh, yeah. The cherry on top," Chelsea said. "Zane used to show up here and 'check up on her' like she was some kind of pet hamster. He didn't even drink. He just loitered."

"What do you mean, 'loitered'?"

"Stood in the corner sipping Shirley Temples like they were single-malt scotches. Eyes glued to her the whole time."

Hayley shivered. "That's more than stalker-adjacent."

"There was one time—I'll never forget it—he confronted her outside. Accused her of cheating on Hank, like it was any business of his. No names were said, but Kylie got in his face. She held her own, but he was furious. I told Randy about it, and he said he'd keep an eye out."

Hayley chewed her lip. "What if Zane was the one who sent those photos of Kylie and Chase to Hank?"

Chelsea's eyes widened. "I never thought of that. But it makes sense. Who else would've known?"

"He had the motive," Hayley murmured. "Hank humiliated him professionally. Kylie rejected him romantically. And now Chase is in the crosshairs."

"Plus, Zane's a diver. Knows the waters. Knows how to approach a boat without being noticed."

Hayley nodded slowly, gears turning. "It's just a theory. But it's starting to make sense."

Chelsea refilled her drink. "You know what they say. Once you eliminate the impossible . . ."

Hayley raised a brow. "You've been reading Bruce's column again."

"I skim," Chelsea said, grinning. "Now, finish your drink. You're gonna need the fuel."

Hayley glanced toward the front door, half-hoping Randy might appear with a box of mementos from their childhood. But the bar remained quiet, save for the snoring regular at the end and the *clink* of Chelsea's shaker behind the counter.

She took a slow sip of her daiquiri. Her mind swirled with suspects, motives, timelines. Doug. Kylie. Zane. The list was not shrinking, and the answers weren't coming any faster.

Somewhere out there, someone knew the truth.

Chapter 16

The dive shop smelled like neoprene and dried salt, a distinct combination of ocean adventure and mildew. Hayley stepped inside, removing her sunglasses as her eyes adjusted from the bright afternoon sun to the dim, cool interior. The only other customer in the shop was a lanky college kid trying to squeeze his size-thirteen feet into fins clearly meant for someone much daintier. He grunted and wobbled, almost knocking over a display of snorkel masks.

Hayley gave him a sympathetic smile and moved farther into the shop. Wet suits hung in rows like deflated bodies, dive logs and waivers scattered across the counter in plastic bins. Behind the glass case up front, there were waterproof cameras, knives, and a display of oddly expensive defogging spray.

She slid behind the counter quickly while no one was looking and scanned the dive logs. Sure enough, under the entries for the night of the fireworks, two tanks and one wet suit had been marked "loaned out."

No customer name.

Just a scrawled note: *returned late.*

Her pulse quickened.

From around the side of the building, Hayley heard the *hiss* of an outdoor shower shutting off, and a moment later, Zane strolled in shirtless, hair wet and slicked back, water glistening down his tanned chest. He spotted her immediately.

"Well, well," he said with a grin. "Didn't expect to see you again so soon. Come to sign up for that dive lesson I keep offering?"

"I was actually thinking about snorkeling," Hayley said breezily, pretending to examine a coral identification chart. "You know, something a little more . . . casual."

Zane stepped behind the counter and reached for a towel, rubbing it over his shoulders. "Snorkeling's for tourists. You want the real experience, you strap on a tank."

She raised a brow. "You offering me the full treatment?"

"Absolutely. First lesson's on the house. I already told you that." He gestured to a clipboard. "I've got a little time this afternoon. Let's get you signed in."

Hayley hesitated. "Is there a liability waiver involved?"

He gave her a bemused look. "Of course. This is Bar Harbor, not international waters. I gotta protect myself from lawsuits and overconfident townies."

She laughed but didn't miss the flicker in his eyes.

"So, what's your policy on returning gear? Let's say, for example, someone borrowed a couple tanks on fireworks night. Would they've needed to log it?"

Zane's smile faded. "Peeking at my dive logs? You're not really here for snorkeling, are you?"

"Curious minds," she said. "Your logs show two tanks and a wet suit checked out that night. You said you weren't diving. So . . . ?"

"I wasn't using them. Returned late."

"By who?"

He leaned on the counter, his gaze hardening. "Look, Hayley. I like you. I do. But you're not press. And you're not police."

"No," she said. "But I am persistent. I just find it odd that you failed to write down any names like all the other entries."

"It was a busy day, what can I say?"

His eyes flicked to a framed photo on the wall. Hayley followed his gaze—Zane and Kylie in wet suits, arms slung around each other, all sun-kissed smiles and summer flirtation.

"Happier times, I imagine," she said lightly.

"That was ancient history," Zane muttered. "She moved on. I moved down."

"Into her favorite hangout, stared at her for a summer, and tried to sell her new husband smoked haddock barbecue sauce?"

Zane didn't laugh. He opened a drawer and pulled

out a waiver form, setting it on the counter in front of her. "You want to dive or not?"

Hayley glanced at the paper. "What's included in the beginner's lesson?"

"Intro pool session, then a shallow dive in the cove. Some practice with your regulator. You'll love it."

She hesitated, then slowly reached for a pen. "Let's do it."

The pool behind the dive shop was surprisingly well-maintained, a rectangular stretch of turquoise bordered by cracked concrete and plastic patio chairs. Zane walked her through the basics—how to clear her mask, purge her regulator, signal when something was wrong.

Hayley bobbed in the water, bubbles rising around her as she practiced breathing slowly through the regulator. She wasn't a natural, but she got the hang of it, and Zane said she passed the beginner's test with "barely enough grace to keep a flounder afloat."

By late afternoon, they loaded the gear into Zane's beat-up Jeep and drove out to a secluded cove near Schooner Head. The trail down to the water was narrow and steep, flanked by scrub pine and wild rosebushes. Hayley carried her wet suit in one hand, mask and fins in the other. Zane had the tanks and gear loaded in a duffel.

"You're lucky," he said as they descended. "It's calm today. Visibility should be excellent."

"Great," Hayley said, trying to sound more enthusiastic than she felt. "What are the chances I run into a jellyfish the size of my torso?"

"Zero," he said. "But if one shows up, I'll be sure to push you toward it."

"Thanks!"

Zane winked at her. "Kidding. You'll be fine."

They suited up on a flat stretch of rock overlooking the cove. Zane helped secure her tank and adjusted the straps on her buoyancy vest.

"Regulator's here," he said, pointing. "Purge valve, alternate air source, pressure gauge. You're good to go."

Hayley took a deep breath. "And we're staying shallow?"

"Fifteen feet, tops. I'll be right beside you."

The water was cold but breathtaking. Once submerged, the world above vanished—replaced by a dreamscape of shifting blues and greens. Shafts of sunlight filtered through the surface, illuminating schools of tiny fish darting like silver confetti. Seaweed swayed like underwater dancers. A crab scuttled across a rocky ledge. For a moment, Hayley was enthralled.

She forgot everything—Hank Desmond, Kylie, even the air tank strapped to her back.

Then came the sputter.

Her regulator choked. Her lungs met resistance.

She tried again—nothing.

Panic surged.

She tapped the pressure gauge. It was flatlined.

Impossible.

She had checked it.

She reached for the alternate air source.

Still nothing.

The serenity of the cove evaporated. Her vision tunneled. She waved wildly, her eyes wide behind the mask, trying not to gulp water in a reflexive gasp. A scream bubbled in her chest.

Zane was just ahead, his back turned.

She kicked frantically, spinning in slow motion. The surface seemed far. Her chest burned.

She waved again—finally, Zane turned.

He spotted her flailing and shot toward her in powerful strokes, regulator already extended.

He shoved it toward her and jammed it into her mouth.

Air.

Sweet, blessed air.

He held her close, signaling for slow, steady breathing. He guided her upward, arm around her like a harness, careful to avoid rapid ascent.

They broke the surface in a rush of gasps and froth.

Hayley clawed off her mask, coughing and sputtering. Zane pulled her to the rocks, dragging her up until she collapsed, face to the sky, her chest heaving.

"What the hell happened?" he demanded, breathless.

She could barely speak. "No air. My tank—empty."

Zane stared at her, stunned. "That's not possible. I checked the tank myself."

"Well, it was dry," she rasped. "I almost drowned."

He ran a hand through his soaked hair, pacing. "Okay, okay—sometimes, if the O-ring isn't sealed properly, you can get a slow leak. It's rare, but it happens. Or maybe the valve wasn't fully open. But I double-checked everything!"

"You handed me a faulty tank," she said flatly. "That's not nothing, Zane."

His eyes snapped to hers. "Are you actually accusing me of trying to kill you?"

"I'm saying it's convenient. You knew I was asking questions. This could've been a warning."

He looked like she'd slapped him. "Seriously? That's what you think of me?"

Hayley didn't answer. She was too busy replaying the suffocating moment when no air came through the regulator.

Zane took a step back, jaw clenched. "You think I'm that unhinged? That I'd risk your life just to shut you up?"

"I don't know what to think," she said, her voice still shaky. "But if this was just negligence, that's bad enough."

"You've got some nerve," he muttered. "I saved your life."

She looked at him, soaking wet and fuming, and didn't say thank you.

Because something about the whole experience still didn't feel like an accident.

Zane packed up in silence, expression tight.

As they climbed back toward the Jeep, Hayley's heart was still racing—not from the dive, but from the realization that someone might be trying to scare her off this case.

If that was the goal, it had nearly worked.

But not quite.

Chapter 17

Hayley spotted Earl lurking behind the hardware store, doing his best impression of a man deeply invested in the workings of a busted vending machine. He had one foot propped on the concrete slab and a notepad in hand, scribbling furiously as he squinted at the soda slot.

"Let me guess," Hayley said, strolling toward him. "Vandals? Or did the machine just refuse to cough up your Mr. Pibb again?"

"Keep your voice down," Earl hissed, glancing toward the street. "You want to get me fired? Maddox has been patrolling this area like a bloodhound. And it's called Pibb Xtra now!"

"Apologies to the rebranding team."

"Don't push it," he muttered, eyes still darting around. He subtly handed her a brown paper bag. "Here."

Hayley peeked inside. A muffin—blueberry—and what looked like an official manila folder folded in thirds.

"You brought me evidence and a snack. How thoughtful." Then she grinned. "I'll make sure Mona hears about this. Anything to keep her from dumping you over the age difference."

Earl scowled. "She says I'm too young for her. Says she needs someone with more life experience and less enthusiasm for chicken wings."

Hayley grinned. "Well, she's not wrong on either count." She pulled out the folder and flipped it open. Her eyes scanned the report.

"You'll want the second page," Earl muttered.

She flipped it and found the ballistic-trajectory diagram. Her pulse quickened. The report detailed the angle of bullet entry—upward, from below the rib cage. The path curved toward the upper thoracic cavity, consistent with a projectile fired from below the victim's position.

"Which means," Hayley whispered. "the shot didn't come from another boat."

Earl nodded gravely. "It came from the water."

Hayley felt a rush of vindication and horror.

"Then it has to be either a dolphin with good aim or someone in a wet suit," Earl muttered, eyes still scanning the alley for any sign of his boss.

She gripped the folder. "Zane. Or Hannah. Or maybe someone else we haven't even considered. But someone used the harbor—the cover of fireworks and the darkness—to get close. What if they were waiting there the whole time? Just beneath the boat, ready to strike?"

Earl grimaced. "It fits. The upward angle, the chaos during the show, all of it."

Hayley looked back toward the sidewalk. "It had to

be someone experienced. Someone who could move underwater, unnoticed. Zane's dive logs show missing gear that night. But Hannah's kayak was out there, too. We just don't know when or where exactly."

Earl opened his mouth to respond—but the crunch of gravel cut him off.

A squad car rolled up in front of the hardware store.

"Uh-oh," Earl breathed.

Chief Caleb Maddox stepped out of the driver's seat, his tailored dark jacket crisp as ever, badge gleaming in the late-morning sun. He looked around, surveying the scene like a man who didn't trust anything that wasn't nailed down.

"Hayley, hide," Earl whispered harshly.

"What?"

"Behind the vending machine!"

"I'm not hiding behind a—"

But Earl nudged her back, and she ducked behind the bulky, sun-bleached soda dispenser just as Maddox approached.

The Chief studied Earl for a beat. "Why do you look so nervous?"

"I'm not nervous," Earl said, too quickly. "Just . . . focused. Serious case of vending machine vandalism."

Maddox frowned, then leaned slightly to the side, squinting toward the vending machine.

"Is someone hiding back there?"

Hayley realized she'd been holding her breath. She stood up slowly, brushing lint from her jacket.

"Hi," she said with an innocent smile. "Just running errands, had to make a stop at the hardware store, must have taken a wrong turn between screws and seed packets."

Maddox raised an eyebrow. "What exactly are you doing back there, Ms. . . . Powell?"

Hayley gestured toward the vending machine. "Uh—honestly, just taking a quick look. I heard about the damage and thought I'd see it for myself."

Earl nearly choked. "She wasn't helping. She just walked out of the store and wouldn't leave."

"Occupational habit of being curious," she added with a shrug.

Maddox narrowed his eyes. "What's in the bag?"

Hayley held it up, thinking fast. "Nails. I'm building a bird feeder. Ran out."

"Bird feeder?" His tone was skeptical.

She nodded enthusiastically. "I'm big on birds. I named a regular goldfinch visitor Goldie Hawn. She's very chatty."

A long pause.

"Well," the chief said at last. "Try not to contaminate the crime scene next time."

"Of course. Wouldn't dream of it."

Maddox turned back to Earl. "I expect a full report on this by tomorrow. I want names. Dates. Surveillance footage, if possible."

"Already working on it," Earl said. "Might be Cody Delvecchio or that Wilburson kid. They're always tagging things. Broke a bench outside the town hall last month."

The chief nodded, glanced back once more at Hayley—skeptically—then started toward the store.

Earl seized the opportunity. "Ms. Powell," he said loudly, "you are not a licensed investigator, and I've told you multiple times to stop interfering in police work. This includes soda-related offenses. You are not above the law."

Maddox, halfway through the hardware store's front door, turned and gave Earl an approving nod.

Hayley blinked. "Did you just scold me for credibility?"

"I'm trying to keep my job," Earl muttered. "You're a liability. Always have been."

She grinned, plucking the muffin out of the bag. "Then I'll just take my baked goods and go."

Earl rolled his eyes. "Don't let Mona know I got soft."

"Too late. I'm texting her a muffin emoji right now."

She sobered as she opened the folder and scanned the report again. "This changes everything. Whoever shot Hank was close. Closer than anyone realized."

Earl nodded. "Be careful, Hayley. Someone went through a lot of trouble to make this look like a drunken brawl gone wrong."

She nodded in agreement. "And I don't think they're done yet."

Chapter 18

The post–Labor Day lull had officially descended on Bar Harbor, casting a sleepy hush over the town's usual bustle. At Drinks Like A Fish, the only customers were a cluster of animated College of the Atlantic students playing darts. They were all fleeces and messy buns, with that particular brand of theatrical energy Hayley associated with theater majors or over-caffeinated podcasters. From her spot behind the bar, filling in while Chelsea was out, Hayley could hear snippets of their conversation: ocean currents, ecosystem shifts, something about algae—and a woman named Tina Whitmore.

Hayley poured herself a ginger beer and leaned against the bar, pretending to study the cocktail specials. The kids were loud enough to eavesdrop on without being too obvious.

"She was definitely off after that swim," one girl with purple streaks in her hair was saying. "I asked how it went, and she just kind of stared through me. Like she'd seen something."

"Came back dripping wet, pale as a ghost," a guy with a backward baseball cap added. "Didn't even towel off—just grabbed her stuff and left."

"She was supposed to take us out to Thunder Hole the next morning, remember?" another chimed in. "Never showed."

"Did you report this?" Hayley asked gently, moving closer with a practiced, disarming smile.

They looked up in surprise. One girl blinked. "Do you work here?"

"Just filling in," Hayley said. "I write the Island Food and Spirits column for the *Island Times*."

"Oh," the guy in the cap said slowly. "Isn't that a cooking column?"

Hayley nodded. "Technically. But I also occasionally investigate crimes."

This time, there were full-on blank stares.

"You probably haven't heard of me," Hayley said with a grin. "That's fine. My glory days peaked with the lobsterman who tried to fake his own death using a mannequin in foul-weather gear. The Coast Guard's still laughing."

A tentative laugh from one of the girls.

"I'm Hayley Powell," she said. "And what you were just talking about? This missing Tina woman? It could be really important."

A girl with a septum ring hesitated. "Tina Whitmore. One of our professors. We told the dean. She said it was being handled."

"Is it?" Hayley asked, her tone soft but serious.

They exchanged uneasy glances.

"Professor Whitmore never showed up for her field class," the boy said. "She was supposed to take us to Thunder Hole to collect algae samples and track ecosystem changes. Nobody's seen her since."

Before Hayley could ask more, the back door swung open with a *bang*, and Chelsea marched in, muttering under her breath and looking thoroughly unimpressed.

"You're back early," Hayley said, stepping behind the bar.

"Don't ask." Chelsea groaned. "He spent the first twenty minutes explaining how he was building a wellness app for cats. I asked what it did, and he said, 'Meditation meows and purring loops.'" She plopped her purse on the counter. "I think I'm officially done dating."

"Been there," Hayley said.

Chelsea noticed Hayley's expression. "What's wrong?"

"I think a professor from the college, Tina Whitmore, is missing."

Chelsea blinked. "Tina? Oh, wow. She hasn't been in lately, but she used to stop by on Fridays for a sauv blanc and kale chips. Always wore those sea-glass earrings. What happened?"

Hayley lowered her voice. "She went for a swim the night of the fireworks. Came back rattled. Then she didn't show up for her algae class. The kids over there say no one's seen her since."

Chelsea looked past Hayley toward the students.

"That's awful. I just thought she was busy doing professor things. You know, tide pools and ocean lectures."

"I've got to follow up on this," Hayley said, wiping her hands. "You're back in charge."

Chelsea gave a mock-salute. "Glad I left my date when I did. Could've been stuck watching feline yoga demos on his phone until midnight."

Hayley left through the front, stepping out into a brisk night. Instead of heading home, she walked the three blocks toward the police station, passing shuttered galleries, dim shop windows, and a pair of raccoons fighting over a discarded sandwich wrapper near the recycling bins.

Both Earl's cruiser and Chief Maddox's sleek black SUV were parked out front. That wasn't a good sign.

Inside, Earl was behind the front desk, flipping through papers on a clipboard and humming to himself.

"Be right with—" He looked up and groaned. "Oh, no. Why is it always you?"

"I need to speak with the chief," Hayley said.

"Nope. No way. He's not in the mood tonight, and I am not your sacrificial lamb."

"It's important. Tina Whitmore—"

"Go home," Earl hissed, leaning forward. "If he sees you here after hours—"

"Is that Hayley Powell I hear?" came a voice from the hallway.

Earl closed his eyes. "And so it begins."

Maddox emerged from his office holding a steaming

mug of coffee and his usual air of reluctant patience. "To what do I owe the pleasure?"

"I just came from Drinks Like A Fish," Hayley said. "A group of COA students told me that one of their professors, Tina Whitmore, went for a swim the night of the fireworks and came back rattled. Then she disappeared. She missed a scheduled class at Thunder Hole the next day. They say no one's seen her since."

Maddox raised an eyebrow. "We've had a missing persons report open on Professor Whitmore since the third," he said. "But this is the first we've heard about her being upset after a swim that night."

Hayley exhaled. "So you're investigating?"

Maddox nodded. "We are. But there's no body. No eyewitnesses. Just a professor who went to collect algae samples and never returned."

"She saw something," Hayley said. "Maybe something she wasn't supposed to see."

"We'll follow up with the students," Maddox said. "Thanks for the tip."

With that, he disappeared into his office, leaving Hayley standing there.

Earl gave her a long-suffering look. "I'm not going to lecture you about boundaries because Mona has already knighted you as the town's official amateur sleuth. But if I lose my job because of your *Murder, She Wrote* routine—"

"I prefer Nancy Drew," Hayley said sweetly. "Younger and hotter."

She exited into the crisp night air and followed the

slope of Newton Street to the Shore Path. The tide was high, and the rocks glistened under the moonlight as she turned the corner toward Randy and Sergio's seaside home. The windows glowed from within, casting warm, golden light over the front garden.

Sergio answered the door in an apron streaked with saffron and parsley.

"*Querida*," he said warmly, kissing her cheek. "You just missed Randy. He's out walking the Shore Path, getting his steps in after my paella."

"I knew I smelled saffron," Hayley said, stepping inside.

She could see boxes were stacked along the living room walls. Bubble Wrap, packing tape, and a half-filled suitcase littered the floor.

The air had that strange, heavy quiet of a home in transition.

"This isn't a social call," she said. "I think something bad has happened. To Tina Whitmore."

Sergio's smile faltered. "She's missing?"

"I think she witnessed something the night Hank Desmond was killed."

"Have you told Maddox?"

Hayley nodded. "He says they're on it. But I can't help feeling there's more to the story."

He rested a hand on her shoulder. "Then you'll find it."

"I'm going to miss you guys."

Sergio smiled. "We'll visit. And you'll visit us. It'll be like *Under the Tuscan Sun*, but with better cocktails."

She hugged him tight, then left and continued up the

hill toward Main Street and eventually her home on Glenmary Road. When she arrived, Leroy barked from the porch and scrambled to greet her as she stepped inside. Bruce met her at the door, already in sweats and a ratty T-shirt, with a stack of junk mail in one hand.

"Any messages?"

"Just an invite to a lawn-mower raffle and another flyer for a psychic reading in Ellsworth," he said. "Also, someone wants to buy our house for cash, sight unseen."

He kissed her cheek as she scooped up Leroy and carried him inside.

"You smell like saffron."

"Do you know a woman named Tina Whitmore?"

Bruce nodded. "She used to guest-lecture at the high school. Rolf Biggs, the science teacher, and my best golfing buddy, said she made plankton sound sexy."

Hayley didn't laugh. She dropped onto the couch beside him, her mind buzzing.

"What did she see that night?" she whispered.

Bruce wrapped his arm around her.

Leroy curled up at their feet.

Outside, the wind picked up. Somewhere in the trees, a bird cried out—shrill, sharp, and out of season.

Hayley stared out the half-open window, unable to shake the feeling that someone out there was still watching.

And waiting.

Chapter 19

The College of the Atlantic campus glistened under the soft haze of mid-morning sun, its oceanfront buildings modest yet elegant, tucked among pines and granite outcrops like an eco-conscious postcard. Hayley, dressed in her most "respectable investigator" outfit—clean jeans, a linen blouse, and her lucky clam-shell necklace—walked past the seawall and main quad toward the marine sciences building with a determined stride. A student on a long board whizzed past her. Another lounged barefoot on the lawn with a biology textbook propped against their knees, earbuds in and mouthing the lyrics to something that clearly wasn't a sea shanty. The campus had that mellow, post–Labor Day energy—school was back in session, but no one was ready to admit it yet.

Hayley hadn't set foot on the College of the Atlantic campus in years, not since a disastrous cooking demo she'd given as part of a local food sustainability panel where she'd nearly set the lecture hall's portable burner on fire. She could still remember the horrified face of the environmental sciences dean as her flambéed blueberry compote shot up toward the sprinkler system.

She found the marine sciences building nestled near the water's edge, a sleek, glass-fronted structure designed to reflect the surrounding bay. Inside, a sandy-haired student in a faded "Save the Whales, Eat the Rich" sweatshirt pointed her to the second floor. Hayley waited in a sun-drenched corridor flanked by posters of marine biodiversity and grainy underwater photography. A janitor buffed the floors with a machine that sounded like a whale giving birth. At precisely 10:03 a.m., a woman emerged from an office labeled DEPARTMENT CHAIR—DR. ELLEN BLODGETT.

Tall, angular, and exuding New England authority, Dr. Blodgett wore a crisp navy blouse and a frown that suggested Hayley had already overstayed her welcome.

"Ms. Powell?" she asked, as though the syllables themselves tasted like vinegar.

"That's me." Hayley extended her hand.

Blodgett shook it briefly, then turned on her heel. "I've only got a few minutes. This isn't a formal investigation, and I have actual responsibilities to attend to."

"Well, I appreciate you taking the time."

Hayley followed her down a hall lined with floor-to-ceiling aquariums, biting her tongue.

"I understand the police have already questioned

staff and students," Hayley said, trying to keep her tone conversational.

"They did," Blodgett said without looking back. "And we answered them. Exhaustively."

"Then I'll try not to be too exhaustive myself."

Before Blodgett could respond, they were intercepted by a sudden crowd of five or six students, among them the same fleecy, rumpled crew Hayley had overheard at Drinks Like A Fish. The girl with the septum ring gave Hayley a quick wave. The boy in the baseball cap held up his phone.

"Is it true you once solved a case involving a poisoned cinnamon bun?" he asked breathlessly.

Blodgett blinked. "Excuse me?"

"It's online," the girl said. "We were googling Hayley Powell after she left the bar last night. She's got a whole Wikipedia page. And an old podcast episode from, like, 2018—'Death of a Blueberry Tart.' She literally solved the cold-blooded murder of the town floozy, who was killed while she was picking blueberries! She was allergic to bees, and the killer injected honey into her skin cream, which attracted a whole hive, and they stung her to death! Isn't that what happened, Hayley?"

"Uh, kind of, but there was more to it than that," Hayley muttered, but the students ignored her.

The students nodded fervently, a few already starting to live stream the hallway drama on their phones for TikTok.

Ellen looked pained. "You do understand this is an

academic institution, not an episode of *Only Murders in the Building*."

"She's trending," the boy in the baseball cap said in awe, showing his phone.

Hayley bit her lip, catching Ellen's glower.

Another student jumped in excitedly. "Didn't you also crack that thing with the karaoke competition and the shrimp scampi?" they asked.

Hayley frowned. "That definitely didn't happen."

"But it says—"

"I think people are just making stuff up now."

A tall boy with film school energy and a lapel mic clipped to his hoodie leaned in closer. "Ms. Powell, would you be willing to come on my podcast? It's called *Murder Maine-ia*. I've been looking for a guest to talk about how small-town corruption intersects with shellfish crimes."

Blodgett massaged her temple like a woman fighting off an aneurysm.

Hayley raised her palms. "Let's all take a breath. I'm just here to look around Professor Whitmore's office."

"And she's got permission," the septum girl added. "My mom donated, like, a whole lab to this place. So . . ."

Blodgett's smile thinned. "Fine. Five minutes."

She unlocked Tina's door, and Hayley stepped into a room that felt more like a well-used cabin than a professor's workspace. Books and charts cluttered every surface. A framed map of the Gulf of Maine was thumbtacked to the wall beside a faded Polaroid of what looked like a lobster boat mid-haul. On the windowsill, dried sea glass sparkled like forgotten candy. A pressed maple leaf, faded but vibrant, was pinned above Tina's desk.

Hayley walked slowly around the room, absorbing the silence. There were no signs of struggle. No overturned coffee mugs. No scattered papers or broken lamps. Just absence. A life suddenly frozen in place.

Hayley moved to the bookshelves. Texts on marine chemistry, whale migration patterns, even a dog-eared copy of *Jaws* by Peter Benchley. Tucked between several volumes was a small, black velvet box. Hayley lifted it—and opened the lid to find a single shark tooth on a chain.

"A gift?" she murmured.

"We don't know," Ellen replied. "But it's not evidence of anything criminal."

Still, Hayley noted the dusty impression where it had sat—untouched for weeks, maybe longer.

Outside the office, the podcaster pressed his nose to the glass. "She's analyzing the tooth necklace!" he hissed to the others. "Classic Powell."

Hayley's cheeks flushed. "I didn't 'analyze' anything," she said firmly, closing the box.

"You're not helping," Ellen muttered through clenched teeth.

The students peered in from the hallway like spectators outside a candy store.

"Is it true you once found a body inside a fondue fountain?" the boy with the podcast mic asked.

"No, I did not," Hayley said.

The group murmured with admiration anyway.

Blodgett stood stiffly near the door, her arms folded. "You realize this is a distraction," she said.

Hayley nodded, still scanning the room. "Probably. But sometimes distractions can lead somewhere productive."

Blodgett stepped forward. "Tina was well-respected. She collaborated across departments, worked with harbor conservationists, even took students on overnight tidepooling excursions. She wasn't flaky."

"No one's suggesting she was," Hayley said gently. "But she vanished."

"She was also a little . . . solitary," Blodgett admitted. "She had friends, but she wasn't the faculty potluck type. Her absence is deeply troubling, and I wish I had answers. But letting civilians comb through her office won't produce them."

Outside the doorway, the podcast guy whispered to another student. "Oh, this is good. This is true-crime tension."

Hayley, trying to mask her growing irritation, offered a tight smile. "I'll wrap up."

The five-minute visit had already ticked past ten. She hadn't found a single useful clue. No notes, no letters, no hint of where Tina might've gone or what she might have seen that night after her swim.

One of the students held up a phone. "Hey, Hayley, quick question. Did you really find a killer by following a trail of spilled margarita salt across a dock in that oyster-shucking murder?"

Hayley blinked. "That . . . okay, that sounds faintly familiar, but I still think someone's embellishing."

"I knew it was real." The girl beamed. "From what I remember, the killer poisoned a margarita by soaking the sea salt in antifreeze!"

The crowd began debating which case was her best, but when someone brought up the fictional "Maple Syrup Heist of '09," Ellen Blodgett finally snapped.

"Enough," she said. "Library. Now."

The students groaned but slowly dispersed under her glare. Before rounding the corner, the podcast boy called back, "You still owe us an interview, Hayley!"

"Sure," she said with a wince. "Let me know if you ever solve the Mystery of the Missing Homework."

As the last of the voices faded, a quiet cough drew their attention.

A man in his late forties stood just beyond the hallway—tall, narrow-shouldered, with silver at his temples and glasses perched precariously on his nose. He wore a soft gray pullover and khakis, giving off the air of a pleasant weather forecaster.

"Peter Baird," he said with a gentle nod. "Oceanography. I just wanted to offer my help, if I can. Tina and I shared lab space last semester. She was . . . collaborative. Quiet, but thoughtful."

Hayley studied him. His voice was calm, his eyes kind, his tone perfectly professional.

"No enemies?" she asked.

He shook his head. "None that I knew of. She kept to herself but never seemed upset. It's all been very sudden. I hope she turns up."

"Thank you," Hayley said, her instincts pinging but not flaring. If he was involved, he hid it well. Just another mild-mannered academic in boat shoes.

Blodgett gave him a nod of acknowledgment and guided Hayley down the hallway and out through the double doors.

"You get what you came for?" she asked curtly.

"More or less," Hayley said.

They parted without further pleasantries. Hayley took a long breath as the wind kicked up from the shore. Her gut told her the cases were connected. Hank's murder and Tina's disappearance weren't random events. Something dark was churning beneath Bar Harbor's calm surface, and it had nothing to do with algae blooms.

When Hayley arrived home, Leroy ran to greet her at the door, barking like she'd been lost at sea for a week. His little Shih Tzu paws tapped on the tile, his tail wagging so hard it threatened to lift him off the ground.

Bruce stood in the kitchen, nursing a coffee and flipping through a catalog offering everything from lobster traps to rustic mailboxes shaped like moose.

"You're back," he said, setting the mug down.

"I'm back," Hayley said. "With absolutely no leads and a mild case of imposter syndrome."

Leroy circled her ankles until she scooped him up and carried him toward the living room, where Bruce followed and gently kissed her hello.

"Tell me what you found," he said, sitting beside her on the couch.

Hayley filled him in—Blodgett's resistance, the students' fervor, the cluttered but undisturbed office. And Peter Baird, the soft-spoken oceanography professor who seemed a little too nondescript for comfort.

"What's his deal?" Bruce asked.

"Too quiet," Hayley said. "He says he barely knew her, but he conveniently shows up just as I'm leaving Tina's office. And not in a 'just happened to be walking by' kind of way."

Bruce raised an eyebrow. "You think he's involved?"

"I think he's wallpaper. But sometimes the wallpaper's hiding a crack."

Bruce whistled. "That's good. I might steal that for the murder mystery I'm working on."

Hayley groaned. "Please don't. You've already got a main character based on me named Kaley."

Bruce grinned. "It's a placeholder."

Hayley didn't even smile. "So many suspects. Blodgett. Baird. Maybe even one of the students. And yet . . . no evidence. No motive. No Tina."

"But no body, either," Bruce said gently. "She could still be out there alive somewhere."

Hayley leaned her head against his shoulder. "I hope so," she said. "I really do."

Outside, the wind picked up, rustling the leaves that hadn't yet turned. Fall was coming—quietly, but with purpose.

And somewhere in Bar Harbor, a killer was still out there.

Chapter 20

The scent of garlic and lemon butter wafted through the Linney-Powell kitchen, a surprising turn of events considering Hayley hadn't lifted a single spatula all evening. Bruce stood at the stove, brow furrowed, wooden spoon in hand, stirring what appeared to be shrimp scampi over linguine. He looked like a man defusing a bomb.

"Okay," he muttered to himself. "Simmer, not boil. Simmer."

Hayley leaned against the doorway, arms folded, watching him with a grin that was equal parts amusement and admiration. "You know, my ex-husband thought saffron was a Fleetwood Mac song."

Bruce didn't look up. "And look how well that worked out."

"Right. He once tried to make chicken Kiev. I spent the next day clinging to a toilet and reevaluating my life choices."

He chuckled but kept his focus on the bubbling pan.

"Well, I googled 'Impressive Meals That Won't Kill a Food Columnist.' This was option three."

"I'm flattered." She stepped closer and inhaled deeply. "Is that . . . white wine? Garlic? Shallots? Bruce Linney, are you seducing me through gastronomy?"

He turned and gave her a wink. "You'll have to wait until dessert to find out."

They sat at the table Bruce had carefully set—real napkins, mismatched but charming dishware, votive candles in jelly jars. A small bouquet of daisies from the yard sat between them in an old maple syrup bottle. Leroy curled at Hayley's feet like a fuzzy footstool.

Hayley twirled a bite of linguine and took her first taste. Her eyes widened. "Okay. That's it. You're officially in charge of dinner every night for the next week."

Bruce beamed. "You're just saying that."

"I'm not. This is . . . better than the shrimp linguine at Café This Way. And they don't have to make out with you after."

"Yet another reason I win."

They toasted with glasses of pinot grigio. The air outside had cooled since sunset. Jazz played softly from the Bluetooth speaker, Ella Fitzgerald crooning about moonlight and love.

Bruce reached across the table and took her hand. "Tell me you're not thinking about the case."

Hayley tried.

She really did.

But the furrow in her brow gave her away.

"It's date night, babe. We agreed."

"I know, I know. You're right. I'm a terrible wife."

"No, you're just a distracted wife."

"Fine. One question," she said. "Then we talk about literally anything else."

He raised an eyebrow. "Just one?"

"Ish." She leaned back. "Zane's looking guiltier by the minute. The dive logs, his proximity on the night of the fireworks, his evasiveness when I asked about the missing wet suit gear . . ."

Bruce twirled his fork. "You still suspect the Larkins?"

"The Larkins had every reason to resent Hank, but that doesn't make them murderers. Plus, given what we know about the bullet's trajectory, they couldn't have fired the shot from their boat. Hannah Holloway? Pretty much the same deal. She was bitter, not bloodthirsty."

"And Doug Marsh?"

Hayley frowned. "He worries me. Nobody knows much about him. He's charming, handsome, a spice merchant on the side when he's not doing your taxes, apparently. But Liddy barely knows the guy. It's a classic Lifetime movie setup."

Bruce sipped his wine. "I spoke to the county DA."

Hayley sat upright. "You what?"

"Casual conversation. At the club. He said they're putting together a case against Chase Wingate. They want something clean. Solid. Stamp it solved and move along."

"Of course they do." Hayley stabbed at her linguine.

"He's rich, powerful, and despised by half the town. That's easy math for a prosecutor."

"Do you think Chase is capable of murder?"

"Sure. But I don't think he pulled the trigger. His brand of cruelty is more . . . drawn out. Calculated. He's more of a killer in the boardroom as opposed to on a boat."

"Then who?"

She sighed. "Doug. Or Zane. But I keep circling back to Tina Whitmore. Her disappearance . . . it's connected. I feel it."

Bruce pushed his plate aside and leaned forward. "Just promise me one thing."

"Anything."

"Don't tell any of this to Liddy. She's already fragile. You cast one shadow over her new romance, and she'll never forgive you."

Hayley held up her hands. "It's not like she isn't already painfully aware of the suspicion circling around him, but I worry she may turn a blind eye to what she doesn't want to see. And that could be dangerous."

Bruce stood and extended his hand. "Okay. Discussion over. It's time for the next phase of date night."

She let him pull her into the living room, where the fire was already crackling in the fireplace. Leroy padded after them, plopping into his usual spot on the throw rug with a satisfied grunt. Bruce dimmed the lights, and they collapsed onto the couch, the kind of old, overstuffed furniture piece that remembered all their seasons together.

"You cooked," she whispered, pulling Bruce close. "Now I clean."

"Not tonight." He kissed her neck. "Tonight, you just . . . relax."

They kissed slowly, melting into each other. Hayley closed her eyes, letting go of everything but the warmth of Bruce's hands, the soft jazz playing in the background, and the rhythmic crackle of the fire. The world narrowed to that moment.

Until the police scanner on top of the fridge jolted them back into reality.

"All units respond—Otter Cliffs. Female, partially submerged. Possible drowning victim. DOA. Repeat, female, wet suit—"

Hayley sat up, heart pounding. "Oh, no."

Bruce was already grabbing his coat. "Let's go."

Hayley turned to Leroy, who barked at the rising tension. "Stay. Good boy. We'll be back soon."

She scooped him up and set him gently in his favorite doggie bed, giving him a treat and a scratch behind the ears. He whined but settled.

The drive to Otter Cliffs was a blur of winding roads, sea mist, and sirens growing louder with every turn. When they arrived, the cliffs were illuminated by a staccato of red and blue lights. Park rangers and first responders buzzed around the scene like a swarm of hornets. Yellow tape fluttered at the perimeter, barely holding back the chaos.

Hayley jumped out before Bruce had even parked. She rushed toward the commotion, but Chief Caleb Maddox intercepted her.

"No."

"Caleb, I'm press—"

"You're a food and cocktail columnist."

"With a long history of investigating crimes in this town!"

"I'm not playing this game with you tonight."

Bruce jogged up behind them, flashing his press badge. "Bruce Linney, *Island Times*."

Maddox exhaled sharply. "Fine. You can cross."

Hayley gaped. "Oh, come on!"

"He's the crime reporter," Maddox said, lifting the tape. "You are not."

Bruce gave her a sympathetic look and ducked underneath.

Hayley clenched her fists. "Sexist p—"

Maddox arched an eyebrow. "I'd be real careful about what word you say next."

Hayley mimed zipping her lips shut.

Earl appeared beside her, exhaustion evident in every line of his face. "Don't do it."

"Do what?"

"Whatever plan you're forming. Stop it. Maddox will fire me, and Mona will dump me."

Hayley sighed and stepped back.

From behind the tape, she caught glimpses of the body.

She knew in her gut it was Tina.

Her wet suit was torn across the chest and side, her mask askew, the plastic visor cracked in two. Her pale arm lay twisted unnaturally beside her. A female forensic tech knelt beside her, snapping photos, while another carefully bagged seaweed-slick evidence.

Bruce conferred with someone near the body, nodding solemnly.

Hayley strained to hear.

"She was a strong swimmer," a ranger said.

"Too strong to drown here," Bruce replied. "This isn't just a slip on the rocks."

Hayley turned to Earl. "You heard that, right?"

He groaned. "Don't quote me. Don't even look at me."

The medical examiner stepped back from the body and addressed Chief Maddox. "Clean tear along the side of the wet suit. Not from a rock. Possibly a knife or other tool. Arm bruising—narrow, elongated. Like grip marks."

Hayley's heart thudded. "She was attacked."

Maddox's expression didn't change. "Or she got tangled on something. Rope. Driftwood. It's not conclusive."

"She didn't deserve this," Hayley whispered.

Earl stared out at the crashing surf. "Nobody does."

Bruce returned, face pale. "It's her. It's Tina."

Hayley nodded, arms wrapped tightly around her middle. "She knew something. Saw something. And now she's gone."

They stood in silence for a long moment, watching the forensics team slowly zip the body into a bag. The *hiss* of the tide, the *click* of cameras, and the rustle of nylon punctuated the night.

As they walked back to the car, the cold wind off the Atlantic pushed hard at their backs, as if hurrying them along.

"She didn't drown," Hayley said quietly. "Someone made sure she'd never tell what she saw."

Bruce opened the passenger door for her. "Then we'll find out who."

Island Food & Spirits
By
Hayley Powell

There is nothing quite like summer in Bar Harbor, Maine. After months of shoveling snow, layering sweaters, and wondering if my car will ever start again, the first warm day of June feels like a national holiday. Sweaters come off, flip-flops come out, and grills emerge from garages and sheds, ready to be fired up.

Now, when I was married to my first husband, Danny, he was always in charge of the grill. Which was fine with me. Charcoal and propane? Not my thing. I was happy to leave that particular fire hazard in his hands.

But then we divorced, and I suddenly realized that if I ever wanted to enjoy a grilled burger or chicken again, I was going to have to conquer my fear and learn to do it myself.

So I did what any sensible woman would do: I invited Mona and Liddy over for moral support, stocked up on vodka, and announced I would be hosting my first-ever solo BBQ. Armed with chicken marinating in the fridge and pitchers of Adult Iced Tea cocktails, I tied on my brand-new apron that read QUEEN OF THE GRILL. Spoiler alert: The apron lied.

Mona offered to help get the fire started, but I waved her off with the false confidence of someone about to make a very big mistake. "If Danny can light a grill," I said, "then so can I."

Step one: charcoal. My logic was simple—more charcoal equals more heat. So I dumped the entire bag into the grill. Step two: lighter fluid. Since I had a mountain of charcoal, I figured the whole bottle of lighter fluid would be appropriate.

Reader, it was not.

I struck a match, tossed it in, and for a second—nothing. Then came a *whoosh* and a roar like a dragon auditioning for a Hollywood blockbuster. Flames shot so high I was pretty sure I'd just signaled the International Space Station.

I froze. Mona and Liddy did not. Mona tackled me to the ground and rolled me back and forth like I was a flaming rotisserie chicken, while Liddy grabbed the garden hose and doused the inferno. After what felt like hours, the flames subsided, Mona stopped rolling me, and Liddy collapsed in the grass, soaked and panting.

"See?" I said weakly. "It could have been worse."

"Say that again after you look in a mirror," Liddy croaked.

I stumbled inside and found one. The sight that greeted me was . . . alarming. My hair, my eyebrows, my arm fuzz—singed to oblivion. I looked like a startled poodle that had lost a fight with a blowtorch. Hats became my go-to accessory for months.

These days, I'm a much better (and safer) griller, though I'm still perfectly happy to hand the tongs to someone else and supervise from a safe distance—with a cocktail in hand, of course.

Speaking of cocktails, here's the recipe for the Adult Iced Tea that kept Mona and Liddy calm enough not to kill me after I'd nearly burned down the yard, followed by one of my all-time favorite chicken recipes—best made with less lighter fluid.

ADULT ICED TEA

INGREDIENTS

2 ounces vodka
1 ounce lemon juice
½ ounce simple syrup
4 ounces iced tea

Fill a tall glass with ice. In a cocktail shaker, combine the vodka, lemon juice, and simple syrup. Shake well and strain into the glass. Top with the iced tea, stir, and serve. Bonus points if you enjoy it before attempting to light a grill.

GRILLED HONEY GARLIC CHICKEN THIGHS

INGREDIENTS

¼ cup honey
¼ cup soy sauce
2 tablespoons apple cider vinegar
1 tablespoon minced garlic
1 teaspoon ground ginger
¼ teaspoon pepper
¼ teaspoon red pepper flakes (optional)
2 pounds boneless, skinless chicken thighs
3 tablespoons olive oil

Whisk together the honey, soy sauce, vinegar, garlic, ginger, pepper, and red pepper flakes. Place the chicken in a resealable bag, pour the marinade over it, and refrigerate at least 1 hour (or up to 6).

Preheat the grill to medium-high, oil the grates, and grill chicken 7–8 minutes per side until cooked through (165°F). Let rest 5 minutes before serving.

Serve with your favorite sides, a tall glass of Adult Iced Tea, and a solemn vow never to use an entire bottle of lighter fluid at one time again.

Chapter 21

Bruce had tied the kayak to the roof of the Subaru earlier that morning, planning to take it out to Eagle Lake after work. But Hayley hovered near the door now, purse slung over one shoulder, her keys jangling.

"You're taking the car, aren't you?" Bruce asked, glancing up from his laptop at the kitchen table, looking every bit the weekend adventurer in board shorts, hiking sandals, and a BAR HARBOR OR BUST T-shirt he swore was ironic.

"I just need to run a quick errand," she said, trying to sound breezy. "I'll have it back in time for your paddle."

He gave her a look. "Does this errand involve tailing suspects?"

"Not necessarily."

"Hayley."

She stopped, turned. "It's just . . . Zane's acting strange. Jumpy. Cagey. He practically runs in the other direction when I say hi."

Bruce sighed. "You're not even sure he's guilty."

"I know. That's what's driving me crazy. He could be innocent. Just scared because he looks suspicious. But if he's guilty . . . then I need to find out before someone else ends up like Hank. Or Tina."

Bruce closed his laptop. "You could be writing about cocktails, you know. Seasonal garnishes. Clam dip tips."

"You love that I'm like this," she said, smiling.

"You're obsessed."

"Pot, meet kettle," Hayley said. "You've been 'working on your column' for days, which is clearly code for 'writing a thinly veiled crime novel starring a version of me who wears less makeup and makes better choices.'"

"It's not a novel," Bruce muttered, looping the straps together. "It's a long-form opinion piece with scenes."

Hayley kissed his cheek. "Mmm-hmm. And I'm not investigating anything. I just happen to be driving in the same direction as a very suspicious man with access to underwater gear."

She winked, grabbed her bag, and headed out.

As expected, Zane's Jeep was parked out front when she arrived at the dive shop. She pulled into a spot across the street, pretending to scroll through her phone while watching through her sunglasses. A few minutes later, he emerged, carrying a duffel bag and a clipboard. He locked the door behind him, threw the bag into his Jeep, and peeled out of the lot.

Hayley followed at a discreet distance.

She wasn't sure Zane was guilty—he might just be terrified. If people believed he was a suspect, he could act guilty even if he wasn't. But that didn't mean she was going to stop following him.

Zane drove through town and took a left down Bay View Street, pulling up outside the Desmond home. The house looked shuttered from the road, its glossy front door closed tight and the porch empty.

He knocked anyway.

When no one answered, he knocked again—harder this time. He pressed his forehead against the door for a moment, then turned and kicked at a flowerpot.

She recognized the tension in his shoulders. This wasn't about logistics or business. It was personal. Zane stood on the porch for a long moment, then turned and stalked off, muttering to himself.

Still holding on, Hayley thought.

He wasn't over Kylie.

Despite everything.

Maybe losing her on top of being accused of murder was pushing him over the edge.

He got back into his Jeep and peeled off toward Main Street.

Hayley followed at a safe distance. Zane spotted Kylie's blue hybrid parked in front of Drinks Like A Fish and double-parked behind her.

Hayley parked across the street in front of the Criterion Theatre, unbuckled her seat belt. She paused for a second, catching sight of Zane outside the bar first—fidgeting, gathering his courage, bouncing on the balls of his feet. Then he pulled the handle of the door with dramatic force and went inside.

Hayley hopped out of her car and had barely stepped into the crosswalk when she nearly got flattened by a cherry-red Buick with a bobbing Virgin Mary on the dash.

"Mrs. Dunphey!" Hayley yelped as she jumped back onto the sidewalk. "Are you out of your—"

"Oh, hi, Mona!" called Mrs. Dunphey, waving cheerfully from the driver's seat. She was ninety-three, wore enormous sunglasses, and steered like a woman possessed by speed and limited depth perception.

Hayley approached the window. "Mrs. Dunphey, you nearly mowed me down."

"I have perfect, twenty-twenty vision." She sniffed. "And that's a lovely blouse, Mona. You've lost weight."

As she hit the gas, Hayley shouted after her, "I'm not Mona! And maybe it's time for an eye test!"

The Buick puttered off, turn signal blinking for three blocks straight.

Shaking her head, Hayley crossed the street and slipped into Drinks Like A Fish. Zane was already mid-explosion at the back table, facing Kylie and—Hayley's stomach tightened—Chase Wingate. Chase had one arm slung over the back of Kylie's chair, the other nursing a pint of some overhyped craft beer. He looked like he owned the place.

Zane hovered menacingly over them. "You're seriously slumming with Prince Trust Fund here?"

Kylie sighed. "Zane. No."

"I thought we were—"

"We're not anything," Kylie snapped. "We ended things. Ages ago. And I moved on. Why can't you?"

Chase raised his glass. "Look, beach boy, don't get your scuba tank in a twist."

"You don't care about her," Zane spat. "You want what Hank had—and now he's conveniently out of the way."

Kylie rolled her eyes. "Zane—"

"You think I don't see it?" Zane's voice was rising. "You're using him. And he's letting you. That's what you do, right, Kylie? You follow the money."

Kylie didn't flinch. "And yet you're still obsessed with me. What does that say?"

Zane flicked his wild eyes toward Chase. "And you—you're not fooling anyone. You think nobody sees through your smarmy act?"

"I'm just here enjoying a drink with a beautiful woman. Why don't you go pretend you're in *Point Break* somewhere else?"

Hayley tensed, ready to intervene. Zane stepped forward, eyes blazing.

"You killed him, didn't you?" Zane spat. "You wanted Kylie for yourself, and so you got rid of Hank."

Chase's smile didn't budge. "Prove it."

"Unless . . ." Zane's jaw flexed. He glared at Kylie. "Unless you're in on it, too."

Chase laughed. "Now, that's entertaining."

Without warning, Kylie picked up her drink and splashed it in Zane's face. "Don't you ever say that to me again."

Zane recoiled, sputtering, fists clenched.

Hayley tensed. This was about to go sideways.

Chelsea appeared out of nowhere like a referee in heels. "Hey there, Captain Wet Wipes," she said brightly to Zane. "You planning to order something? Or are we loitering with intent?"

Zane threw down a napkin, turned on his heel, and stormed out of the bar.

As he left, Chelsea looked over and spotted Hayley. "You okay?"

"I've been better," Hayley said.

"Jack and Coke on the house?"

"Rain check."

Hayley exited the bar quickly, just in time to see Zane slam his Jeep door and take off down the street again. Hayley followed as he drove along the coastal road into Acadia National Park and swung into the public lot near Thunder Hole. He hoisted a dive bag over his shoulder and disappeared down the path that curved toward the cliffs.

Hayley parked at the far end and lifted Bruce's kayak off the roof rack. It was clumsy, heavy, and probably not built for stealth, but it was all she had. She locked the car, grabbed her paddle, and made her way down to the shoreline.

The sky was already shifting to late-afternoon gold, the waves churning in slow, foamy slaps against the jagged rocks. Zane had vanished from view, but she noticed damp footprints on the granite—then caught the unmistakable glint of a mask just before a figure slipped beneath the water.

She counted thirty seconds.

Then a minute.

Then five.

He wasn't coming back up.

Hayley dragged the kayak to the edge of the surf. She wobbled as she climbed in, nearly tipping it on the first try.

"Get a grip," she muttered, bracing with the paddle. She pushed off, dipping the oar in and paddling along the shoreline.

She fought the current as the kayak spun left and then veered right. One wave slapped the front hard, and she shrieked as water splashed over the bow.

"This was a terrible idea," she grunted, adjusting her grip. "You're not an action hero, Hayley."

Eagle Lake had been a breeze compared to this. The wind pushed hard, the current tugged, and her paddle technique was—generously speaking—haphazard. She spun in a wide circle, nearly capsized, and at one point smacked her own forehead with the paddle.

"Yes, this was definitely a big mistake," she hissed, salt spray hitting her face.

But then she saw it—a narrow break in the rocks ahead. A sliver of black between jagged granite walls.

She angled toward it, muscles burning, fingers aching.

The kayak scraped through the tight passage and emerged into a hidden cave.

Inside, it was eerily quiet. The cave ceiling loomed

above her, slick with condensation. She spotted a ledge and paddled closer.

Pulling herself out of the kayak, she saw evidence of recent use: two air tanks, one standing upright, the other still damp. A crumpled blanket. Protein bar wrappers. A phone in a waterproof case. Someone had been using this spot as a base—possibly for weeks.

She picked up the phone case.

Aqua-blue cover.

Initials *TW*.

Tina Whitmore.

Could this phone belong to Tina Whitmore?

Then she heard it.

Splash.

Footsteps.

Hayley froze.

A figure emerged from the far end of the cave. Fully suited in black neoprene, dive mask still on, fins dragging as he stepped onto the stone.

Hayley crouched behind a boulder, pressing herself into the shadow, her heart hammering like a bass drum.

The figure moved with deliberate care, peeling off his gloves, exhaling loudly through the regulator. Hayley crouched, trying not to breathe, but her foot slipped on a slick patch of rock and dislodged a pebble, which clattered across the stone floor.

The diver stopped.

He turned toward the sound, head tilted.

Hayley pressed herself flat against the rock, trying to disappear.

She could hear his breathing now, the slow in-and-out *hiss* of oxygen.

The sound grew louder.

Closer.

She squeezed her eyes shut.

Don't move.

The footsteps stopped inches away. She could see the rubber edge of a fin.

Then, mercifully, a distraction—something small and skittering across the cave floor. A crab, maybe.

The diver turned, stared at it for a moment, then slowly retreated.

Hayley stayed frozen for a full minute after the splash.

Only when she was sure he was gone did she stand, trembling, pocket the waterproof phone case she had found, and carefully make her way out of the secret sea cave.

She climbed back into the kayak and pushed off.

The ocean felt wider now. Darker. She was far from shore, muscles aching, salt in her eyes.

She paddled slowly, each stroke harder than the last.

She wasn't sure she had the strength to make it back.

But she knew she had to try.

Chapter 22

Hayley gritted her teeth and dug her paddle into the waves, breath ragged as she powered the kayak forward. The entrance to the sea cave shrank behind her, swallowed by shadows as she fought her way out into open water. The adrenaline that had propelled her out of hiding was ebbing fast, leaving behind a buzz of nerves and the sticky fear of what she'd just narrowly avoided.

Don't think about the diver.

Just focus on getting back.

The waves had grown more unruly in her absence. Swells slapped the hull of the kayak and sprayed her with cold salt water. She shifted her weight and paddled harder, aiming toward the distant line of trees along the cliff where she'd launched.

Then the kayak shifted slightly—not sharply, not dangerously, but enough for her to sense something was off. She frowned, adjusted her balance, then glanced behind her.

The anchor line.

It wasn't trailing in the water.

She leaned closer. The end near the stern was cleanly severed—no fray, no tearing, just a smooth slice.

Her breath caught.

A chill unrelated to the ocean breeze ran down her spine.

The diver.

She wasn't supposed to make it back.

"Come on, Hayley," she whispered, gripping the paddle. "You can do this."

But the current was shifting. The water churned beneath her with sudden force, dragging the kayak sideways. She adjusted quickly, digging in again—but she wasn't making progress. In fact, she was being pulled out.

Panic flared.

She changed tactics, aiming for the nearest outcropping of rock, hoping to gain a temporary hold. But the surf was relentless. Her kayak slammed into a rising wave, lurched, then listed dangerously to one side. She overcorrected, heart pounding—

And flipped.

The ocean's chill wrapped around her like a fist.

She hit the water with a gasp, the kayak rolling away like a capsized leaf. Her limbs flailed. Up. Kick up. She broke the surface sputtering, salt in her throat, eyes burning.

The tide shoved her again. She turned toward shore but saw only jagged rocks and dark water. She kicked, arms slicing the sea in frantic strokes, but her muscles were already exhausted. The weight of her soaked clothes dragged her down.

She wasn't going to make it.

A lobster buoy bobbed nearby—red and white, thick rope dangling beneath it. Hayley lunged, fingers scrabbling until they caught hold. She wrapped both arms around the buoy, clinging as if it were the last thing tethering her to the living world.

Which, at that moment, it was.

She coughed, head pressed to the cracked paint, vision blurry. "Help," she croaked, though she knew no one could hear her over the wind and waves.

And then, just as her strength began to fail, something moved beneath the surface.

A ripple.

Then a splash.

A figure broke through the water beside her, surfacing like some aquatic avenger—goggles, snorkel, and a head of damp, sandy-blond hair.

"Zane?"

He yanked off the mask and stared at her, breathless. "What the hell are you doing out here?"

"Trying not to die," she managed.

Without another word, he grabbed her arm. "Come on. Kick with me."

They swam in tandem. He steadied her when she slipped. She gasped and sputtered, but slowly, painfully, they inched toward the rocky shoreline. The jagged coast tore at her legs, but she didn't care. Land meant survival.

Zane pulled her up onto a boulder, then collapsed beside her, chest heaving. "Jesus, Powell. Are you insane?"

She coughed again. "Only on weekends."

They sat in silence, drenched and shivering, the sea crashing just beyond their feet.

After a moment, Hayley turned. "You were diving?"

He nodded. "Checking visibility. I didn't expect a passenger in distress."

Hayley stared at him, trying to gauge the truth. "There's a cave."

Zane blinked. "What?"

"A sea cave. West of Thunder Hole. I followed you. Saw you go in the water. I found the cave. Someone's been using it—dive gear, food wrappers, even a phone case."

Zane's expression closed off instantly.

"You know what I'm talking about."

"No," he said too quickly. "I don't."

"You're lying."

"I'm not."

She searched his face, but the fear she saw there didn't feel like guilt. It felt like recognition.

"When I came out, my anchor line was cut. Someone wanted to sabotage me. It wasn't you, was it?"

Zane shook his head. "I wouldn't hurt you."

"But you're scared."

He stood. "I have to go."

"Zane—"

He looked over his shoulder. "Whatever you think you saw—don't go back there. It's not safe."

And with that, he bolted for his Jeep, peeling out of the dirt lot before she could stop him.

Hayley staggered back to her car, hands trembling as she fumbled with the keys.

The drive home was a blur.

The waterproof phone case she'd pocketed from the cave pressed against her thigh, a reminder that this wasn't over.

Not even close.

Bruce was pacing in the driveway, looking like he was ready to call the Coast Guard. When she pulled in, he ran to the car and yanked open her door.

"Where the hell have you been?"

Hayley stepped out, drenched, hair plastered to her skull. "I lost the kayak."

"I don't care about the kayak!"

He wrapped her in a hug so fierce she almost burst into tears.

"Get inside," he said. "Shower. Now."

Later, wrapped in a blanket and cradling a cup of tea, Hayley sat on the couch while Bruce listened to the full story, his expression growing darker by the second.

"Someone tried to kill you."

She nodded. "I can't be sure, but that cave—it's a hideout. Someone's using it regularly. And they didn't want me finding it."

Bruce ran a hand through his hair. "You have to tell Earl."

"I plan to."

They drove to Mona's house, where the porch light was on and they could hear Alanis Morissette's voice wailing through the speakers in the house like an anthem for women who'd had enough. Hayley understood how she felt.

Mona answered in sweatpants and a lobster bib, clearly mid-dinner, but ushered them in without question. Earl appeared behind her, flannel shirt unbuttoned over a T-shirt that read LOBSTER: THE OTHER WHITE MEAT.

Hayley launched into her story again—Zane, the cave, the sabotage.

Earl whistled. "You sure the line was cut?"

"Clean slice. No fray. Someone used a blade."

"Could've been a fishing boat nearby," Mona offered.

"I didn't see one. And the diver was waiting."

"What diver?" Earl said.

"I saw someone. In a wet suit, full gear. Too tall and broad to be Zane. I don't think it was him."

"But Zane knows something," Bruce added.

Mona sat, brow furrowed. "It rules out Kylie. Hannah. Mrs. Larkin."

"Unless they're hiring help," Hayley said.

"Which means we're missing someone," Earl muttered. "Someone hiding in plain sight."

Hayley reached into her coat and pulled out the

waterproof phone case. "I found this in the cave. Maybe there's something inside."

Earl examined it. "We'll get it opened and scanned. Carefully."

Mona snatched it out of his hand. "Allow me to take a crack at it before we go handing it over to Chief Grumpy."

Hayley raised an eyebrow. "I didn't know you could hack into phones, Mona?"

"My sons taught me everything I need to know."

Hayley nodded, suddenly exhausted. "I'm scared, Earl. For the first time, I really think I might be in over my head."

"You've been in over your head before," he said gently. "You always manage to kick your way to the surface."

Bruce reached over and took her hand. "You're not alone in this."

Hayley glanced at them—Bruce, Mona, Earl—and felt a shaky breath escape her lips.

"Good," she said. "Because we're going to need all the help we can get."

Because the next time, she might not be so lucky.

Chapter 23

Hayley had dried off and changed hours ago, but she still felt chilled to the bone. Not from the water—but from what she had seen inside that cave.

Now she stood with Mona and Bruce in the warm glow of Mona Barnes's kitchen, clustered around her butcher-block island, where the waterproof phone case lay like an artifact pulled from the deep. It looked like a rubber brick. Opaque. Sealed tight. Potentially holding the last clues Tina Whitmore might have left behind.

Earl hovered nearby, arms crossed, clearly conflicted. "I should take it to Maddox," he said. "Chain of evidence, proper channels—this is important."

"I want a crack at it before it disappears into the evidence locker forever," Mona repeated evenly, giving him that flinty-eyed stare that had stopped grown men—and nine unruly children—in their tracks for decades.

Earl hesitated. "Mona, you know I'm already on thin ice with the chief. He's suspicious of me just for being around Hayley when she opens her mouth."

"I respect that," Mona said. "So I don't expect you to help us. Just pretend you left the case on the kitchen table. Maybe go watch the Patriots game in the living room and forget we ever had this discussion."

Bruce checked his phone and then glanced between them. "That game's already in the fourth quarter," he said, tempted.

"I swore I wouldn't leak anything to Hayley," Earl whined.

"Then don't," Mona replied, wiping her hands on a dish towel. "Just go relax, enjoy the game."

"I can't just—"

"Yes, you can."

Hayley bit her lip, watching the two of them square off.

"I respect your integrity," Mona added, softening just a touch. "And I don't expect you to break the rules. But you also know me. You're not going to stop me, and I love you for not trying."

Earl sighed. Long and theatrical. Then he opened the fridge, and said. "Okay, but like Bruce said, the game's in the fourth quarter. You two better work fast."

"Earl—" Hayley started.

But Earl had already reached into the fridge, grabbed a beer, and cracked it open. "Don't make me feel worse," he said gruffly as he retreated down the hall.

Bruce lingered. "Do you need me?"

Hayley arched an eyebrow. "Seriously?"

"I mean, I want to help, but it's fourth and goal."

Bruce looked genuinely torn. "If you find anything good, you'll tell me, right?"

"I'll give you a full play-by-play," Hayley promised.

"Then I'm out," Bruce said, grabbing a beer and following Earl. "Go, Pats!"

Mona was already scooping up the phone case and striding toward her cluttered back office. "Mona Barnes. Lobsters by day," she muttered, "digital locksmith by night."

Hayley trailed behind, stepping over a pile of oyster traps and a laptop propped up on a stack of old clamming licenses. Mona's desk looked like Radio Shack had exploded on it—cables, drives, a soldering kit, even a tiny drone missing one blade. A tangled mess of cords, monitors, and half-assembled computer towers filled every corner. Old fishing charts and novelty mugs shared shelf space with networking gear and a stack of overdue water bills.

Mona booted up a tower that made an ominous whirring noise, then slapped the side of it like she was waking up an old dog.

"Your boys taught you this?" Hayley asked, watching as Mona expertly connected a cable from her laptop to the phone case.

"They owe me for the roof I put over their heads," Mona said. "Now, let's see what Tina Whitmore has been up to lately."

She slid in the SIM card from the phone and tapped a few keys with surprising finesse. "Boys taught me a few tricks. This program bypasses pattern locks by triggering a file system corruption that opens recovery mode. Little bit of digital voodoo. The phone will think it's been bricked and open up just enough to let us look inside."

"I'm impressed," Hayley said.

The connection wasn't immediate. The waterproof case had done its job, but some of the files were corrupted. Mona muttered to herself, fingers flying across the keyboard. She pulled up an interface that looked like something out of a spy movie—lines of code blinking as she bypassed the password lock.

"Boom," Mona said with satisfaction. "She didn't stand a chance."

The screen flickered and began to populate with data.

"Okay," Hayley breathed, leaning in. "Let's see what we've got."

The first video was of Tina on a boat with students, collecting seaweed samples. The next was some kind of department outing—a clambake with professors toasting with plastic cups and laughing over paper plates. One was just a blurry shot of a lecture hall, the camera tilted sideways, the audio full of static.

"Nothing useful," Hayley said, deflating.

"Patience, Grasshopper," Mona muttered.

Then another file loaded—a video, time-stamped the night of the fireworks. Tina's voice was faint, drowned by the distant boom of shells overhead. The footage was grainy and jerky, the phone jostling as if she was swimming with it.

The screen jittered, filled with static. Then it cleared.

A burst of fireworks lit up the sky above Frenchman's Bay.

The camera jostled—Tina had clearly propped it on a rock or maybe wedged it into her dive gear. Waves slapped against the hull of a boat just out of frame.

Then, a shape broke the surface.

A diver.

Hayley held her breath.

The footage was too grainy to make out a face. But the figure rose from the water in the distance, maybe twenty feet away from a recognizable boat: the *Slaughterhouse*.

"That's Hank's boat," Hayley whispered.

"Sure is," Mona murmured.

The diver pulled something from a watertight satchel. He moved strangely—broader than Zane, heavier in the shoulders. The image shook again as a firework crackled loud enough to rattle the mic.

Then the clip ended.

Hayley stared at the screen. "Someone used Zane's gear. Or planted some to throw us off. That cave wasn't just a hideout. It was a setup."

Mona sat back, rubbing her chin. "You think Tina saw too much. And someone made sure she couldn't talk about it."

Hayley nodded, heart pounding. "Whoever planted the gear in that cave—this wasn't random. Zane knows more than he's saying. He has to."

Earl appeared in the doorway, Bruce right behind him, looking sheepish.

"Did you find anything?" Bruce asked.

Hayley held up the phone. "Yeah. And I need to get it to Maddox."

"Not sure where he is," Earl said, then hesitated. "Actually, I do. He's having dinner with Randy and Sergio."

Hayley blinked. "Seriously?"

"You're not going over there now, are you?" Bruce asked. "They're in the middle of a dinner party. You'll look like a nosy journalist."

"I *am* a nosy journalist," Hayley shot back.

Bruce frowned. "Hayley, I can't go. Maddox barely tolerates me as it is. I don't want to burn that bridge."

"You afraid of a little confrontation?" she teased. "Coward."

"I'm a pragmatist," he said. "Bring me leftovers."

Hayley stuffed the phone into her purse. "Wish me luck."

"If it gets ugly, text me a safe word," Bruce muttered as she left.

The porch lights were on when Hayley reached Randy and Sergio's place near the Shore Path. She hesitated before knocking, her stomach in knots. The windows glowed with the cozy amber of pendant lights, laughter spilling faintly through the glass.

She knocked once, then again.

Sergio answered, wearing a crisp button-up and a broad smile.

"Hayley! Come in. We're just about to have dessert."

"I won't stay long," she said quickly. "I know I'm interrupting."

"Don't be silly. You're always welcome."

She stepped inside, self-conscious as the conversation around the table hushed. Caleb Maddox turned slowly in his seat, his expression polite but guarded. Randy stood with a dessert plate in one hand and a smug look on his face.

"Well, well," Randy said. "Look who finally decided to visit her favorite brother."

Hayley glanced around. "Looks like quite the spread."

"You missed the garlic-rosemary chicken," Sergio said.

"And the roasted corn salad. But you're just in time for my bourbon pecan pie bars. Or should I say *your* pecan pie bars. I used one of your recipes, by the way," Randy added. Then, turning toward Maddox, he said, "She's a regular Ina Garten, this one."

Hayley smiled thinly, but her eyes were scanning the room.

Maddox sipped his coffee, watching her like a hawk.

"I actually just came from an impromptu kayaking trip," she said.

Sergio's eyes widened. "You went what now?"

Randy's jaw dropped. "*You? Kayaking?*"

"I'm more athletic than I look," she replied primly.

"You tripped over your own welcome mat last week," Randy reminded her.

"One time!"

Maddox set his mug down. "Kayaking where?"

"Acadia," she said. "Near Thunder Hole."

Randy furrowed his brow. "That's a weird spot to just go paddling."

Hayley shrugged. "I was clearing my head. Ended up near a small cave in the rocks. And that's when I found something."

The table stilled.

"What kind of something?" Maddox asked.

Hayley hesitated, then slowly reached into her purse and pulled out the waterproof phone case. "It belongs to Tina Whitmore."

Maddox narrowed his eyes. "You just . . . found it?"

"I didn't know what it was at first," she said, floundering. "I saw a glint, went closer . . ."

"And found that? In a sea cave?" Maddox interrupted.

"Not just this. I found other evidence," she shot back. "That cave had gear in it. Tanks. A blanket. Snack wrappers. And that phone. But then someone showed up when I was there. I managed to hide without being seen. But it wasn't Zane. This guy was taller, beefier, probably the same guy on the video."

Maddox sat back in his chair. "What video?"

Oops.

"Um, well, we . . . I mean, *I* managed to gain access to the phone, and there was a video from the night Hank

Desmond was shot and killed, and well, you should probably watch it and see for yourself."

Maddox rubbed his forehead. "You realize this is obstruction, Hayley. You're interfering with an active investigation."

"Yeah, I can see that now," Hayley squeaked.

"So if it's not Zane in the video, then who is it?" Randy asked.

"Could be Chase Wingate," Sergio said. "He's got a large build. Roger Larkin, too."

"But Wingate was already onboard the *Slaughter-house*, and Larkin was supposedly on his own boat yards away," Randy said.

"It's definitely not Zane," Hayley repeated. "He's either being framed, or more likely, he knows who's been using his equipment and that cave as a base of operations."

Maddox sighed. "I'll send officers out to Thunder Hole first thing in the morning."

By 8 a.m., Hayley and Bruce were already parked at the overlook near the cliffs. The two police cruisers down by the service road told them Maddox was ahead of schedule.

In the distance, a Bar Harbor PD skiff puttered back toward shore.

"They're back," Bruce said, shielding his eyes.

They waited until they saw the boat glide in from the sea, carrying Maddox, Earl, and another officer.

When they returned, Maddox climbed out and walked over.

"We found the cave," he said. "Just a hole in the rocks. No gear. No tanks. No dive logs. Waste of time."

"That's impossible," Hayley said, heart pounding. "It was all there. Someone must've—"

"Only thing in there was a disturbed-looking crab," Maddox added. "Offended we didn't bring snacks."

He turned on his heel and walked back to the boat.

Bruce watched him go, then turned to Hayley. "You know what this means, right?"

"Someone cleaned it out," she said. "They knew I'd been there."

"Zane?"

"He knew the cave. He knew someone was using his gear. He's scared, Bruce. He definitely knows more than he's telling."

Bruce didn't argue. "You really think he'll open up to you now?"

"I have to try," Hayley said, staring out at the crashing surf. "Because I'm not letting this go."

Chapter 24

The dive shop was dark.

Hayley stood on the sidewalk, staring through the glass at the dim, empty interior. The CLOSED sign dangled slightly crooked in the window, and just beneath it, a piece of printer paper had been Scotch-taped to the door.

Gone diving. Back soon.

But it wasn't soon.

She rattled the handle gently. Locked. A rack of wet suits stood undisturbed in the far corner. The air tanks were lined up behind the counter like silent sentinels. A potted plant in the window looked under-watered and limp, the dirt bone-dry.

A gull screamed overhead, and Hayley startled. She turned to scan the quiet street—and caught the faintest flicker of movement across the way.

A curtain twitched in the window of the small white cottage directly opposite the dive shop.

Hayley narrowed her eyes, then crossed the street. She was about to knock when the door creaked open and Mrs. Dunphey emerged, one hand adjusting a comically thick pair of glasses that looked like they could pick up satellite signals. The other hand was pressed against the chest of a hyperactive pug, who was barking and snorting like he was on a one-dog mission to protect the homestead.

"Oh, Mona, I thought that was you!" Mrs. Dunphey called out cheerfully, squinting.

"It's Hayley, Mrs. Dunphey," Hayley said, offering her most patient smile. "You almost ran me down in the street the other day."

"I thought that was Mona."

"No, it was definitely me. Hayley. Hayley Powell." She took a deep breath. "You've known me since I was a little girl."

"I have? Well, I'll be dipped in chowder." She gave the pug a firm heel command. "Martin, hush now, it's just Mona's friend."

"Hayley," Hayley repeated, enunciating.

"Right, right. Haley Joel Osment. You were great in that ghost movie." She cackled at her own joke and waved Hayley to a wicker chair on her porch. "Come sit."

Hayley stepped cautiously past Martin, who immediately latched on to her ankle with his teeth—not biting so much as mouthing, like a baby testing out teething options.

"He's harmless," Mrs. Dunphey said, patting the dog's head. "He just has trust issues. Like his mother."

"Good to know," Hayley muttered, carefully prying Martin off with the toe of her shoe. "I assume you saw me peering in the dive shop window across the street looking for Zane?"

"I saw someone milling about, but I couldn't quite make out who it was. I would have opened the window and waved hello if I knew it was you, Mona."

"Hayley."

"Right. Hayley."

"Do you happen to know when he left today?"

Mrs. Dunphey beamed. "Oh, I don't see much anymore. My eyes are mostly decorative at this point. Don't tell the DMV. But I heard him. Loud and clear. Arguing with someone last night."

Hayley perked up. "Arguing?"

"Ugly tone," Mrs. Dunphey said, lowering her voice dramatically. "And not from him, either. The other one did all the yelling. Zane was quieter. Defensive."

"Did you hear what they were saying?"

"Well, I'd already taken my hearing aids out for the night," she said with a sheepish shrug. "But I caught a few things. Something about 'ruining everything' and 'you'll regret this.' Then Martin started howling—he's very sensitive to tension—and I lost the rest of it."

Hayley tried not to glance down at the pug, who was now licking her shoelaces with mournful resolve.

"Did you recognize the other voice?"

"Could've been Jesus himself for all I know. Like my eyes, my ears are practically ornamental, too." She leaned closer. "But it didn't sound like a friend, I'll tell you that much."

Hayley nodded, filing it away.

"I hope he's okay," Mrs. Dunphey added, almost wistful now. "Zane's a nice boy. Got a permanent whiff of low tide about him, bless his heart, but he always offers to carry my groceries."

"Thanks, Mrs. Dunphey. This was helpful."

"Tell Mona I said hi," the old woman called as Hayley stepped off the porch. "And that her weight loss has not gone unnoticed."

Hayley stared at her. "Weight loss?"

"When I saw her the other day crossing the street, it looked as if she'd lost thirty, maybe forty pounds."

"That was—" Hayley stopped herself. Why keep this conversation going ad nauseam? "I will," she said. Martin barked twice, as if issuing a formal goodbye.

Hayley drove over to the Desmond house to drop in on Kylie one more time. She rang the bell and waited.

When Kylie finally opened it, she looked tired. Her flannel shirt was buttoned unevenly, and her leggings were spattered with coffee stains. Her hair was yanked back in a ponytail, but her fingers kept tugging at the loose ends as though she needed something to hold on to.

"Hayley," she said softly. "Hi."

"I didn't mean to intrude," Hayley said gently. "I just wanted to see how you were holding up."

Kylie nodded, then stepped aside. "Come in."

The living room was shadowed, blinds drawn to block the glare. Hayley sat down slowly on the couch.

Kylie perched across from her, curling her legs beneath her, arms wrapped around her midsection like she was holding herself together.

"It's hard," Kylie said after a long pause. "Losing him. Even with everything . . . it's still hard."

Hayley nodded. "I can imagine."

"I try to keep it together, you know? Be the strong one. People expect me to be fine because we were on the verge of splitting up. But it's not that simple."

"No, it's not."

"I miss him," Kylie said, her voice barely a whisper. "Even when I hated him, I loved him."

It was the same routine Hayley had heard before—every word perfectly timed, every sigh in place. A matinee performance of Bar Harbor's favorite tragic widow.

"I appreciate you coming by to check on me."

Hayley felt a slight pang of guilt.

That was not why she was here at all.

After a long pause, she attempted as naturally as she could to ask, "Have you seen Zane lately?"

Kylie shook her head. "I only saw him once in passing after he confronted me and Chase at the bar the other day. But now he's suddenly gone quiet."

"That's not like him."

"No," Kylie murmured. "It's not."

Then a door opened down the hall.

Chase Wingate entered the room like he owned it, his button-down half-tucked, a phone in one hand, the other adjusting the watch on his wrist.

"Sorry to interrupt," he said, not sounding sorry at all.

Hayley stood. "I was just asking Kylie if she's heard from Zane recently."

Chase chuckled. "No, and you can bet she won't. It's obvious the guy ran off to avoid facing a murder charge. Probably halfway to Nova Scotia by now."

"There's no evidence he left town," Hayley said calmly. "Or that he's a murderer."

Chase waved a hand. "He's a mess. Always was. My guess? Guilt finally caught up with him."

"I wasn't aware you even knew Zane that well," Hayley said, eyes narrowing with suspicion. "Other than what Kylie told you about him."

"I signed up for some diving lessons one summer a few years back. Zane had the glassy stare of a man who mistook lobster butter for vape oil the whole time, so I didn't go back. That was way before he got all hot and bothered over me and Kylie getting together."

Kylie sat up, defensive. "Hayley, if you think Chase had anything to do with Zane's disappearance—"

"I didn't say that."

Chase shook his head. "The cops are closing in, the kid got scared and blew town, end of story."

"You seem awfully sure."

"I've got a good gut," he said, tapping his stomach. "Helps with business. I'm flying to New York tomorrow for a deal that could be huge. I don't have time for small-town drama."

Hayley tilted her head. "You were involved with Kylie before Hank died, weren't you?"

Chase's smile vanished. "Everyone in town knows

that. But it wasn't like that. And for the record, I didn't even know about that gun onboard. I'm sick and tired of everybody trying to pin that shooting on me! The only thing I'm guilty of is having too much to drink that night. I had no beef with Hank. I was going to invest with him. What Kylie did was up to Kylie, not me."

Kylie sat up straighter, suddenly stiff. "Chase—"

"No, I'm just saying," he said, holding up his hands. "I never pressured you. I always said it was your choice. You were the one who wanted out of your marriage."

"I made the decision," Kylie said firmly, but her tone had flattened.

"I supported her," Chase added. "Which is more than Hank ever did."

The silence that followed was thick and sour.

Hayley crossed her arms. "Seems like you've made yourself right at home here."

Chase bristled. "What's that supposed to mean? Are you saying I'm shacking up here now? I don't need to crash anywhere. Did you see my Florida home featured in *Town and Country* a few months ago? How dare you suggest—"

Kylie stood. "Chase, could you run to the pharmacy? I got a text that they have that prescription ready my doctor called in."

Chase blinked. "Now?"

"Yes. Please."

He looked like he might argue, but then thought better of it.

"Fine," he muttered, grabbing his keys and walking out. The door clicked shut.

Kylie let out a long, shaky breath. "He gets defensive. I'm sorry."

Hayley watched her carefully. "You okay?"

Kylie nodded. "Chase was right about one thing. The last time I saw Zane, he was scared. He said someone was after him. That he was being framed."

"Did he say who it was?"

"No names. Just . . . that someone wanted to ruin him. Personally, professionally. That he couldn't trust anyone."

Hayley stood slowly. "If you hear from him—"

"I'll call you. I promise."

Hayley hesitated at the door, one hand on the knob. "Do you believe him?"

Kylie looked down. "I don't know what to believe anymore."

Hayley stepped out into the crisp air, her mind spinning.

Zane's disappearance could indicate his guilt.

But it could also mean something much worse.

He might be running for his life.

Chapter 25

Leroy had barricaded himself in the laundry room again, proudly chewing on one of Bruce's socks like he'd just killed a wild animal and was celebrating with a victory feast. Hayley stood in the doorway, arms folded, watching him with the disapproving glare usually reserved for uncooperative teenagers and celebrities who put ketchup on lobster rolls.

"That's not a chew toy," she said.

Leroy looked up, tail wagging, eyes gleaming with pride, then clamped down harder on the sock like it might escape. Hayley was about to lunge for it when her phone rang on the kitchen counter. She backed out of the laundry room, snatched up the phone, and saw Chelsea's name on the screen.

"Tell me you're calling to invite me to breakfast," Hayley said, answering with one eye still on Leroy.

"I found something outside behind the bar," Chelsea replied. Her voice was tight. "Something big. You need to see it."

Ten minutes later, Hayley pulled into the alley

behind Drinks Like A Fish, wearing jeans, a hoodie, and mismatched socks—thanks to Leroy. The alley still smelled of last night's fryer oil and the faint scent of beer, mingled with the morning fog rolling off the harbor. Chelsea stood by the back dumpsters, her arms crossed, lips pursed.

"Over here," she said, nodding to the space between the recycling bins and a giant pile of cardboard.

Hayley stepped closer and saw them immediately—two silver scuba tanks, spotless and gleaming, stacked like an offering. Stenciled letters that spelled ZANE'S COASTAL DIVES were unmistakable, faded but readable on both.

"They weren't here when I closed up last night," Chelsea said. "I took the trash out myself. These showed up sometime after midnight."

Hayley crouched beside the tanks. They were almost too clean. No scuff marks, no ocean residue, not even dust from the alley. They'd been rinsed and placed there deliberately, like a trap laid by someone who knew she'd be looking.

"Where'd they come from?" Hayley asked.

"Last order for the shop," Chelsea said. "Zane was running his mouth about it one night in here, after a few beers. Said he hated dealing with bills and receipts. Tyler—the guy who helps him with his books—was the one who actually placed it."

Hayley glanced up. "Tyler? You dated him, didn't you?"

Chelsea rolled her eyes. "I've dated most of the

eligible bachelors in Hancock County between the ages of twenty and thirty-five. Occupational hazard. Tyler's harmless—crunches numbers, eats nothing but kale, and has the emotional range of a whiteboard. But he's smart. And he logs everything."

Hayley snapped a few photos of the tanks, then rose to her feet. "Where is he now?"

"Liddy scooped him up for her real estate office," Chelsea said. "He's doing her books now. Keeps a spreadsheet on commission splits and avocado toast consumption."

Inside the bar, Hayley refilled her travel mug with fresh coffee—just coffee—and thanked Chelsea, promising to follow up soon. As she stepped out the front entrance, she saw the morning sun had finally broken through the clouds, burning off the fog and turning the harbor water to silver. She was halfway down the sidewalk when a familiar voice rang out.

"Well, if it isn't Bar Harbor's resident gumshoe."

Nancy Larkin appeared, striding briskly toward her in a white visor and matching tennis skirt, a tiny dachshund trotting beside her at the end of a leash. The dog looked like he regretted every life choice that had led him there.

"Morning, Nancy," Hayley said, forcing a smile. "You're out early."

"Roger likes his breakfast sandwich hot," Nancy said, then lifted an oversized latte. "And I like a little cardio with my caffeine." Her eyes flicked toward the alley beside the bar. "Busy morning?"

"Just coffee," Hayley said, keeping her tone breezy.

Nancy's gaze lingered on the alley, curious. "Hmm. Thought I saw something shiny back there." She smiled, all innocence. "Bar Harbor's getting messy these days. You never know what people will dump where."

"Guess not," Hayley said, watching her carefully.

Nancy took another sip and tugged on the leash. "Well, enjoy your coffee, dear."

Hayley watched her walk off, the dachshund dragging its feet.

Something itched at the back of her mind. Roger was probably already at their diner, the Fryer Side Chat, across town getting ready to open up for the breakfast rush—he could make his own breakfast sandwich, for heaven's sake. So, why was Nancy fetching one here, blocks away, right after the scuba tanks appeared?

Her eyes drifted back toward the alley.

Nancy hadn't come to buy breakfast.

She'd come to make sure the evidence she'd planted had been found.

Hayley made a mental note: Keep a closer eye on Nancy Larkin. And her husband, Roger, for that matter—who could have easily fit into that wet suit.

Hayley parked outside the *Island Times* office to find Bruce already at one of the outdoor café tables next door with a laptop open, blueberry scone half-eaten beside his coffee.

"Good morning," he said. "You're up early."

"Someone left me a present behind the bar," she said, pulling out the chair across from him.

Bruce arched an eyebrow. "What kind of present?"

"Two scuba tanks. Clean. Labeled. Practically gift-wrapped with Zane's name on them."

Bruce whistled softly. "Someone's trying to build a narrative."

"That Zane's ditching evidence," Hayley said. "And they're working fast."

Bruce nodded, then opened a file on his screen. "Got another update. Tina's sister is flying in. Wants to finalize things, clear out her apartment."

Hayley exhaled. "So she knows."

"She knows Tina drowned, yeah. But there's more. She told me Tina emailed her two days after the fireworks. Said she recognized someone while swimming the night of the fireworks and it freaked her out. Wouldn't say who, just that she didn't feel safe. Her sister said she sounded 'off.' When she wrote her back asking her to give more details, Tina never responded."

Hayley's stomach sank. "That's the day she vanished."

Bruce nodded. "She might've seen too much."

Hayley sipped her coffee and felt her suspicion harden.

Tina had definitely seen someone.

And that someone was in the video on her phone.

Someone connected to Hank.

Now she was dead.

And Zane was being lined up to take the fall.

Hayley's next stop was Liddy Crawford's real estate office. The storefront looked like the inside of a coastal-themed Pinterest board—everything whitewashed wood and ocean blues. Inside, Liddy glanced up from her laptop.

"Well, well," she said, surprised. "You here to buy that adorable bungalow in Otter Creek or just to sweep me off my feet for a decadent early lunch?"

"Tempting," Hayley said. "But I'm actually looking for Tyler."

Liddy fanned herself with a property brochure. "Your loss. I was planning on lobster mac and cheese and a chocolate martini. Don't tell my trainer."

Hayley laughed, then walked past the lobby into the back office, where Tyler was typing at lightning speed while sipping something the color of pond scum through a metal straw.

"Hayley!" he said brightly. "Want a protein ball? They're quinoa-based."

"I'll pass."

She explained what had been found behind the bar.

Tyler immediately frowned.

"I placed that tank order," he said. "Four total. Two

went to the shop. Zane took the other two to clean at home. That's the last I saw of them."

"You think someone could've gotten into his house or the shop?"

"Totally. He keeps meaning to install better locks, but his budget goes toward dive gear and fish-themed T-shirts."

Hayley nodded. "Anyone suspicious hanging around lately?"

"There was one guy. Ball cap, sunglasses, trying way too hard to look casual. Just loitered outside the shop when I was there helping with the books. Never came in. Couldn't get a good look at him."

"Could you describe him at all?"

"Not really. That's the thing—he looked average. Almost . . . intentionally forgettable."

Hayley made a note. "Could've been casing the place."

Tyler shrugged. "I thought he was a tourist. But now?"

Liddy popped her head in. "Lunch? Last call. I'm heading to the Wharf for a basket of fried clams and a side of slaw."

Tyler recoiled like she'd threatened to eat roadkill. "Fried clams? Liddy, that's a week's worth of sodium and saturated fat in one sitting."

She waved a dismissive hand. "Relax, Mr. Muscles. Not all of us survive on green powder and chia seeds. Some of us enjoy life—and food that's actually fried."

"It's not food—it's a cry for help," Tyler muttered, shaking his head.

"You know what's a cry for help?" Liddy shot back. "Your lunch. It smells like a compost bin at a yoga retreat."

Hayley laughed. "Rain check," she said, waving them both off.

She stepped outside. Her thoughts churned.

Two tanks, most likely planted.

A dead marine biologist who'd sent a frightened email.

A nosy local who might've staged a casual run-in.

And someone out there who was suddenly moving fast.

Zane was being framed.

And whoever was behind it?

They were getting sloppy.

Which made them dangerous.

And desperate.

Hayley tucked her notepad away and crossed the street. She had a sinking feeling that the next clue wouldn't be so clean.

Or so easy to find.

She just hoped she'd find it before someone else disappeared.

Chapter 26

The Bar Harbor Farmers Market was already buzzing by the time Hayley arrived. Vendors snapped open pop-up tents while customers jostled through the aisles, baskets swinging. Overhead, seagulls circled like thieves, screeching for free samples.

Hayley navigated the crowd with a coffee in hand and her hair shoved under a Red Sox cap, doing her best impression of someone who hadn't agreed—again—to help Mona sling lobsters on a weekend. She spotted the red BARNES LOBSTER CO. canopy near the harbor-facing edge of the market. A giant white cooler sat front and center, propped open to display live culls snapping lazily in their crate, beside a chalkboard that read FRESH LOBSTERS $5/LB. LIMIT 10. DON'T BE GREEDY.

Mona was mid-lecture to a red-faced teenager attempting to bag a lobster with salad tongs. "Angle them down or they'll turn and nip your fingers clean off!"

Earl stood nearby in his day-off uniform: a slightly faded CRUSTACEAN NATION T-shirt, flip-flops, and cargo shorts that had definitely seen better summers. He was watching the chaos with an expression of serene panic and holding a roll of mesh bags like he didn't know whether to offer help or hide behind them.

Hayley grinned and stepped behind the card table to man the old-school cash box. "Tell me again how this is my day off?"

"You're the one who said you missed the smell of bait," Mona shot back.

"Did not."

"Well, you implied it with your eyes."

Earl approached with a small mesh sack. "I bagged three without injury."

"You want a trophy or a juice box?" Mona muttered, but Hayley caught the twitch of a smile on her face.

They got through a dozen sales before Hayley spotted something unusual across the market square. Liddy was weaving through a flower stand in a turquoise blouse, big sunglasses perched atop her head. Walking beside her, close but not quite touching, was Doug Marsh—tall, neatly dressed, looking like he was trying not to look like her date.

Hayley paused, a bag of mussels halfway to a customer, and watched. Liddy laughed at something he said and playfully nudged him with her shoulder. Doug flushed, clearly charmed, but didn't reciprocate.

They didn't hold hands.

They didn't flirt.

It wasn't romantic—at least not yet, given recent events—but Hayley saw something simmering under the surface.

A connection.

Or maybe tension.

She wasn't sure which.

Perhaps Doug's hesitation had something to do with all the attention on him from the Hank Desmond case.

That had to be taking a toll.

That's when she noticed him.

Ten or so paces behind Liddy and Doug, a man in a forest-green baseball cap hovered awkwardly between booths. He kept glancing in their direction, then away.

Wraparound sunglasses. Windbreaker. Broad-shouldered, lanky, posture like he wanted to disappear into his own shoes.

Her skin prickled. He looked vaguely familiar. Could it be the man who'd entered the cave after her? The same build. The same head tilt.

She stepped back from the table, ignoring Mona yelling about a lobster trying to escape into an empty stroller, and began weaving through the booths to get a better look.

She passed a table of herbal tinctures, ducked behind a wood-fired pizza cart, and turned a corner—only to find the green-capped man was gone.

"Damn it," she muttered.

"Well, that's not how I imagined our reunion."

Hayley turned and saw Sergio Alvarez dressed in linen and looking relaxed while holding a tiny compostable smoothie cup. Randy stood beside him with a bunch of rhubarb under one arm and an expression that screamed, *Why am I awake so early?*

"Sergio," Hayley said. "Shouldn't you be packing for your big tropical adventure?"

"I don't pack until the night before," he said. "Randy packs six weeks early and still forgets his socks."

Randy raised an eyebrow. "Bold of you to assume I wear socks." He paused. "Or underwear, depending on the pants."

"TMI!" Hayley blurted.

A moment of awkward silence passed.

"So," Hayley said. "You guys excited?"

"Thrilled," Sergio said.

"Terrified," Randy said at the same time.

Sergio gave Randy a sideways glance. "You're not having second thoughts, are you?"

"No, of course not," Randy said.

Hayley watched her brother, trying to determine whether he was lying or not.

"You know, Hayley," Sergio said, trying to recover. "you could come for an extended stay. Write your columns from Brazil."

"Absolutely," Randy said quickly. "The spare room has air-conditioning and mosquito netting and everything."

Hayley tried to picture herself in Brazil in a sundress, holding a caipirinha, and immediately had a vision of her sunburned and crying in a hammock. She then shook her head. "The restaurant's busy even in the winter. I can barely get a week off without Betty threatening a mutiny."

Randy opened his mouth like he wanted to say

something, then closed it. The silence between them stretched just a beat too long.

"But I'll . . . think about it," Hayley said gently.

Back at the lobster booth, Earl was trying to wrangle a runaway crustacean while Mona yelled, "That's what you get for naming it!" at a child crying over "Larry the Lobster."

Mona then turned to see Hayley slip back behind the booth. With both hands on her hips and a look that could've curdled milk, she shouted, "You just abandon your post in the middle of a rush?"

"There was a man in a green hat," Hayley said.

"Is that supposed to mean something?"

"He was following Liddy and Doug. I think he's the same guy Mrs. Dunphey saw outside the dive shop, and the one I saw in a wet suit at the sea cave. Same build."

Earl perked up, shifting the tongs to his other hand. "Green cap, sunglasses, kind of hunched over? Yeah, I know who that is."

"You do?" Hayley said.

"Billy Downs," Earl said. "Lobsterman. Works alone. Real quiet. Spends most of his time out past Little Cranberry. Awkward as hell."

"Why would he be trailing Liddy and Doug?"

Mona frowned. "Wait. Is that the guy who used to show up at Liddy's open houses and just . . . loiter?"

"I thought he was interested in the properties," Earl said.

"He once asked if one had a walk-in freezer. For

fish," Mona said. "She told me she started bringing pepper spray."

Hayley's pulse ticked upward. "Where does he live?"

Earl shrugged. "Down near Otter Creek. Big blue house with a boat ramp in the backyard. You want me to pay him a visit?"

"No," Hayley said. "I will."

But as it turned out, she didn't have to. She spotted him again—standing near a produce booth, half-hidden behind a stack of onions.

Hayley handed the cash box to Earl and slipped away.

She heard Mona calling after her, "Where the hell are you going now?"

This time, she didn't lose him. She tracked him past the kettle-corn stand, through a row of potted succulents, and finally caught up with him as he ducked behind the town hall's loading ramp.

"Hey!" she called.

The man stopped, startled.

"Why are you following Liddy and Doug?" Hayley demanded.

His sunglasses hid his eyes, but the faint dip of his chin told her she'd hit a nerve. "Don't lie. I've seen you twice now. You've been trailing them."

He took off his hat and rubbed the back of his neck, revealing a sunburned, weathered face. "I didn't mean nothing by it."

"So, what did you mean?"

He sighed. "I like Liddy. Have for a long time. I saw

her with that guy, and I got . . . jealous, I guess. Thought he might be sniffing around her."

Hayley narrowed her eyes. "That's why you've been creeping around corners like a stalker?"

"I didn't mean to scare anybody," he said. "I'm just . . . not good at this kind of thing."

Hayley softened just a little. "You're Billy Downs?"

He nodded.

"I'm Hayley—"

"I know who you are."

Sergio and Randy reappeared, the latter still holding produce and the two of them them clearly mid-stroll.

"Everything okay?" Sergio asked, eyeing Billy.

"Fine," Hayley said smoothly. "We were just discussing lobster supply and small business licenses. Billy's thinking of setting up a booth like Mona's. Right, Billy?"

Billy looked alarmed, then caught on and nodded quickly. "Yeah. Thinking about it."

Sergio smiled. "Smart. Direct-to-consumer is the future."

Randy and Sergio wandered off again, and Hayley turned back to Billy.

"I thought you might be the guy I saw in the cave," she admitted. "But I don't think you are. Which means you're off the suspect list."

Billy let out a breath like he'd been holding it all morning.

"Go home, Billy," she said. "Don't follow Liddy

anymore. And if you like her? Maybe try talking to her. Like a human."

He nodded. "Thanks. Sorry."

Hayley watched him go, then looked out across the market. The crowd was still bustling. Music played softly from someone's Bluetooth speaker. Kids ran past, sticky with jam.

Another potential suspect off the board.

But the one who mattered?

Still watching. Still hiding.

And Hayley was running out of places to look.

Island Food & Spirits
By
Hayley Powell

After my divorce, I had finally mastered the art of barbecuing without setting myself—or my lawn—on fire. Unfortunately, according to my best friends, Mona and Liddy, it was time for me to "get back out there."

I told them I'd rather alphabetize my spice rack.

But Mona and Liddy were relentless, and after a few too many of Liddy's Aperol Orange Spritzes, I found myself agreeing to a setup with one of her Realtor friends. There were, however, two conditions.

First, the date had to take place at my house. The last thing I needed was to become the topic of breakfast gossip at Jordan's Restaurant. I could just picture it: half of Bar Harbor analyzing my date between bites of blueberry pancakes. Hard pass.

Second, Liddy and her latest boyfriend, Mike, would be joining us. I needed backup. If the date went south, at least I'd have witnesses.

So, date night arrived. Liddy and Mike showed up—with my date, Joe, in tow. I'd gone all out:

spicy jalapeño poppers, BBQ pork chops, loaded baked potato salad, and my triple-threat chocolate cake for dessert. I figured that even if the date flopped, at least the food wouldn't.

I handed out cocktails and went to fetch the appetizers—crispy, bacon-wrapped jalapeño poppers stuffed with pimento cheese (a new twist I was particularly proud of). But when I offered Joe a plate, he just stared at me like I'd tried to hand him a live grenade.

"I can't eat those," he said, clutching his stomach. "Spicy food sends me straight to the ER."

I apologized profusely, ran inside, and threw together a plate of cheese and crackers instead. Liddy and Mike raved about the poppers, so at least someone appreciated them.

Dinner went no better. I plated everything beautifully and presented Joe with the biggest pork chop, extra potato salad, and a big smile. He took one look, gasped dramatically, and shouted, "Are you trying to kill me?"

Apparently, he was allergic to pork. And therefore to the bacon bits in the potato salad. And, possibly, to joy itself.

As if that wasn't enough, when I suggested dessert instead, he declared that chocolate cake would send his blood sugar "through the roof" because—surprise!—he had diabetes.

By then I was seeing red, and not just from the grill. Fortunately, Liddy recognized my look and quickly intervened. She and Mike gently suggested Joe call it a night before I needed medical attention for myself.

He finally stormed off, muttering about dietary sabotage, and the three of us just stared at each other in stunned silence before bursting into laughter.

I told Liddy I wasn't ready to date again anytime soon, but when I was, I planned to meet the next guy in the grocery store—so I could check his cart for red flags before agreeing to dinner.

The rest of the night was perfect: good friends, good food, and no medical emergencies. Speaking of which, here are the recipes that survived the date from hell—Liddy's Aperol Orange Spritz and my trusty BBQ Pork Chops.

Aperol Orange Spritz

Ingredients

1½ ounces Aperol Orange Aperitif
5 ounces prosecco
Splash of orange juice
Splash of soda
Orange slice, for garnish (optional)

Add a few ice cubes to a wineglass. Pour in the Aperol, prosecco, orange juice, and a splash of soda. Add the orange slice if desired. Sip slowly while contemplating why you ever agreed to blind dates.

BBQ PORK CHOPS

INGREDIENTS

4 to 6 thick-cut boneless pork chops
Salt and pepper

BBQ SAUCE

1 cup ketchup
⅔ cup brown sugar, packed
3 tablespoons Worcestershire sauce
3 tablespoons apple cider vinegar
2 tablespoons Dijon mustard
1 teaspoon garlic powder
Salt and pepper to taste

In a saucepan over medium heat, combine the BBQ sauce ingredients. Bring to a boil, then reduce to low and simmer 5–6 minutes, stirring constantly. Remove from the heat and set aside.

Preheat the grill to medium heat and oil the grates. Season the pork chops on both sides with salt and pepper. Place on the grill and cook 3 minutes. Flip, brush generously with sauce, and cook another 5–7 minutes. Flip again, brush with more sauce, and cook an additional 5–7 minutes, or until the internal temperature reaches 140°F.

Remove the chops from the grill and let rest, covered, for 5 minutes before serving.

Add your favorite sides, a chilled Spritz, and maybe a reminder to ask about food allergies before planning the menu.

Chapter 27

Hayley parked in front of a small, weathered clapboard house tucked on a quiet side street just beyond downtown Bar Harbor. Tina Whitmore's house—modest, gray-shingled, with a rickety porch swing and a flower bed overtaken by early autumn weeds—looked like the kind of place meant for privacy.

Or invisibility.

A FOR RENT SOON! sign leaned against the mailbox, the hand-scrawled lettering as subtle as a sledgehammer.

The front door was propped open, and cardboard boxes lined the steps. Hayley knocked on the door frame and called inside. "Lacy?"

From within came a rustle and then a voice: "Back here!"

Hayley stepped into the narrow front room. The interior was sparse—no photos on the walls, no knickknacks or clutter, just plain furniture, functional shelves, and the ghost of someone who never meant to stay long.

Lacy Whitmore emerged from the hallway, a roll of

packing tape in one hand and a tired smile on her face. She was in her late thirties, with chestnut hair pulled into a ponytail, wearing jeans and a windbreaker with an L.L. Bean logo on the sleeve.

"You must be Hayley," she said. "Thanks for coming."

"I wish it were under better circumstances," Hayley said. "How are you holding up?"

Lacy gave a small shrug. "It's weird. We weren't that close. Tina was . . . private. Didn't share much. Even when we were kids." She gestured around. "She never decorated. Never put down roots. She didn't even have a will, so I'm stuck trying to sort this all out while some cranky landlord breathes down my neck."

Hayley looked around at the nearly bare room. A bookshelf with marine biology textbooks. A small desk with nothing but a lamp and a box of paper clips. The television was old, the armchair mismatched. It was less a home than a hideout.

"Can I look around?" Hayley asked.

Lacy nodded. "Knock yourself out. Maybe you'll find something I missed."

Hayley moved quietly through the house. The bedroom was just as sparse—neatly made bed, dresser with two framed pictures on top: one of Tina and Lacy as kids, and one of a beach at sunset. The bathroom had nothing but drugstore shampoo and a nearly empty tube of toothpaste. No journals, no notes. Nothing personal. It appeared her real home was her office at COA.

"She didn't talk about anyone from the college?" Hayley asked when she returned.

"Never," Lacy said. "Whenever I asked about her job or if she was seeing someone, she just said she was too busy with research or students. I think she liked keeping us at arm's length."

Hayley frowned. "No names? Not even a favorite student or coworker?"

"Not a one. She kept that part of her life completely walled off. And she rarely visited us in Freeport. I mean, she'd send birthday cards to my kids, but that's about it. I'd invite her every Thanksgiving, every Christmas, but she rarely ever showed."

Before Hayley could press further, there was a heavy knock on the screen door. A man stood on the porch in an ill-fitting windbreaker and khakis, holding a clipboard and looking more annoyed than mournful.

"Speak of the devil," Lacy muttered under her breath.

Hayley opened the door with a half smile. "Terry Osgood. Still squeezing every nickel out of every rental in town?"

Terry Osgood, class of '93, had once been voted "Most Likely to Charge His Grandma Late Fees." His sandy hair was thinning, and his forehead was deeply etched from decades of frowning at other people's belongings.

"Hayley Powell," he grunted. "Didn't expect to see you playing moving company."

"I'm here for moral support," she said sweetly. "But I see you're still allergic to compassion."

He ignored her. "You wrapping this up today?" he asked Lacy.

"I told you I'd be out by this afternoon," Lacy said calmly. "We're on track."

"I've got painters scheduled," Terry replied. "And an eager tenant waiting. Just want to keep things moving."

Hayley stepped between them. "You ever hear of giving someone five minutes to grieve?"

Terry frowned. "I'm not stopping her. Just checking in."

"You live across the street, right?" she asked.

Terry squinted at her. "Yeah. Why?"

"I'm just wondering—what kind of relationship did you have with Tina?"

He snorted. "Didn't really have one. She kept to herself. Always acted like she was above the rest of us."

Hayley tilted her head. "Above you how?"

"Wouldn't say hi. Never came to the block cookout. Even ignored the town's Fourth of July potluck last year—brought out a folding chair and sat in her yard like she couldn't be bothered. One of those types who thought just 'cause she worked at the college, the rest of us were bumpkins."

Hayley nodded slowly. "But she paid her rent on time?"

"Every month," he admitted. "Didn't make noise, didn't complain about repairs. But she kept her distance."

She studied him. "So she never caused you any problems . . . but she rubbed you the wrong way?"

He crossed his arms. "What are you getting at?"

"I'm just asking questions."

"Well, maybe ask 'em to someone who knew her

better," he snapped. "I didn't do anything to her, if that's what you're implying."

Hayley raised a hand. "Relax. I'm not pointing fingers. I just figured since you live nearby, you might've noticed something. Visitors. Arguments. Anything strange."

Terry exhaled, shoulders still tight. "Only strange thing was that guy."

Hayley's eyes widened. "What guy?"

"Just a guy. I don't know, tall, maybe mid-thirties, early forties. Broad shoulders. Came around late one night knocking on her door."

"When?"

"Day or two after the fireworks, maybe? She was definitely home. I'd seen her go in earlier. But she didn't answer. Lights all went out. Like she was hiding."

"Did you see his face?"

Terry shook his head. "Nah. Too dark. Baseball cap, I think. But he looked frustrated when she didn't come out. Pounded on the door a few times, then left."

Hayley felt the hairs on her arms rise.

Another man in a baseball cap.

Another shadow.

It couldn't be a coincidence.

"Thanks for the info," she said tightly.

Terry gave a half shrug and turned to leave.

"Give your mother my best," Hayley added. "And tell her I said you turned out exactly as she feared."

He didn't reply.

Lacy returned from the bedroom, shaking her head. "What a peach."

"Did Tina ever mention someone bothering her?" Hayley asked.

"Not really. But . . . that email. The one I told your husband, Bruce, about."

Hayley leaned in.

"She sent it the morning after the fireworks. Said she saw someone in the water that night. Someone she recognized. She didn't say who. But it clearly rattled her. She kept saying something wasn't right. And then she vanished."

Once everything was boxed up, the house felt even emptier. A shell inside a shell.

"She didn't have much," Lacy said quietly. "No clutter. No mess. I guess that made this easier. But it still feels . . . sad."

"You want some lunch?" Hayley asked. "I know a place."

Lacy sighed with relief. "I'm starving. Skipped breakfast thanks to your friend Terry and his ticking clock."

They headed to the Dockside Café, where the view of the harbor stretched wide and bright beyond the deck railings. The interior was cool and airy, with hanging string lights and a quiet hum of lunchtime conversation. A waitress with pink bangs and a joyful bounce in her step greeted Hayley with a hug.

"Hey, stranger! You back for the haddock sandwich?"

"Not today, Missy," Hayley said. "We're keeping it light."

She glanced at Lacy. "This is Tina's sister."

Missy's smile softened. "I'm so sorry. She was a sweet customer. Always ordered the same thing."

Lacy looked surprised. "She never mentioned this place."

"She came alone. Sat near the window with a book. Never said much, but she always tipped well."

They also chose to sit near the window, the water glittering just beyond the glass. Lacy ordered a grilled cheese and chowder; Hayley got a Caesar salad, though she doubted she'd eat more than half.

"She really didn't tell me anything," Lacy said, stirring her chowder. "Not about work, not about friends. Just sent short emails every few weeks. And then that last one . . ."

Hayley leaned in. "Do you still have the email?"

Lacy nodded and pulled out her phone. "I saved it. I don't know why, but . . . something about it gave me the chills."

She tapped a few times, then handed the phone across the table.

Hayley read: *I went swimming during the fireworks last night. The cold water clears my head. I set my phone on the rocks to catch the show—you'll see the clip. Someone surfaced near Hank's boat, pulling something from a satchel. What you won't hear is the shot. It was quick, sharp—not a firework. And in the bursts of light I saw him climbing onto the rocks in a wet suit. I know him. He saw me, too. The way he looked at me . . .*

it wasn't friendly. It felt like a warning. I can't stop shaking.

The message ended there. No signature. No follow-up.

Hayley stared at the screen, her heart thudding. Tina had recognized someone. Someone she hadn't expected to see. Someone she feared. And now she was dead.

She passed the phone back slowly. "She didn't just feel unsettled. She was terrified."

Lacy nodded, voice barely above a whisper. "And she didn't tell me who it was. I wrote her back immediately to find out more, but I heard nothing from her after that. And then . . ." Her eyes welled up with tears. "The worst possible thing happened . . ."

Hayley reached out and took Lacy's hand. "I'm so sorry."

"Excuse me for a moment." Lacy sniffed, snatching up her napkin to dab at her eyes as she hurried off to the bathroom.

Hayley looked out at the harbor.

Although she still didn't have the name of this mystery man, one thing was certain.

Whomever Tina saw—it was the same person who had killed Hank Desmond.

And they'd made sure Tina never spoke again.

Chapter 28

Bruce had already left for the *Island Times* newsroom—he was tracking down a lead on a rash of vandalism at local heritage sites, including someone rearranging lawn flamingos at the Historical Society into anatomically inappropriate positions. That was the kind of story Bruce lived for: a crime with character.

Hayley, however, had more pressing crimes in mind. Her plan was to stop by the Desmond house again—see if Kylie had heard from Zane or if Chase had made any new power moves—but as she turned onto Main Street, something caught her eye.

Kylie's white Lexus—recognizable by the vanity plate KDESMOND and the glittery decal that read BAR HARBOR BARBIE—was parked crooked in front of Portside Bridal & Formalwear. The boutique wasn't open for walk-ins until noon, which meant this was a private appointment.

Hayley parked across the street, curiosity piqued. She peeked through the window and saw Kylie inside, standing in front of a three-way mirror in what looked suspiciously like a second-wedding dress. Ivory satin, off the shoulder, tasteful sparkle. Hayley's stomach turned.

Inside, the boutique was a chilly perfume box of chiffon and tulle. Maureen, the owner—a bustling woman with red glasses on a chain and the vocal discretion of a megaphone—lit up when she saw Hayley.

"Oh, are you here to help the bride choose?" She beamed. "I was just about to bring out the mermaid-cut with the illusion neckline—very popular with younger second wives!"

Kylie's eyes widened in horror. "Maureen!"

Hayley blinked. "Second wife?"

Kylie, catching her reflection, turned coy. "I'm just . . . trying things on. Nothing official."

"Yet," Maureen chirped, bustling off to fetch another gown. "But she's glowing like a woman about to lock down her next retirement plan!"

Kylie stepped off the riser, holding up the train of the dress as she moved. "It's for a charity gala."

Hayley raised an eyebrow but kept her tone neutral. "In a dress like that?"

"It's not what it looks like," Kylie said, slipping behind the curtain. "Okay, maybe it is. But Chase and I . . . it's been a hard few weeks. He's been supportive. He's been there."

Hayley hesitated, unsure how far to push. She'd

questioned Kylie before—twice, in fact—and come away unconvinced she was involved in Hank's murder.

But still—this?

So soon?

Kylie's voice was muffled as she wriggled out of the dress. "Hank and I—were complicated. You know that, Hayley. We've talked about it."

Hayley nodded slowly. "I'm just surprised how quickly you're moving on."

Kylie peeked her head around the curtain. "Grief doesn't have a schedule. And Chase has been . . . kind."

Not a word Hayley would ever use to describe the man.

Maureen returned with a blush-toned gown and began hanging it on the door. "Kind and handsome! And generous. He insisted on the rush order himself!"

Hayley gave her a look.

Maureen smiled, completely unbothered. "This one's got a bit of sparkle in the train—very flattering for aisle photos."

Hayley turned back to Kylie. "What about Zane? Have you heard from him since we last spoke?"

Kylie exhaled, leaning on the fitting-room door frame. "No. I told you. Not since he closed up his shop and disappeared. The only person I know who might have seen Zane is Rufus."

"Rufus?"

"Rufus Bickford. They've been inseparable since middle school. Zane's little sidekick. Rufus is a total burnout, but Zane always looked out for him. Gave him jobs, kept him from completely going off the rails. If anyone knows where Zane might've gone, it's Rufus. Go talk to him."

"Why didn't you mention this to me before?"

"You didn't ask."

Kylie's patience with Hayley was at an end.

"Where can I find him?"

"Try the back of a bait shack," Kylie muttered. "Or anywhere that smells like bong water."

Rufus Bickford was exactly where Kylie had predicted—behind a bait shack at the edge of the marina, perched like a sunburned gremlin on a plastic bucket and mid-debate with a seagull over a half-eaten Whoopie Pie. He wore mismatched flip-flops, swim trunks with cartoon sharks on them, and a ripped hoodie that read I PAUSED MY GAME TO BE HERE.

Hayley approached cautiously, trying to avoid stepping in fish guts.

"Hey, Rufus?"

He squinted up at her, red-eyed and smiling. "Whoa. You're the food lady."

"Among other things. I'm looking for Zane."

"Me, too, man. We were supposed to meet for a drink at Drinks Like A Fish a few nights back. I even showered for it. He never showed." He pulled a vape pen from his hoodie and took a long drag that smelled like mango and gasoline.

"Have you heard from him since?"

Rufus shook his head. "Total radio silence. But that's Zane, you know? He gets into these moods—off-grid, brooding, like Batman but with less money and more unpaid bar tabs."

Hayley blinked. "Try to focus, please. Did he say where he was going?"

"He mentioned his storage unit. Said it needed purging. He gets sentimental about stuff—dive logs, gear, even his old surfboards. It's out on Crooked Road, next to that bait distributor with the dead pelican sign."

Hayley made a note. "Thanks, Rufus."

"You got it, lady. If you see him, tell him I've got his vape charger."

Mona was up to her elbows in scallops when Hayley burst into the lobster shop. Earl was already there when Hayley arrived—wearing a faded T-shirt with rubber boots and peeling potatoes like he was auditioning for *Downeast Downton Abbey*. It was his day off, but he'd dropped in to help Mona fill a bulk order for a tourist clambake party—ten pounds of scallops, two dozen live lobsters, and enough mussels to make her swear off seafood for good.

When Hayley launched into her latest theory, Earl's face did something between a wince and a sigh. "You want to break into a storage unit?"

"It's not breaking in if we're just . . . checking on a friend," Hayley offered, badly.

Mona didn't even pause as she weighed a sack of steamers. "She's buying me dinner. Baked haddock. Blueberry ale. And not from the tourist menu."

Earl groaned. "You two are like gasoline and an open flame."

"You're coming, then?" Hayley asked.

"Someone has to keep you from getting arrested," he muttered. "But I'm driving. And when we get there, I'm staying in the truck. I want zero part in whatever borderline felony you're about to commit."

The storage facility on Crooked Road was bleak and boxy, hemmed in by cracked asphalt and a few dying maples. The desk was manned by a bored teenager with a phone in one hand and a bag of Flamin' Hot Cheetos in the other. Hayley leaned over the counter, peppering the teenage manager with inane questions about pest control, flood insurance, and whether any of the units had wonky padlocks she should avoid. His eyes glazed over—half-listening, half-scrolling on his phone.

Out of the corner of her eye, she spotted Mona slip around the far row of units, tool kit in hand.

Hayley gave the manager a final smile, muttered something about comparing rates, then casually drifted away, circling the row and joining Mona just as she knelt beside Zane's unit.

Three false starts.

The lock stuck.

Footsteps crunched past—Mona and Hayley ducked behind a row of lockers as the manager paused, squinted, then kept walking.

The lock was stubborn.

Hayley coughed loudly to cover the *click* as the boy wandered past again from a suspicious bathroom break.

A minute later, Mona clicked the bolt open and tugged Hayley inside.

The storage unit was cool and dry. Too clean. Too curated.

On a crate in the middle sat a pink dive fin. Folded beside it, one of Hank's monogrammed towels. Inside a mesh dive bag—folded gloves, snorkel, wet suit.

Mona whistled low. "That's a hell of a coincidence."

Hayley stared at it, stomach sinking. "It's not a coincidence."

Mona tilted her head. "What do you mean?"

"This isn't a storage unit. It's a set piece."

"'Set piece'?"

"Someone planted this," Hayley said. "On purpose. This isn't evidence left behind. It's a display. A message. Like someone's building a case against Zane from scratch—one prop at a time."

Mona frowned. "Framing him?"

Hayley nodded. "Someone who knows him. Knows how to make it look real. But it's too perfect. No way he'd leave a pink fin that likely belonged to Tina and Hank's towel just sitting out like this."

Just then, a voice barked: "You can't be in there!"

The teenage manager stood at the doorway, filming them on his phone. "Smile! You're going on TikTok."

Chief Caleb Maddox arrived five minutes later, lights flashing and boots crunching across the gravel. Earl was right on Maddox's heels, hands raised like he was surrendering at a roadblock.

"It's not what it looks like," Earl wailed, trying for a calmer tone.

"It looks like trespassing, tampering with evidence, and dragging Mona into it, as well" Maddox snapped.

"They just wanted to check on Zane's things," he offered quickly. "That's all. I told them it was probably a bad idea, but—"

"You *drove* them here?" Maddox turned on him, incredulous. "Earl, you're supposed to be a law enforcement officer, not the president of the Hayley Powell Fan Club."

Earl looked like he wanted the gravel to open up and swallow him. "It's her. You try saying no when she gets that tone."

"You're on probation," Maddox snapped. "One more ride-along stunt like this, and you'll be directing traffic at the turkey trot."

Hayley stepped forward. "This wasn't Earl's idea. It was mine. Don't punish him."

"I told him to keep you out of this," Maddox shot back. "And instead he plays Uber driver to your felony field trip."

Hayley held up the pink fin. "Please. Just check the

security footage. If I'm wrong, I'll leave. If I'm right, then Zane's being framed—and this is the smoking gun."

Maddox exhaled, nostrils flaring. "Fine. One look. But after that, we're done."

Inside the cramped office, the manager cued up the footage. The time stamp blinked: 12:03 a.m., three nights earlier. A tall man wheeled a black suitcase over to Zane's unit. He moved with practiced ease, kept his head turned, wore a cap pulled low. Opened the lock with a key. Disappeared inside. Reemerged empty-handed.

"Not Zane," Hayley said. "This guy's taller. Broader frame."

Maddox grunted. "Could be anyone."

Hayley leaned forward. "I told you I saw someone in a wet suit in that sea cave the other day. Broad shoulders, same build. Could be him."

"Yes, and we searched that cave," Maddox said. "Found nothing. No dive bag, no gear. Are you sure you didn't imagine it?"

"I didn't imagine the man standing ten feet from me," Hayley snapped. "He moved like this guy. Same size. Same confidence. He wasn't hiding. He was checking something."

Mona added, "He's built like Roger Larkin. Or Chase Wingate. Doug Marsh, maybe."

Maddox crossed his arms, watching the screen. "None of them have rock-solid alibis."

"Exactly," Hayley said. "Any one of them could've

done this. Any one of them could've planted that evidence. You need to stop treating this like it's random. This was deliberate. Whoever this is—he planted that evidence. To sink Zane."

Maddox stared at the screen a moment longer, the edges of his jaw tight.

Hayley didn't say it, but she could tell: She'd finally gotten his attention.

Chapter 29

Hayley stood on the dock pretending to take scenic shots for her next *Island Times* column—a piece about Maine's most picturesque clam chowder pairings—but her real focus was the gleaming yacht tied up just ahead.

The Daily Catch.

As if summoned by tension alone, Nancy Larkin appeared on the gangplank, jangling her pearls and waving a tall glass of something icy and orange.

"Well, if it isn't Bar Harbor's busiest busybody," she called cheerfully. "Come aboard, darling. We're setting sail for the sunset booze cruise."

Hayley hesitated. Roger followed Nancy onto the deck in mirrored sunglasses and a breezy button-down. He raised his glass. "Plenty of room and plenty of rum."

"I was just—uh—taking photos."

"You can photograph your cocktail," Nancy said, already ushering her aboard. "That counts, doesn't it?"

Hayley climbed the gangplank, uneasy. The sun was

still bright, but shadows had started to stretch across the water. Something about this invitation felt . . . off.

Forced.

Or rehearsed.

Once onboard, Nancy pressed a glass of bubbly into her hand. "Mimosa? Or do you need something stiffer? We've got everything but scruples."

"This is fine," Hayley assured her.

"We hit the harder stuff once we're out to sea," Nancy said with a wink.

Hayley accepted the drink, scanning the deck.

Cushy, serene.

Too serene.

The engine purred to life.

Nancy was already at the helm, halfway into a story about someone at the Chamber of Commerce allegedly having cosmetic procedures done in Bangor under a fake name.

Roger raised his glass. "To fresh air and a fresh start."

Hayley sipped cautiously. She hadn't eaten lunch, and she didn't trust either of them to not try to push her overboard.

It wasn't so much paranoia as pattern recognition.

Roger settled beside her, smiling too widely. "You're not here just for the view, are you?"

Hayley feigned surprise. "Whatever do you mean?"

"You think I'm the man in the wet suit. The one sneaking around the cave and the storage unit."

Nancy laughed lightly as she gripped the wheel.

"That would require Roger to put on neoprene. Do you know how much he sweats in polyester?"

Hayley blinked. "So you've heard about the man I saw in the sea cave?"

Roger nodded. "Caleb Maddox came around this morning. Asked if I'd ever been scuba diving near Thunder Hole."

Nancy let out a snort. "Roger? Scuba diving? He nearly drowned once using a snorkel at Sand Beach."

Roger chuckled. "He showed me a still from the footage. Tall guy, broad shoulders, avoids the camera. I told him it wasn't me."

Hayley sipped. "And he believed you?"

"He checked the times. You were in that cave during the day—I was home watching *Naked and Afraid* reruns. Nancy made popcorn. The night someone broke into that storage unit? I was at poker night at the VFW. Ask anyone."

"I even picked him up afterward," Nancy added. "So he could drink without guilt."

Hayley tried to smile, but her grip on the mimosa glass had tightened.

The Larkins were being oddly forthcoming.

Too forthcoming.

Or were they just innocent and being honest?

It was hard to tell.

Roger leaned closer. "But tell me this—why are you really investigating all this, Hayley? Hank Desmond wasn't your friend. You've got no badge. Why keep digging?"

Nancy's tone turned airily sharp. "Unless, of course, you think you're the only one in Bar Harbor who knows the truth about people."

Hayley laughed nervously. "I just . . . care about justice."

Roger refilled her glass. "And we care about not being accused of murder."

Nancy took a seat beside her. "It's exhausting, frankly. The whispering. The sideways glances. It's starting to feel like we're in one of those true-crime documentaries where the locals decide the couple with a nice boat must have done it."

"Yeah," Roger added. "We were planning a quiet life. Instead, we've been drafted into your little murder mystery as red herrings."

Hayley looked out to sea. The coast was getting smaller behind them. The air cooler. The bubbles in her stomach weren't just from the champagne anymore.

"Guys," she said slowly. "if this is your way of telling me to back off—"

Roger held up a hand. "Relax. I told you. I'm not the man in the wet suit. I've got nothing to hide."

Hayley exhaled shakily.

"Roger's right," Nancy added, her tone softening. "We're not murderers. Just overworked people who barely have time for a night out, let alone participating in a conspiracy."

Hayley clinked her glass. "Fair enough."

Still, she made a mental note to check how fast she could swim in jeans.

Dinner at The Fig & Fern was exactly the kind of romantic, softly lit, overpriced fantasy Bar Harbor couples indulged in when they wanted to pretend the world wasn't full of secrets and lies. Which is why Hayley felt like an absolute jerk when she spotted Liddy and Doug Marsh at a window table, framed by candles and lilac centerpieces, and knew she had to interrupt.

She hesitated outside for several seconds. Liddy was laughing—really laughing—and Doug was holding her hand across the table like they were in a Nora Ephron movie. Hayley hated herself, but she couldn't walk away.

She entered, smiled at the hostess, and made a bee-line over to their table.

Liddy's smile faltered. "Hayley?"

Doug didn't even try to look pleasant. "Of course."

"I know, I know," Hayley said quickly. "Worst timing ever. But I need to talk to you both. Just two minutes."

Liddy, ever gracious, gestured to an empty chair. "What's going on?"

Hayley sat. "There's been new evidence. Surveillance footage. A man in a wet suit—seen in a sea cave and again breaking into Zane's storage unit. He avoids cameras, knows the layout. Someone is trying to frame Zane."

Liddy frowned. "A wet suit?"

Doug's posture tensed. "And you think it was me?"

"I'm saying it could've been anyone—someone tall, broad. Like Roger Larkin. Like Chase Wingate. Like you."

Liddy blinked. "Wait. Are we suspects again?"

Hayley pressed. "Doug, the gun used to kill Hank—it came from your home. You said it was stolen. Do you have any idea when that could have happened?"

Doug's jaw tightened. "Like I said before, I didn't even realize it was gone until the police told me where they'd found it. I kept it locked in a safe." He paused, shifting in his seat. "The only time I took it out was during a cocktail party I hosted the week before Labor Day. I showed it off—stupid, I know. A few people saw me open the safe."

Hayley frowned. "Who was there?"

"A dozen people or so. Friends, acquaintances. Some I don't know well. They came and went."

Liddy arched a brow. "I wasn't invited."

Doug turned to her, startled. "Because I hadn't met you yet. You had yet to steal my heart."

The line was sweet, but the moment was brittle. Liddy looked down, her fingers still on the wineglass stem.

"You didn't tell me about the party," she said.

"I didn't think it mattered."

"It matters if someone at that party took your gun and used it to kill your friend," Liddy said.

Doug's voice broke, quieter now. "You think I'm lying?"

Liddy didn't answer right away. Her lips parted, then pressed shut again. She looked like someone trying to solve a puzzle with one piece missing. "I don't know what to think," she admitted. "You told me the gun was stolen . . . and I believed you. But now, with everything else . . ."

Doug's jaw tightened. "I didn't realize I had to build a whole case file in order to date you. You said you trusted me."

"I want to," Liddy said softly. "I want to believe every word you've said. But now there's footage. There's this man sneaking into storage units, matching your build. And then there's the fact that Hank is dead. And you had a motive. We both know that."

"I didn't kill him," Doug snapped. "I didn't sneak into a cave or plant evidence or—" He shook his head. "God, this is insane."

Liddy's voice trembled. "But what if it's not?"

Doug turned toward Hayley. "Is this going to be your next headline? 'Hayley Powell Destroys a Relationship in Three Easy Steps'?"

Hayley raised both hands. "Doug, I'm not trying to hurt anyone. I'm just trying to get to the truth."

"Well, maybe next time you try a little harder not to bulldoze everything else in the process." He turned to Liddy one last time. "I was honest with you. But if that's not enough, maybe nothing will be. Whatever happened to innocent until proven guilty?"

He stood abruptly, his chair scraping across the floor loud enough to make the couple two tables over glance in their direction. He tossed a fifty-dollar bill on the table and walked out, his shoulders rigid, his stride tight.

Liddy sat frozen for a moment, eyes wet but unblinking.

Hayley hesitated. "I'm sorry. I didn't mean to make things worse."

Liddy finally looked at her. Her expression was soft, sad, tired. "I know. You're just doing what you always do. Looking out for people. Even when they don't want you to."

Hayley gave a small, awkward smile. "You'd think I'd have figured that out by now."

Liddy exhaled, brushing a napkin across her cheek. "You probably have. But it wouldn't be you if you didn't get tangled in it."

They both let out a breath that wasn't quite a laugh.

Liddy stared out the window toward the sidewalk where Doug had disappeared. "He says he didn't do it. And I want to believe that. I really do."

Hayley reached across the table. "I'm sorry."

"He's not a bad man," Liddy said. "Just a man who's afraid the world will stop seeing him as good."

Hayley didn't answer.

But she understood.

If Doug was telling the truth, that left one name.

Chase Wingate.

* * *

By twilight, Hayley was parked across from the Desmond home, slouched low in the seat of her Subaru, camera balanced on her knee. Chase had seemingly moved in already. His BMW was in the driveway. The porch light flicked on just before eight.

Kylie opened the front door in silk pajamas, hair pulled back, holding what looked like a martini as she checked her mailbox. Chase appeared in the doorway, a glass of wine in hand. He stepped forward to kiss the back of her neck.

Hayley snapped a photo.

Then another.

She wasn't even sure what she was trying to get on camera.

Maybe some kind of clue.

Or slipup.

Something that might prove Chase was the man in the wet suit and on the security footage.

Her phone buzzed.

Bruce.

She answered, trying to keep her voice casual. "Hey."

"Hey yourself. Where are you? You said you had a book group tonight."

"I do."

"Uh-huh. Are you there now?"

Hayley hesitated. "Um, yes?"

There was a pause on the other end.

She could never lie to Bruce.

He could always tell.

"Right. I just passed you. You're parked outside Kylie Desmond's house, aiming your camera like a PI on a Netflix docuseries."

Hayley slumped lower. "You're supposed to be covering copper theft."

"You're supposed to be at Caroline Pryor's house discussing *Where the Crawdads Sing*."

She sighed. "Touché."

Suddenly a sharp knock on the driver's-side window made her jump.

Chief Caleb Maddox.

Of course.

She rolled it down halfway.

"Evening, Chief."

"What are you doing, Hayley?"

"Research. For my column."

He peered into the car. "This part of your culinary tour? Scoping out suspects between appetizers?"

"It's for a piece called 'Ten Great Spots to Catch a Killer Between Courses'."

"Cute."

He leaned on the door frame. "I'm going to say this once. You're not subtle. And I know you're getting information from inside the department."

Hayley blinked. "Excuse me?"

"I don't mind you playing detective, Hayley. But when you start quoting things from autopsy reports?

That's not guesswork. That's a leak. Which makes me wonder who is setting your place at the evidence table."

She crossed her arms. "Maybe someone is. But it's definitely not Earl."

Maddox's eyes narrowed. "I never said it was."

Hayley cursed silently.

She tried to recover. "There are plenty of people in the department. You think I'm that persuasive?"

He scoffed. "No. I think someone's letting their guard down around you." He stepped back. "You want to keep playing detective? Fine. But if someone loses his badge because of you, that's on you."

Hayley drove straight to her restaurant.

At Hayley's Kitchen, the dinner rush had faded into the soft hum of clinking forks and low conversation. She spotted Earl and Mona in their usual booth near the back, Earl hunched over a steaming bowl of clam chowder and half a turkey BLT, Mona methodically working through a plate of sweet potato fries and sipping a cranberry spritzer.

Hayley slid into the booth, silent.

Earl looked up, instantly reading her face. "He's still on me, isn't he?"

She hesitated, then nodded. "Yeah. He didn't say your name outright, but it's clear he's made the leap."

Earl groaned and dropped his spoon. "Dammit. I knew it. I should've just kept my mouth shut."

Mona looked back and forth between them, brow raised. "What did he say, exactly?"

Hayley kept her voice low. "He knows I've been getting information no civilian should have. He suspects someone inside the department is leaking it to me. He's focused. Angry. Like he's got something to prove."

Earl leaned back in the booth, blowing out a breath. "I'm already on probation. And now he thinks I'm leaking autopsy reports and scene notes to my friend, the food columnist."

"You didn't leak anything," Hayley said quickly. "You told me a few things. Gave me a little context. That's all"

"I showed you parts of the preliminary report on Hank's wound pattern," Earl said flatly. "I didn't just drive the getaway car, Hayley. I gave you report summaries, discussed lab results. You think Maddox won't nail me for that? That's not 'a little context,' Hayley. That's grounds for suspension—or worse."

Mona reached across the table and took his hand, firm. "You were helping her. You weren't feeding a tabloid. You were doing the right thing."

Earl gave her a tight smile, but there was no humor behind it. "The 'right thing' doesn't carry much weight with Maddox. All he sees is insubordination."

Hayley's stomach twisted, guilt curling in her gut. "This is my fault."

"You didn't twist my arm," Earl said. "I offered."

"I pushed. I insisted. And you—" She swallowed. "You're the one who might lose his job."

Earl sat forward, rubbing his hands over his face. "Hell, maybe I should just beat him to the punch. Turn in my badge and open a fudge shop. Least then I'd still be able to keep the damn lights on."

Mona let out a dry laugh. "I'll help with the packaging. We'll call it 'Internal Affairs and Toffee.' Think it has a ring to it?"

But Hayley didn't laugh. She looked at them both, hands trembling slightly. "I'm serious. I didn't think it would spiral like this. I just wanted the truth. For Zane. For Tina. For Hank—even if he didn't deserve sainthood." She paused, voice lowering. "But I didn't think about what it could cost you."

Earl looked at her, softer now. "You were just trying to help people. Same as me."

Hayley nodded. "But people get burned when I go digging. They always do."

They sat quietly for a moment, the lull in conversation louder than anything else in the restaurant.

Finally, Hayley broke the silence. "I ruled out Roger. I think I've ruled out Doug, too, even if I didn't get a clear alibi. Liddy would've covered for him if she could. She didn't. That means . . ."

Mona finished her fry, chewed slowly, then said. "That leaves Chase."

Hayley exhaled, leaning back against the booth. "No alibi. No timeline. Just a smug look and a glass of wine on the porch like nothing ever happened."

"And let's not forget he was discovered at the scene of the crime," Mona added.

The windows of the restaurant caught their reflections—tired, worn down, and not nearly as confident as they'd been at the start of all this.

Hayley looked at Earl again, really looked at him—the deep worry in his eyes, the strain around his mouth—and felt something sink inside her.

"What if I've already cost you your job?" she whispered.

Neither of them answered.

Because it was entirely possible she had.

Chapter 30

Hayley tugged her jacket tighter as she stepped onto the boatyard lot, the tang of diesel and salt water thick in the crisp morning air. Fog hovered just above the waterline, slowly lifting to reveal lobster boats bobbing at their moorings. The boatyard was a maze of rigging, rusting trailers, and stacked buoys. She sidestepped a coiled hose, eyes scanning for someone who looked young, a little too wiry to be a seasoned fisherman, and possibly still mooning over her daughter.

She found him crouched near a flatbed, elbow-deep in a tangle of fireworks wire and fuse cable, muttering to himself as he tried to untangle a rat's nest of cord.

Aiden Meeks. Mid-twenties, freckles, curly brown hair under a backward Celtics cap, and a T-shirt so scorched it might have caught fire mid-show. When she said his name, he startled so hard he smacked his head on the trailer's edge.

"Oh—uh—hi! Mrs. Powell!" He scrambled to his feet, trying to brush off his shorts and not look like he'd just tased himself.

"Hayley," she said with a smile. "You were in Gemma's class, weren't you?"

His ears turned beet red. "Yeah! AP Chem. God, she was . . . like, brilliant. She made covalent bonds sound . . . sexy. And nice. And so pretty. I mean, not that you aren't also—uh—" He flailed. "Sorry."

"She's engaged," Hayley said gently, amused.

"Oh. Yeah. Sure. Of course." He gave a weak shrug. "But I can still pine a little, right?"

"You and every sous chef on the Eastern Seaboard."

"Yeah, I heard she was a really big deal at the Flavor Network these days."

Hayley leaned against a piling. "Listen, I'm looking into something from the fireworks show on Labor Day. You were on the pyro team?"

Aiden nodded quickly. "Yeah, mostly running cue checks and backup fuses. Nothing glamorous."

"Did you notice anything strange? During the finale?"

He paused, lips pressing into a thin line as he rocked back on his heels. "Actually . . . yeah. I didn't report it or anything, because I figured it wasn't a big deal."

"Try me."

Aiden glanced around like someone might be eavesdropping from behind the nearby stacks of traps. "Right near the end of the show—like, during the last big volley—I saw something in the water."

Hayley's heart gave a quick jolt. "Something . . . what?"

"A person. Or at least I think it was a person. Floating

out near the barge. Maybe fifty yards off? I caught it in my peripheral—only saw it because the fireworks were backlighting the bay. Looked like a head, shoulders, maybe in a wet suit. Just hovering there."

"Not moving?"

"No. Like they were treading water, facing the boats."

Hayley straightened. "Did they swim away? Surface? Anything?"

"I turned to check a fuse error and when I looked back, they were gone." He shrugged helplessly. "I just figured it was a marine bio student from COA. They do weird stuff in the water all the time, right?"

She didn't answer. Her mind was spinning. The location—fifty yards off the barge—would've put the diver within clear range of Hank's boat. The timing—right during the finale—lined up exactly with the bullet trajectory Earl had described. And Tina's video had shown fireworks at the same moment she'd heard the shot and when the man in the wet suit reached the shore.

Whoever that figure was, they'd waited in the water, used the finale's sensory overload as cover, and fired.

"Thanks, Aiden," Hayley said, distracted. "That's . . . really helpful."

"Hey," he said, shy again. "If you see Gemma, tell her hi for me?"

"Sure thing," Hayley said.

"And tell her that when she gets bored with that undeserving fiancé of hers, I'll always be here waiting!"

"I will," she lied, already walking away, head buzzing.

By early afternoon, Hayley was back at the house, flipping through her notebook at the kitchen table. A fresh cup of black coffee steamed beside her, ignored. Leroy curled up on the floor next to her foot, snoring softly.

Aiden's story was specific and disturbing. A figure in a wet suit, hovering in the water fifty yards from the fireworks barge, perfectly positioned to shoot Hank. The timing matched Tina's video and Earl's ballistics estimate. That person in the water hadn't been watching the show—they were waiting.

Planning.

The trajectory.

The timing.

The sound cover from the fireworks.

This wasn't a heat-of-the-moment murder. It was a surgical strike.

Which left her with three possibilities.

Three men.

Three question marks.

Doug Marsh owned the gun found in the melted cooler. His fingerprints were on it. He claimed it had gone missing after one of his cocktail parties, and she couldn't yet confirm—or deny—that story. Doug had left Liddy's side during the finale, claiming he needed to check on a phone call. Could he have made it out to the water and back in time? Maybe. It'd be tight. But possible.

Chase Wingate's prints were on the bullets. Not the gun. Why weren't his prints on the weapon itself? And if he was passed out below deck, like Kylie had insisted, then he couldn't have been in the water.

That left Zane, who'd gone completely off the grid. A trained diver. Strong swimmer. Familiar with the currents and depth of the bay. He had motive. Maybe he wasn't running from a setup—maybe he was running because he was the one who'd pulled the trigger.

Hayley rubbed her temple. As much as she disliked the idea, Zane was starting to look more likely than Doug.

At least for now.

But she couldn't completely rule Doug out, either.

Not yet.

Liddy's office was a burst of color and fragrance when Hayley walked in. A crystal vase of wildflowers sat on her desk, and she was humming to herself as she rearranged Post-it Notes on a wall calendar.

"You!" Liddy sang out. "Is this a peace offering or just a social call?"

"A little of both." Hayley shut the door. "I need to talk to you about Doug. Again."

Liddy gave her a look, then turned toward her sideboard with flair. "Well, if we're going to dredge up unpleasantness, we'll need some alcohol."

She opened a paneled cabinet and swung out a hidden bar cart stocked like a speakeasy—gin, vodka, bourbon, amaretto, even a half-used bottle of Goldschlager. She tossed a scoop of ice into two tumblers and looked back over her shoulder. "Gin rickey or something stronger?"

"I should say no," Hayley murmured, "but it's been a day."

Liddy handed her a vodka cranberry with a twist of lime, then clinked glasses. "To forgiveness. And possibly libel."

Hayley explained what Aiden had told her—about the silhouette in the water, the location near Hank's boat, the perfect timing. Yet another account of a wet-suited shooter near the *Slaughterhouse*. She admitted she'd wondered if Doug had been the one in the wet suit.

Instead of getting angry, Liddy barked out a laugh and reached into her desk. "Honey, if Doug tried to dive, you'd hear him screaming from here to Castine." She pulled out a folded sheet of paper and handed it over. "Medical exemption. He gets barotrauma from shallow swimming pools."

"Why didn't you tell me this before?"

"Oh, I just found out! Doug's been planning a surprise trip to Belize—some sort of diving excursion he wanted us to do together. Very *Eat Pray Love*. Anyway, he had to get a medical screening for the scuba package, and *boom*—inner-ear drama. Barotrauma? Something like that. The poor man can't go deeper than a swimming pool without feeling like his head's going to explode. Total romance buzzkill."

Then she handed Hayley the paperwork. "He was embarrassed. I think he thought I'd find him less sexy if I knew he couldn't dive. As if I care about that macho nonsense. I like a man who stays on dry land and mixes a good cocktail."

Hayley read the document. It was official. Doug Marsh couldn't dive more than six feet without risking a burst eardrum. He was medically disqualified from every dive-training program on the coast.

One more door closed.

One more theory shot to hell.

Hayley drained the rest of her drink in a single gulp.

Dusk was settling by the time Hayley left Liddy's office and started back toward home. The sidewalk gleamed with the sheen of recent rain, and the sky was slashed with orange and pink streaks. As she rounded the corner near the Desmond house, she stopped short.

Chase Wingate stood leaning against the split-rail fence.

Waiting.

His sleeves were rolled to his elbows, and his expression was unreadable.

"I saw you watching the other day," he said.

Hayley kept her tone light. "I like to people-watch. Occupational hazard."

"You were spying."

"You were making out with Hank's heartbroken widow on the front porch. Pretty sure even the squirrels stopped to stare."

Chase stepped forward. "Kylie doesn't need this crap. Especially from you. She's grieving."

"And you?"

"I grieve differently," he responded.

Hayley folded her arms. "Chase, your fingerprints were found on the bullets."

Chase let out a sharp breath, almost a laugh, but there was no humor in it. "Yeah, I've heard. Over and over. Every cop in town's shoved that in my face. And I still don't know how the hell it happened."

"Think harder," Hayley pressed. "Prints don't just appear. You handled those rounds somewhere."

He shook his head, pacing a little. "No. I never loaded that gun. Never fired it. It was Doug's, not mine. Why would my prints be all over his ammo?" His voice cracked with frustration. "None of this makes sense."

"Unless it does," Hayley said quietly. "Unless you're remembering wrong—or leaving something out."

That landed. He stopped mid-stride, frowning. His eyes narrowed as though a door was creaking open in the back of his mind.

"Wait," he said slowly. "Doug's cocktail party. The week before Labor Day."

Hayley stayed silent, letting him fill in the gap.

"He brought the gun out of the safe—was showing it off. There were bullets on the table, I remember that.

People were passing them around, making jokes. I picked up a couple. Just goofing." His voice quickened, eager now. "That's it. That has to be it. That's how my prints got on them."

"Convenient memory," Hayley said.

"It's the truth," he snapped. His exhaustion bled through. "I didn't shoot Hank. Somebody used that party to set me up."

"Doug?" she asked.

"Who else? It was his gun."

Hayley shook her head. "Doug's out. He couldn't have been anywhere near the water that night—the doctors made that clear. But you?" She leaned in. "You were right there. On Hank's boat. At the scene of the murder. And your fingerprints are on those bullets."

Chase faltered, mouth working. Then he started grasping at straws. "But . . . are they even sure? One shot fired—are they positive it matched?"

Hayley's eyes stayed locked on his. "It matched."

Chase froze.

Hayley's stare didn't soften. "If you're lying, Chase . . . it's going to come out. And when it does, it won't just be the cops breathing down your neck. You'll be finished."

"I'm not lying," he shot back, voice rising. "I told you what happened. The party, the bullets, that's it. Why don't you believe me?"

"Because you're not exactly a picture of honesty," Hayley said evenly. "You were sleeping with Kylie behind Hank's back. The man's dead, and you expect me to take your word at face value?"

His jaw tightened so hard she thought his teeth might crack. Color rose in his face as he stepped closer—too close.

In a sudden, sharp movement, he seized her arm.

"You need to stop asking questions," he hissed. "You're just going to make things worse for me."

Hayley didn't flinch.

His grip tightened. "People get hurt when they don't know when to quit."

Then he let her go, turned on his heel, and stalked up the path. The screen door slammed behind him.

Hayley stood rooted to the sidewalk, the chill of the evening creeping into her bones. Chase had given her his story, but the fear in his eyes told her even he didn't believe it would hold.

And that scared her more than anything.

This wasn't just about clearing someone's name anymore.

This was about survival.

Chapter 31

Hayley had just taken a peach cobbler out of the oven—it was for Bruce, but she'd already eaten a spoonful when it was still molten and regretted nothing—when her phone rang.

The screen lit up with Lacy Whitmore's name.

"Hayley? Sorry to bother you. I was cleaning out Tina's office at COA this morning," Lacy said, sounding brisk but drained. "There was something . . . odd. I didn't want to text it. I thought maybe I should show you in person."

Hayley straightened. "I can meet you there."

"I'm actually back at her house now. Trying to finish the last of it."

"I thought you were supposed to be out days ago."

"I was. But Terry's been a lot more accommodating since he walked in on me bent over a box in yoga pants. I think I broke his ability to form full sentences for a solid minute."

"Sounds like he's got a little crush."

"If I don't finish soon, Terry might ask me to move in instead of move out."

Hayley laughed. "I'm on my way."

Outside Tina's cottage, it looked like a well-picked-over yard sale. The porch railing was draped in a beach towel that had probably been left out since July, and the front lawn was dotted with recycling bins, cardboard boxes, and two folding chairs that didn't match.

Inside, the living room was a mix of sealed boxes and folders left open mid-sorting. Hayley stepped around a stack of books and an unplugged microscope to find Lacy seated cross-legged on the hardwood floor, binder rings open, papers fanned out like cards in a magician's act.

"I told myself I'd be out by Monday," Lacy said without looking up. "That was how many days ago?"

"I think you've earned a grace period," Hayley said, dropping her purse on a chair. "Especially if you've got Terry Osgood under your spell."

"I couldn't get through her desk at COA. It was like a paper hoarder's version of Narnia. I opened one drawer and found an unpaid parking ticket from 2014, two granola bars, and a field guide to mollusks. And then . . ."

Before she could finish, the front door creaked open.

Terry Osgood, the landlord, poked his head in. "Knock knock," he said sheepishly. "Just checking in on the timing."

Hayley turned, trying not to smile, muttering under her breath, "Speak of the devil."

Terry had slicked his thinning hair back and was holding a brown bag with what looked suspiciously like takeout from the new Thai place on Cottage Street.

Lacy stood. “I’m sorry, I know I promised today—”

“No rush,” Terry said quickly, then looked bashful. “I, uh, brought you some pad thai. Thought you might not have had dinner yet. You’ve been working so hard.”

Lacy blinked, surprised. “Oh! That’s . . . very kind.”

“I can come back tomorrow. Or Thursday. Friday at the absolute latest.” He glanced at Hayley and cleared his throat. “You’ve got my number.”

When he left, Hayley raised an eyebrow. “Well, well. I didn’t realize we were in the presence of Bar Harbor’s Most Eligible Landlord.”

Lacy gave a mock-groan and dropped back onto the floor. “He offered to help me Bubble-Wrap Tina’s microscopes earlier. I thought it was just small-town kindness, but now I’m reasonably sure it was the yoga pants thing.”

“Or maybe he just thinks pad thai is the language of love,” Hayley quipped, crouching beside her. “Now—what did you find?”

Lacy reached into a manila folder labeled 2023 ALGAE COMPARISONS—MID-JUNE SAMPLE SET, and pulled out a neatly folded piece of paper. “This was tucked between two sheets of graph paper. At first I thought it was trash.”

She held up a folded glossy flyer—the kind you’d

find at a local food expo. The paper was soft and worn at the edges, the ink slightly faded.

"It was shoved in the back of a drawer marked for algae comparison charts," she explained. "But obviously . . . not that."

Hayley unfolded it carefully.

Across the top was a bold, retro-style banner: "Smokin' Hot Shellfish Cocktail Sauce!" Below it, a photo of two men standing shoulder to shoulder, arms slung around each other, grinning like old drinking buddies. Hank Desmond was unmistakable, a big man with a booming presence, beaming in his signature apron. The man beside him was none other than Dr. Peter Baird.

Hayley stared. She had only met Baird recently—after Tina's drowning—but he had talked about Tina, not Hank.

Not once had he mentioned a friendship—or any connection—with Hank Desmond.

Lacy watched her carefully. "You recognize him."

"I met him at COA after Tina died," Hayley said slowly. "He talked about how much he liked Tina. I had no idea he even knew who Hank was."

"Well, they clearly knew each other. Intimately enough to pitch shellfish sauce."

Yet another person in Hank Desmond's orbit hoping to replicate his enormous success in the barbecue industry. This wasn't just a pattern; it was an epidemic.

Hayley traced a finger along the flyer's edge. "Hank

made a fortune with his sauces. People were furious about being cut out. Doug. Zane. Maybe even Kylie. Word is, she signed an iron-clad prenup. But Baird's name never even came up."

Lacy nodded, her voice low. "You remember that email Tina sent me—the one where she said she saw someone recently who unsettled her? She didn't say who. Just that it was someone she knew . . . and it shook her. Do you think—?"

Hayley stared at the flyer in her hand.

"She was talking about Baird," she murmured. "She must've seen him that night—coming out of the water." Hayley's fingers tightened around the flyer. "It was him. It had to be."

She folded the paper and tucked it into her bag.

"Thanks for calling me," she said quietly.

That afternoon, Hayley slipped into a back seat in the COA lecture hall. The room was a sleek mix of exposed wood and glass, with sunlight cutting through the windows and gleaming off rows of laptops, tablets, and one student discreetly recording audio into her smartwatch.

Peter Baird stepped up to the podium, squared his notes, and launched into his lecture: "Predator Behavior in Coastal Ecosystems."

He spoke with the practiced ease of a man used to controlling a room—not dynamic, but assured. His tone was clinical, but his metaphors landed.

"True predators," he said, "don't announce themselves. They don't bare their teeth or growl. The most effective predators blend in. They adapt. They observe. They strike only when the conditions are perfect."

Hayley felt a cold shiver trace her spine.

"They lurk. They wait," he continued. "They become the thing you're not afraid of—until it's too late."

He paused. His eyes scanned the room.

"Predators," he said softly, "blend in."

Hayley's skin prickled. She didn't look away.

He was talking about predators in the ocean. Or was he?

When the lecture ended, Hayley lingered until the students had packed up and drifted out in lazy clumps. Baird gathered his notes and unplugged a flash drive from the podium. When he noticed her approaching, he offered a faint smile of recognition.

"Ms. Powell. Back again."

"I'm making a habit of it," she said lightly. "Your talk was fascinating."

"Glad to hear it."

There was a pause. Then Hayley tilted her head.

"Can I ask—did you know Hank Desmond?"

Baird blinked. "No. Not really. Why?"

Hayley reached into her bag. "Because this says otherwise."

She handed him the flyer.

He looked down—and froze. Not dramatically, not theatrically. Just a subtle change in posture. A catch in his breath. A flicker in his expression.

Then he smiled. Controlled. Careful.

"Oh. That." He handed it back like it was meaningless.

Hayley waited patiently for him to explain.

It took a moment.

It appeared as if his mind was racing.

Then his face relaxed.

"We met a few times," he said easily. "Hank was trying to brand a few of his sauces. He asked for help with the label design—layout, fonts, things like that. I dabble in graphic design. Side projects. I lent him a hand, he slapped my design on the flyer, and that was that. It never went anywhere."

"Except it did," Hayley said. "He launched a whole line. It's sold all over New England."

Baird raised his eyebrows, feigning surprise. "Really? Huh. I guess I didn't keep tabs."

"So you did know him. Rather well, in fact."

"That was years ago," Baird said. "It wasn't a partnership. I did a mock-up or two and moved on. He got what he needed and ran with it. I honestly forgot he even used the design."

Hayley gave him a small nod, eyes never leaving his face.

There was a long pause.

Hayley tucked the flyer away and nodded. "Well, thanks for clearing that up."

She turned, feeling his hot gaze on her back, and walked out of the building into the cooling air, her boots crunching over the gravel. Goose bumps crawled up the back of her neck.

She didn't believe a word of it.

His story was too polished. His voice too even. And his eyes . . . they'd given it away.

Inside her bag, the flyer crackled as she walked.

In her mind, Baird's voice echoed: "Predators don't announce themselves. They blend in."

And suddenly, Hayley wondered just how long this particular predator had been circling.

Chapter 32

Leroy was snoring on the couch, his back legs twitching like he was chasing something in his sleep—probably a rogue meatball—when Hayley's phone buzzed against the kitchen counter.

She picked it up and saw Bruce's name flashing.

She answered. "If this isn't about dinner, it better be about murder."

"It's better," Bruce said, breathless and triumphant. "It's motive."

She sat upright. "Go on."

"I found a small-claims case filed by Peter Baird against Hank Desmond."

Hayley's heart skipped. "Where?"

"Rockport, Massachusetts. Just under ten years ago. Right before Hank's sauce really blew up."

"I'm coming. And I'm bringing Leroy. He's been cooped up in the house all day. Besides, if this turns out to be about a parking ticket, he can sniff out the real story—or at least the nearest sandwich."

* * *

The *Island Times* office hadn't changed in years—still too many leaning stacks of old issues, still the faint hum of a printer that sounded like it was dying dramatically. The newsroom buzzed with quiet chaos, reporters hunched over keyboards and muttering into headsets, the air still faintly scented with burnt coffee and the musty paper smell of old editions that refused to be thrown out.

Hayley pushed through the front door, Leroy trotting dutifully at her side, sniffing every corner like he expected cheese to be hiding under the recycling bin. She made her way to the back bullpen and Bruce's office.

Bruce waved her in as an excited Leroy skittered across the floor and stood on his hind legs, desperate for attention.

"Hey, buddy," he said, giving Leroy a quick scratch. "Don't let your mom distract me from serious journalism."

Hayley dropped her purse beside a filing cabinet and leaned in. "Tell me everything."

Bruce held up a highlighted printout. "Peter Baird filed a small-claims suit in Rockport. Claimed Hank owed him five thousand dollars for design services—branding, label work, product mock-ups. Said they had a verbal agreement for royalties if the sauce took off."

"Did they?"

Bruce flipped the page. "Doesn't matter. Baird signed a waiver. Classic boilerplate—work-for-hire, no royalties. The court tossed it. But get this—Sal covered it at the time. Just a blurb in his column, but it proves there was history."

Hayley blinked. "Sal wrote about it?"

Bruce smiled. "You might want to bring an offering."

Hayley groaned. "I didn't bring him anything."

Leroy barked once, as if shaming her.

Sal's office door was slightly ajar, so Hayley knocked and stepped in. Sal looked up from a molasses Whoopie Pie—half-eaten and precariously close to a pile of press release printouts. His eyes immediately narrowed.

"You came empty-handed."

"Nice to see you, too."

"No muffin? No lemon square? No peanut butter bar?"

"I brought Leroy," she offered weakly.

Sal gave the dog a squint. "Can he be filled with raspberry jam?"

Leroy growled, insulted.

Hayley sighed and pulled out the court file. "I'm here on business. You wrote about this case—Baird suing Hank Desmond in Rockport."

Sal snatched the page and read with one raised brow. "Well, well. I remember this. Hank had just started pushing his new sauce in stores up and down New England. Baird flipped when he saw it on a grocery shelf—Shaw's in Gloucester, I think."

"So Hank used Baird's design."

Sal grunted. "A modified version. Baird helped

create the look—color, tone, font. Hank launched with it and cut him out."

"Why didn't the lawsuit go anywhere?"

"Because Baird had no case. He signed away his rights. But that's the thing—he didn't let it go. I heard from a mutual friend that Baird couldn't stand seeing Hank's face in the condiment aisle. Would go out of his way to avoid it."

"And then he moved to Bar Harbor not too long ago."

Sal leaned back and sucked sugar off his fingers. "Right when Hank was considering expanding distribution, not just throughout New England, but nationwide. You think he moved here on purpose?"

Hayley looked down at Leroy, who was chewing on a rubber crab he'd found under Sal's desk.

"I think he's been blending in. Waiting."

Back in the front office of the *Island Times*, Hayley slid into the desk that used to be hers, back when she juggled office management, vendor invoices, and reporters who thought deadlines were more of a suggestion. The desk technically belonged to Tucker now—the overzealous twentysomething who labeled everything in emojis and once tried to pitch a TikTok series about bar trivia night—but Bruce had waved her over like she still owned the place.

She didn't argue.

It still felt like hers.

Leroy, having grown bored of his rubber crab, emerged from beneath the copy desk with a cracked ballpoint pen in his mouth like it was a victory cigar. Hayley stared down at him.

"Well, that's comforting," she said. "He's escalated from plush toys to office supplies."

Bruce leaned against the desk, arms folded. "Let him express himself. We've all chewed a pen or two under deadline pressure."

Hayley gave him the side-eye. "Is that how you write your ledes now? Gnawing on a Bic until inspiration strikes?"

"Only the retractable kind," he said. "I like a little danger."

She reached into her bag and pulled out the old flyer, smoothing it across the desk. Hank and Peter Baird grinned up at her, their arms slung around each other like two guys about to take over the condiment world. She scanned the image, eyes narrowing at the bottom corner.

J.C. Media. Light. Tilted. Faint, but unmistakable.

A slow smile crept across her face. "Well, look who left his signature."

Bruce leaned in. "That our local auteur? The Spielberg of Bar Harbor?"

"Jeff Campbell," she said. "Who else would watermark a seafood label like it was a Criterion Collection DVD?"

Bruce groaned. "Please tell me you're not going over there. The last time I saw Jeff, he tried to get drone footage of the Chamber of Commerce picnic. He almost decapitated a selectman."

"I am going," she said, already folding the flyer and stuffing it back in her bag.

"Alone?"

Hayley looked at him. "If you come with me, he'll try to cast us as a married couple in one of his tourism videos. Next thing you know we're slow-dancing in soft focus to a L.L. Bean jingle."

"Fair," Bruce muttered.

She turned to Leroy, who was now curled up under the desk, lazily gnawing on the pen like a chewed straw. "You stay here with your dad. Try not to rewrite his column."

Bruce raised an eyebrow. "If he starts talking about capturing your 'essence against the golden light,' run."

Hayley grabbed her bag. "Not until I see how flattering the golden light actually is."

The Campbell Studio was nestled behind an art gallery that had been "closed for renovation" for five years. Jeff's garage door was open, revealing a space filled with tripods, umbrellas, light reflectors, drones, and two mannequins dressed like "romantic lobstermen." On the wall were framed photos of Jeff himself with various celebrities who had visited the island. The one with local Maine author Stephen King looked suspiciously photoshopped.

Jeff himself was perched on a stool, wearing a billowy scarf over a T-shirt that read AUTEURS DO IT IN ONE TAKE.

He probably wears that on dates, Hayley thought to herself.

"Hayley Powell!" he shouted as if she were royalty arriving at Cannes. "You're just in time. I'm storyboarding my next tourism short—*Bar Harbor: Tides of Wonder*. It needs more emotion. More woman with a past."

"I brought one," Hayley said, stepping in. "But she also brought questions."

"Ooh. Intrigue." He adjusted his scarf. "Go on."

She handed him the flyer.

Jeff gasped. "Ohhh, vintage Jeff! That font! That framing! That's mine. I shot this on a dock in Southwest Harbor at sunset. Hank wanted 'dockside authenticity.' I gave him art. This was part of my 'Rustic Flavor Profiles' series. God, Hank was a nightmare about lighting—insisted on 'golden hour' but didn't understand cloud cover. And Baird? Baird was wearing boat shoes with no socks. A crime."

Hayley fought a grin. "Did they seem to get along?"

"At the time? Sure. Baird was thrilled. He said Hank was considering his design. I remember him pacing, saying, 'This could change everything.' Kept smoothing his shirt between takes. Told me Hank was 'on the verge of a massive rollout' and his label design was going to be 'the look that launched a thousand oysters.'"

Hayley blinked. "That's . . . vivid. And did Hank use it?"

Jeff shrugged. "Not the exact file, but close. Practically identical. Baird never got credit. Hank told people he designed the final version himself—said it better reflected 'his brand.' Classic Hank. Loud. Confident. Totally shameless."

Hayley leaned in. "And Baird?"

"He was furious. Next time I ran into him—months later, after the launch—he said Hank had ghosted him. Acted like they'd never spoken. Pretended the whole thing was Hank's idea from the start. Then one day he just . . . disappeared. Moved to Massachusetts, I think, to teach environmental sciences, or something boring like that."

"Only to reappear here at COA."

Jeff waggled his eyebrows. "You think he came back for revenge?"

"I think he didn't come here for the tide pools."

Jeff leaned in. "If this becomes a limited series, I want to direct the pilot. And I want you in it."

"In the murder story?"

"No, no. In my Bar Harbor promo video. You, cooking something rustic in a seaside kitchen while drone shots fly overhead. The people want authenticity, Hayley. They want salt air and sass."

Hayley laughed. "We'll talk."

Maybe.

Someday.

At home that night, Hayley laid it all out on the dining table—Jeff's flyer, Bruce's court documents,

Sal's grumbling quotes. Leroy snoozed beneath her feet, belly-up and snoring softly.

It was all there:

Peter Baird had been part of Hank's rise.

His design, his branding, had helped sell the sauce.

But Hank had cut him out, lied, and profited.

Like he had done to so many others.

But Baird sued.

And lost.

Then watched the sauce become a sensation in his own hometown. Then statewide. Regionally. And, eventually, about to be nationwide.

He vanished, reemerged in Bar Harbor, and slid neatly into the edges of the town.

Teaching at the College of the Atlantic.

Quiet.

Patient.

Watching.

Hayley opened her notebook and scrawled two words at the top of the page:

He's hunting.

And in her mind, she heard it again—Baird's voice in that lecture, calm and certain:

"Predators don't announce themselves. They blend in."

Only now, Hayley realized—he wasn't talking about fish.

He was talking about himself.

So, what happens, she wondered, *when a predator stops blending in?*

And starts to bite?

Island Food & Spirits

By

Hayley Powell

Last night, while Bruce and I were devouring his BBQ ribs (the famous ones, according to him), we started laughing about the first time he ever made them for Randy and Sergio. It's one of those stories that gets funnier every time we tell it—though Bruce didn't think so at the time.

Now, for those of you who don't know, Bruce and I go way back. We met in high school, and let's just say sparks did not fly. If anything, I wanted to use those sparks to light his hair on fire. Later, when we both worked at the *Island Times*—me writing my food column, him covering the crime beat—we still couldn't stand each other. Love came much later, after years of verbal sparring, eye-rolling, and me insisting that he was the most infuriating man in Bar Harbor. Turns out, I was half right.

Anyway, by the time we finally started dating, Bruce decided to impress my brother, Randy, and his husband, Sergio, with a backyard BBQ. He was already friendly with both—Randy from the bar, and Sergio from his police beat reporting—

but this was his big chance to show off his "world-famous ribs." (I hadn't heard of their fame before that day, but sure.)

Bruce spent a week preparing. He hunted down the perfect racks of ribs, crafted his secret spice rub (not Hank Desmond's, which he eschewed as too peppery), and bought enough charcoal, lighter fluid, and weather apps to survive a grilling apocalypse. So, of course, when Saturday rolled around, we woke up to pounding rain and gusting wind.

"Maybe you could just do them in the oven?" I suggested.

Bruce gave me a look that said I'd just insulted his manhood. "If I let a little weather stop me, I don't deserve to man the grill."

So out he went, determined and soaking wet, setting up his grill like a castaway making fire. Meanwhile, I stayed inside mixing Appletinis and saying silent prayers.

By the time Randy and Sergio arrived, the rain had turned into a full-on deluge. When I pointed Bruce out through the kitchen window, Randy and Sergio both sprang into action—grabbing coats and umbrellas and running out to "help."

"Leave him," I called after them. "He'll come in when he's ready!"

But, of course, they didn't. Randy and Sergio both have that heroic streak—Sergio's literally a cop, and Randy just likes an excuse to play one.

Within seconds, they were flanking Bruce like bodyguards, holding umbrellas over him and his grill while he stubbornly flipped ribs in the downpour.

There they stood—three drenched men huddled around a flaming grill, laughing like it was a beach party. Then a gust of wind picked up and launched all four foil-wrapped veggie packets into the air like flying saucers. Sergio's umbrella followed, soaring into the sky and disappearing forever.

Next thing I knew, the baked beans went airborne, the pot clattering across the patio and splattering brown splotches against my kitchen window. It looked like a scene from *Twister*—if that movie had been about grilled side dishes.

That was my breaking point. I flung open the back door and yelled, "Get inside! Now!" loud enough for the entire neighborhood to hear.

To his credit, Bruce grabbed the ribs before abandoning ship, and honestly? They were the only survivors of the storm. We finished cooking them in the oven, poured another round of Appletinis, and ate dinner with what was left of the baked beans. The guys were laughing, soaked to the bone, already turning the disaster into legend.

And that was the night I realized Bruce wasn't just stubborn—he was my kind of stubborn.

APPLETINI

INGREDIENTS

2 ounces vodka
1½ ounces sour apple schnapps
1 ounce simple syrup
½ ounce lemon juice

Fill a cocktail shaker halfway with ice. Add all the ingredients, shake well, and strain into a chilled martini glass. Sip while watching someone else fight a losing battle with a grill.

Easy Oven BBQ Ribs

(For when Mother Nature has other plans)

Ingredients

2 racks baby back ribs
Seasoning of your choice (I use salt, pepper, and garlic granules)
1 bottle of your favorite BBQ sauce

Preheat the oven to 350°F. Remove the membrane from the back of the ribs (a paper towel helps with grip). Season generously on both sides and place, arch side up, in a large baking pan. Cover tightly with foil and bake 2½ to 3 hours, until fork-tender.

Remove the ribs from from the oven, uncover, and slather with BBQ sauce on both sides. Broil for a few minutes to caramelize. Slice and serve.

Perfect for rainy days, first impressions, and anyone who insists their ribs are "world famous."

Chapter 33

Hayley spotted him the moment she stepped onto the Village Green—the most conspicuous inconspicuous man in Bar Harbor.

Earl was seated stiffly on a slatted bench beneath a fading maple tree like he was in a second-rate John le Carré spy thriller. He wore a battered windbreaker zipped all the way up despite the warm breeze, a pair of reflective aviator sunglasses that screamed off-duty mall cop, and a floppy beige fishing hat pulled low over his forehead. If his goal was to blend in with the few remaining tourists, he had failed spectacularly—he looked like someone trying to escape a federal indictment.

Hayley approached with two iced coffees in hand from ChocoLatte and deadpanned, "I see you've activated Operation Overkill?"

Earl tilted the *Boating Monthly* he was holding—upside down—and peered at her from over the top. "You're late."

"I had to wait for them to foam the cold brew," she

replied, plopping onto the bench beside him and handing him a cup. "What's with the getup? Did you lose a bet with the Coast Guard?"

"Caution," Earl said, accepting the drink with mock-gravitas, "is the better part of valor. Especially when your boss already has you on probation for consorting with civilians."

"You consort with me every morning over breakfast sandwiches," Hayley muttered.

From inside his windbreaker—after a series of overly dramatic glances left, right, and up into the branches as if expecting an NSA drone—Earl pulled out a slightly crumpled manila envelope, expertly swaddled in a page from the *Island Times* classifieds, like it contained nuclear codes, or worse, Caleb Maddox's browser history. He leaned in, voice lowered to a conspiratorial stage whisper. "As requested," he said, eyes darting again toward a passing golden retriever like it might be wearing a wire.

Hayley tore into the package with the urgency of someone opening their SAT scores. Inside was a thin forensic file, the one she'd been waiting on. Her eyes scanned the top page and narrowed.

"I thought Chief Maddox said the cave was empty. Nothing there."

"He believed that at the time," Earl said, casually sipping his coffee as two teens raced by on skateboards, one of them gripping a giant inflatable clam and yelling. Earl stared after them. "Shouldn't they be in school?"

"Earl, focus," Hayley pleaded.

Earl snapped to attention. "Right. The hair sample wasn't found until later. One of the forensics guys did a second sweep. Found it tucked way in the back, near a coral shelf pocket."

"So Maddox just didn't bother to tell me?"

"He didn't know," Earl said. "The report just came in. And you know Maddox isn't exactly in the habit of calling you with hourly updates on every twist and turn in the case. That's why you've got me."

Hayley shook her head, grumbling. "So basically, the cave *wasn't* completely empty. It was just searched by people who needed stronger prescription lenses."

She scanned the page more carefully now. A single coarse gray hair, embedded in the fibers of a wet suit fragment recovered from sediment near the back of the cave. The lab confirmed it had been exposed to seawater and heat. Microscopic remnants of neoprene were still clinging to the follicle. The texture was wiry, the color silvery-white. Recently dyed at some point, the report noted—perhaps to mask aging.

Hayley read the line twice, then muttered, "So, whoever it belonged to didn't just have gray hair. They tried to cover it up."

Earl leaned in, peering at the page. "Someone's been using Just for Men. Probably whatever shade is one step up from midlife crisis."

Hayley didn't smile. "This came from the wet suit. Which means it had to be from the man I saw in that cave. The one who killed Hank. And most likely drowned Tina, too."

"So, who do you think it is at this point?"

"Zane's got a head full of golden surfer curls," she muttered. "And Roger Larkin's been bald since Bush was in office. The first one."

Earl nodded. "So I guess, unless your killer stole someone's toupee—"

"This isn't Zane," she said. "And it's definitely not Roger."

Earl scratched his stubbly chin. "Doug Marsh? Possible. His hair was a similar salt-and-pepper mix."

Hayley shook her head. "No. A man who gets dizzy during swim lessons could never pull off a cold-blooded dive-and-shoot mission."

She held the report between them like it might whisper the answer. "Someone older. Someone smart. Someone who blends in."

"It sounds like you already know who that hair belongs to."

"I do. Peter Baird."

And she had now found even more incriminating evidence.

Before Earl could respond, a familiar voice screeched across the Green.

"*Aha!*"

They both turned.

Mrs. Dunphey was bearing down on them at full throttle, her garden cart rattling behind her like a one-woman parade. She wore a wide straw hat with a fake sunflower the size of a salad plate stuck to the brim, and her wraparound sunglasses gave her the look of a paranoid beekeeper.

"I knew it!" she shrieked, jabbing a gloved finger in Earl's direction. "I knew something was going on!"

"Mrs. Dunphey," Hayley said, standing halfway. "Nice to see you."

"You thought you could fool me, Hayley Powell!" she accused. "But I knew that wasn't your husband. I know my eyesight isn't perfect, but that's definitely not Bruce Linney. I saw you two canoodling from across the street and thought maybe Bruce got a new haircut and took up fly-fishing, but I was wrong. This one's new. Who is he?"

Earl turned awkwardly away, pretending to examine his *Boating Monthly*. "I'm not new."

"You most certainly are," she said. "Unless you're hiding from someone. Are you in witness protection? On the lam? Canadian? Oh dear lord, is Hayley having an affair with a Mountie?!"

"Ma'am—" Earl started.

She peered at him closer, leaning in until her nose almost touched his cheek. "Wait a second . . . you look vaguely familiar. Do you work as a bag boy at the Shop 'n Save?"

"No, Mrs. Dunphey, I'm—"

She pointed an accusing finger in his face. "You're the one who always packs my eggs in the bottom of the bag, which is why they always get crushed!"

With an exasperated sigh, Earl yanked off the sunglasses and tugged the floppy hat off his head, revealing his unmistakable face.

"Earl!" she gasped. "You scoundrel!"

Earl gave a tiny, embarrassed wave.

Mrs. Dunphey gasped again, more theatrically this time. "You're stepping out on Mona Barnes? With her best friend?"

"Oh, for the love of—" Earl tried to protest.

Hayley choked on her iced coffee. "He's not stepping out on anyone!"

Mrs. Dunphey raised her chin. "Well, I don't know what sort of arrangements you people have, but I think it's shameful. Poor Mona. She's out there hauling lobster traps with her bare hands while you two sneak around the Village Green playing dress-up like it's some kinky *Mission: Impossible*."

And with that, she spun her garden cart around and stomped off, her pug—decked out in a Red Sox jersey—snorting behind her.

"Should I call Mona and explain?" Hayley asked.

Earl looked mortified. "Let me disappear first."

And just then, as if summoned by fate, a Bar Harbor police cruiser rolled past on Main Street. Chief Maddox was behind the wheel. His eyes scanned the Green. For a split second, he locked eyes with Earl—disguise-less and thoroughly exposed.

"Do you think he saw you?" Hayley asked.

"Oh, he saw me." Earl groaned, sinking low into the bench. "Cover officially blown." Earl drained the last of his iced coffee. "So, what now?"

"We need Maddox to request a hair sample from Peter Baird so the lab can test it and see if it's a match."

"Baird's not even on his radar at this point for the Hank Desmond murder."

"Then I need to get him pointed in that direction."

"And how are you going to do that?"

Hayley looked at the forensics report again, fingers resting on the page. "The cave wasn't empty. Not completely. They missed something once. What else did they miss?"

"You're not seriously thinking of going back out there—"

"I have to," she said. "There could be something else. Something bigger. Something that proves irrefutably it was Peter Baird who wore that wet suit. And why."

Earl muttered, "You know what else you need? Supervision."

"Too late for that."

She patted his shoulder, tucked the folder under her arm, and turned toward the parking lot.

Earl called after her. "Just don't die. It'd be hard to explain to Maddox!"

Hayley glanced back with a grin. "Then don't wear the hat."

And with that, she strode off, her mind already back in the cave, retracing every step, every missed shadow—hoping the next one would finally give her the truth.

Chapter 34

Bruce stood barefoot in the kitchen, sipping coffee and scribbling in a reporter's notebook with the manic focus of someone determined to finish a deadline piece before breakfast. Leroy, bored with the lack of attention, had decided to root through the recycling bin and was now parading a crushed Diet Dr Pepper can around the living room like it was a trophy from the Westminster Kennel Club.

Hayley tightened the strap on her shoulder bag and called out, "If I don't make it back, tell the world I died heroically. Possibly surrounded by seaweed."

Bruce didn't look up. "Noted. Just be sure to return the new kayak. I have plans for Eagle Lake tomorrow."

She kissed him on the cheek. "Unlike the last one, you'll have it back in one piece. Can't promise the same for myself."

He glanced at her then, eyeing her sneakers and windbreaker. "You're really going back to that cave?"

"I need to see it again. Earl says the hair the forensics

guy found didn't come from the first sweep—it showed up later, tucked behind some coral shelf in the back."

Bruce finally set the notebook down. "You sure about doing this alone?"

"No, actually I'm not. I'm bringing backup. Hannah Holloway."

He blinked. "Hannah Holloway? The one who still resents you for not writing about her eco-tour business in your 'Hidden Gems of Bar Harbor' column?"

"Yes, she didn't buy my explanation that I only write about food and cocktails," Hayley said, grabbing Leroy's leash and tethering him to the banister. "I'm banking on the fact that she's got a thing for Zane. I saw them last summer—kayaking around Bar Island at sunset, laughing like a pair of teenagers on a first date. She claims they're just dive buddies, but I've seen less chemistry in a bottle of seltzer. I'm hoping her crush outweighs her mild hatred of me."

Bruce smirked. "You're a master manipulator."

"Flattery will get you dessert when I test recipes tomorrow." She opened the door, then paused. "If I'm not back by dinner, investigate my murder. And when Netflix calls, make sure they cast someone at least ten pounds lighter to play me."

Bruce gave her a deadpan look. "You know I'm going to be the first person they arrest, right?"

Hannah Holloway was tightening a life vest on a mannequin near the front window of her kayak shop, earbuds in, bobbing her head faintly to music Hayley could only assume was something instrumental and vaguely Scandinavian.

When Hayley walked in, she didn't look thrilled.

"Oh," Hannah said flatly. "It's you."

"Good morning to you, too," Hayley chirped. "I come in peace. And bearing caffeine." She handed over a large iced latte. "No milk, half sugar, weird mushroom powder. Just like you take it."

Hannah narrowed her eyes but accepted the drink. "So, what do you want, Hayley?"

"A guide," Hayley said, stepping up to the counter. "I've already got a kayak strapped to my roof like a giant hood ornament. I just need someone who knows the tides—and doesn't mind questionable company."

"Last time you went kayaking, you nearly drowned, or so I heard. You had no business taking a kayak into the choppy Atlantic. You were bad enough on a smooth lake."

"True. Which is why I need someone competent. Strong swimmer. Knows the water."

"And you thought of me? Wow. Desperate times."

"Look, I wouldn't ask if it wasn't important. You know what's going on with Zane, right?"

Hannah stiffened. "Not really. I mean . . . I haven't seen him."

"But you used to, right? Kayaking together, maybe some diving? Maybe a little post-paddle flirtation?"

"Okay, sure. But that proved to be a dead end. He

was way too into Kylie, and I wasn't into being sloppy seconds."

"I really need you, Hannah."

Hannah crossed her arms. "So where do you want to go? Let me guess. This is about that sea cave everyone's been whispering about at the marina?"

Hayley nodded. "You heard about that, too?"

"Hard not to. Bar Harbor's been buzzing about it ever since the cops came up empty. So, what—now you want to poke around the scene they already cleared?"

Hayley smiled sweetly. "What can I say? I'm stubborn, and mildly obsessed. And you—have excellent core strength and a crush on Zane."

Hannah colored slightly. "I teach people how to stay upright in a kayak. That's it."

"Uh-huh." Hayley leaned on the counter. "You're worried about him. I can tell."

Hannah hesitated just long enough to give herself away.

"I think he's in trouble," Hayley said gently. "I think someone scared him. I also think you're the kind of person who wants to help when she can."

Hannah looked at her for a long moment. Then gave a sigh worthy of an Oscar.

"Fine, but just promise to follow my instructions to the letter this time, and if you hum the *Jaws* theme at any point, we're done."

"Cross my heart."

* * *

The paddle out was brutal.

Wind whipped across the surface of the water, chopping the waves into shards that slapped against the kayaks. Hayley's hands were already cramping, her thighs aching, her stomach doing slow backflips.

Hannah sliced through the water like a human motorboat, calm and in command.

Hayley, in contrast, gripped her paddle with white knuckles. Hannah, in the back, seemed to sense the tension.

"You okay?" Hannah called over.

"Define okay!"

But she kept paddling.

The last time she'd been out here, she'd almost died—and every gentle lap of water against the hull felt like a whispered warning.

They coasted past lobster buoys and seaweed-laced rocks, hugging the shore and ducking beneath an outcropping where cormorants blinked at them from their nests. The cliffs loomed higher than she remembered, streaked with shadow and seaweed.

"Did you tell anyone where you were going?" Hannah asked.

"Bruce," Hayley said. "And Leroy, but I don't think he grasped the details."

The approach to the sea cave came into view—those same dark rocks slick with spray, the opening like a mouth waiting to swallow them. Hayley tamped down her fear and pushed forward.

Inside, the cave was cool and echoing, every drip of

water off a stalactite sounding like a gunshot. Hayley felt the hairs rise on her arms, even under her windbreaker.

The police had found nothing here a week ago.

But now . . .

She pulled out a waterproof flashlight and swept the beam across the floor.

Hannah pointed her flashlight at a crumpled sleeping bag in the corner, a pile of empty granola bar wrappers, and a half-crushed can of Bud Light.

"Someone's been back here after the cops," she whispered.

They paused.

Hayley stopped breathing.

A sound. Soft. Indistinct. The faintest shuffle behind a rock shelf, barely louder than the drip of seawater off the cave walls.

Hannah turned slowly, the beam of her flashlight quivering. "Did you—"

"Shhh." Hayley's whisper cracked in the thick air.

She raised her flashlight again, sweeping the rocky crevices. Shadows danced across wet stone and seaweed. The cave had a way of playing tricks—echoing back your own movements, making still things seem to flicker.

But this . . . this was something else.

There it was again.

A scuff.

Closer this time.

"Is someone there?" Hayley called out, trying to

sound firm, but her voice warbled, echoing off the cave walls with eerie distortion.

Silence.

Then movement. A subtle shift, just past a curtain of limp, kelp-like algae hanging from a rock face.

Hayley took a step forward. "We know someone's in here," she said, louder this time. "We're not leaving."

No reply.

The shadows thickened behind the curtain of seaweed—then twitched. Hayley and Hannah both jerked backward, instinctively huddling closer.

The seaweed rustled. Slowly.

Then—something emerged.

A figure stepped through the green veil of algae fast and low, arms raised, face wild in the sudden beam of the flashlight.

Both women screamed. Hannah nearly dropped her light.

"Whoa—stop! It's me!"

Zane.

Wet-haired, stubbled, eyes wide with panic and exhaustion. He froze with his hands in the air, wincing as if expecting to be tackled.

Hayley staggered backward, clutching her flashlight like a weapon.

"Zane?" she breathed.

"I thought you were the cops," he said, shoulders sagging. "Or worse."

"Worse than the cops?" Hannah said, breathless. "Like who, the Coast Guard?"

Hayley scanned him. "You look terrible."

"Thanks. Been living off gas station jerky and rainwater. I can't go home. They think I did it."

Hayley's eyes were still locked on Zane. He looked like hell—like he hadn't slept in days, with a week's worth of beard and eyes like a cornered animal. His clothes were damp, his hair was clumped, and a fine red mark ran along the edge of his jaw, like he'd been scraped or struck.

"Explain. Now," she said.

"I've been hiding out here," he said simply. "Waiting for things to cool down, for the cops to finally realize I didn't kill anyone."

Hayley narrowed her eyes. "You didn't clear out the cave before the cops came?"

He shook his head. "No, that wasn't me. I came back after. I figured I was safer here than anywhere else."

"'Safer'?" Hannah echoed.

"Yeah, I was reasonably confident the person trying to set me up for two murders wouldn't think to come here looking for me, especially after the cops searched it."

Hayley braced herself. "What person are we talking about?"

"I know who did it," Zane said. "I've known all along. But I can't prove it."

Hayley crouched down, scanning the area again. She spotted something partly buried under a granola bar wrapper—a crumpled slip of paper. She tugged it free.

A marine supply invoice.

She flipped it over.

The initials at the bottom: *PB*.

Her stomach dropped. "Peter Baird rented this gear?"

Zane nodded grimly. "He asked me to help him get equipment a few weeks ago. Said he wanted to dive solo, do some underwater photography. I didn't think anything of it—he was Tina's colleague at COA."

Hayley's voice dropped. "And when the gear turned up behind Drinks Like A Fish?"

"I knew," Zane said. "I knew I was being framed."

"What happened when you confronted him?"

Zane looked at her, then Hannah. "He said that if I talked, I'd end up like Tina."

They were silent a long moment.

Then Hannah stepped forward, softly. "I was worried about you."

Zane gave a tired, grateful smile.

Hayley exhaled and tucked the slip into her jacket. The truth was finally forming. Baird had motive, means, and now a pattern of silencing anyone who got in his way.

It was time to turn the tide.

Chapter 35

Hayley had sautéed a lot of onions in her life. She's flambéed shrimp in a blizzard, caramelized scallops in the back of a moving RV, and once brûléed bananas during a blackout while using a lighter and a paring knife.

But this was the first time she'd attempted a lobster mac and cheese demo while being grilled about murder—and her hot husband.

"Be honest," a girl in a crop top and COA hoodie whispered from the back of the college's airy teaching kitchen. "Is Bruce Linney really your husband? Because he looks like if sexy Hemingway did CrossFit."

Hayley stirred her roux and tried not to blush. "He's mine, and I've got the wedding photos to prove it."

"Can he come next time?" someone else called.

She'd been invited by the Student Sustainability Club, though it became immediately clear the real draw was her reputation as a murder magnet. One student joked that COA should rename the kitchen "The Scene of the Thyme." Another offered her a Tupperware container of seaweed chips and whispered, "You're so much cooler than our forensics professor."

A guy with gauged ears and an apron that said WHISK TAKER leaned over the island. "If this ever becomes a streaming series, who do you want to play you? My vote is Julianne Moore. No question."

"She's too classy," another student said. "I vote for the girl from *Poker Face*."

Hayley held up a whisk like a traffic cop. "Wow. An insult and a compliment all in one. My husband and I were just talking about this. But we're here to talk about food. Unless one of you thinks the killer used lobster shells as a weapon—"

"I mean," said a nonbinary student with a silver nose ring and a sardonic smile, "you could probably gouge an eye out with one of those claws."

"Not helpful, Sage," Hayley said.

"Helpful-adjacent," she said.

She sprinkled in shredded cheddar, trying to steer them back toward dairy and away from death, but it was no use. The room buzzed with true-crime excitement.

"I heard Tina was wearing a wet suit when she disappeared."

"Do you really think Zane killed anyone?"

"Rumor has it you nearly drowned when you were out investigating that sea cave. What was it like on the edge of death? Was there a light? A tunnel?"

"Do you know you're trending on local TikTok?"

Hayley groaned. "Why didn't I just bake cookies?"

Sage edged closer. "Okay, real talk. You didn't come here just to cheese up our lunch, did you?"

Hayley hesitated, then lowered her voice. "No. I need to get into Peter Baird's office. I was hoping for a little extracurricular help."

Sage's eyes lit up. "You're my hero."

Within seconds, a student-led distraction plan was set in motion with the kind of coordinated chaos that could only come from a campus that had turned Earth Day into a three-day festival involving interpretive dance, ethically sourced glitter, and a surprisingly effective petition to outlaw plastic forks.

Someone spilled a kelp smoothie in the hallway. Another faked an allergic reaction to quinoa. A pair of wannabe drama majors debated the ethics of marine forensics in increasingly louder voices until Peter Baird finally stormed out of his office, muttering, "This campus is a circus."

Sage gave Hayley the signal—a subtle tip of the head toward the anthropology wing.

Hayley tucked a pot holder into the oven door, whispered "Stir that every thirty seconds," and hustled down the corridor, her heart pounding.

Baird's office was dim and musty, the walls plastered with maps of predatory migration patterns, an academic certificate, a signed poster from a Maine PBS special entitled "The Predator's Mind," and dive photos in which Baird stared intently at the camera like he was auditioning for *Jacques Cousteau: The Musical.*

Hayley snapped photos with her phone—of his desk

calendar, of a corkboard covered in notes about Tina's research, and a scribbled diagram of dive sites near Thunder Hole. Nothing jumped out at first glance, but she knew how often little things became big ones later.

She tugged open a few drawers—paper clips, brochures, an old flip phone, a small bottle of beard oil. Then, tucked in the back of a lower drawer, a black-handled hairbrush.

She reached in carefully. Gray hairs were snarled in the bristles—coarse and thick. She pulled two loose ones out with tweezers from her purse, dropped them into a Ziploc baggie, and started to close the drawer—

When the door handle turned.

Hayley froze.

There was nowhere obvious to hide, so she dropped behind a tall, metal bookshelf next to the window, curling herself into a crouch.

Peter Baird entered, sighing as he muttered to himself. "If I wanted to grade TikTok monologues, I would've gone into performance studies."

He crossed the room and sat at his desk. Hayley remained perfectly still, biting her lip. Her phone vibrated in her back pocket. She didn't dare check.

Any sudden move and he would sense her presence.

She had to remain absolutely still.

How was she going to get out of here undetected?

Then, mercifully, came a knock.

"Professor?" Sage's voice rang out, perfectly indignant.

"I need to discuss my grade. I worked so hard on that paper. You only gave me an A?"

Baird sighed. "That's a very high mark, Sage."

"Not when you factor in how brilliant I am. I made a predator–behavior-to-*Drag Race* comparison that slayed. And you said although impressive, it still lacked depth?"

"Which explains the A and not an A plus."

As Sage stormed into the office, waving papers, throwing Baird off-guard, Hayley seized the opportunity to slink along the wall and slip out the side door, barely breathing while Sage had him distracted. She bolted down the hallway and back into the kitchen, where someone had added bacon to the mac. The pot was threatening to boil over.

She stirred quickly and lifted the lid off the Dutch oven.

"Did you get it?" Sage asked, returning with a triumphant grin and a water bottle labeled UNFILTERED STUDENT RAGE.

"Oh, I got it," Hayley whispered. "Thanks to you."

"I feel like Holmes to your Watson. That's so lit!"

That afternoon, Hayley met Earl behind the Bar Harbor Post Office, where the only thing more sacred than federal mail was plausible deniability. And if anyone asked, they were just two concerned citizens discussing stamp prices—nothing more.

Earl arrived in his off-duty windbreaker, sunglasses on, head ducked like he was part of a B-movie spy ring. At least he'd upgraded from his last attempt at undercover—a neon boat hat that could've guided planes to safety. He handed her a coffee from Choco-Latte as she held up the plastic bag with Baird's hair sample.

Earl, glancing around to make sure no one was watching, carefully took the Ziploc bag with a sigh. "You got this from his office?"

"While you were probably out doing actual police work."

"I was, in fact, investigating a suspicious seagull-related trash bin fire this morning, thank you very much," he muttered. "Had to chase a gull off a flaming pizza box behind Finback's. This is what my career has come to. It's only going to get worse the more I hang around you."

"I'm sorry, Earl," Hayley said, genuinely remorseful.

"It's okay. It makes Mona happy, and I'll do anything to keep my baby girl happy."

Baby girl?

Hayley decided not to mention that Mona was nearly twenty years older than Earl.

He held the strands up to the light, squinting. "I'll hold on to it, Hayley. But Maddox isn't gonna authorize a DNA test without a court order, a witness statement, or divine intervention from Saint Forensics. He's still ticked we used departmental resources to search that cave and turned up nothing but one random hair sample—not even found at the crime scene, mind you."

Hayley bristled. "It was near the crime scene."

"It was in a cave. Caves are not jurisdictionally promising."

"Jurisdictionally. That's a big word. Someone's been studying."

"What can I say? I have ambition. I want to be the best I can be for Mona."

"Then help me crack this case. That will surely impress your woman." She yanked out her phone and pulled up the photos she'd taken in Baird's office. "Look. It's Baird's calendar. The week before the shooting? A note that says 'Doug M's cocktail party. Bring wine and charm.' That was the night when Doug's gun went missing."

Earl's expression shifted. He leaned in. "Wait, really?"

She angled the screen toward him. "Right there. You can see it under his scribbled note about dive profiles and that doodle that looks suspiciously like a harpoon."

Earl rubbed his jaw. "So, Kylie, Chase, and Baird were all at that party."

"Exactly. But only one of them is bitter enough, trained enough, and creepy enough to swim up to a boat in the dead of night, shoot a man through the ribs, and then try to frame someone else for it."

"Okay, I'll talk to the chief. But I'm not making any promises."

* * *

Hayley stopped by the Desmond house just before dinner. A silver Mercedes was parked in the driveway—Chase Wingate's, she was sure. The plate read WNG8—because of course it did.

Kylie answered the door barefoot, wearing a silky wrap dress in lemon yellow that clung like it had been steamed onto her. Her toenails matched the coral cocktail she carried in one hand. Behind her, smooth jazz drifted from a Bluetooth speaker. Her days of playing the grieving widow were officially over.

"Oh. You again." Kylie's eyes narrowed, irritation winning out over surprise. "Haven't we covered this enough? Because I'm really not in the mood for another exhausting interrogation."

Hayley caught the edge of the door before it shut. "I'm not here to build a case against Chase," she said quickly. "I'm here to do the opposite. But I need you to hear me out."

Kylie hesitated, lips pressed thin, then finally pivoted on her heel and stalked toward the back patio. Kylie dropped into a cushioned lounger, stretched her legs, and went to work on the hem of her dress, tugging it smooth and then rough again, like she was trying to pull herself together by force of will.

She let Hayley stand there in silence for a beat. Then another. The gulls overhead filled the gap with their shrill complaints. Finally, with a dramatic sigh, Kylie lifted her chin.

"Fine, go ahead," she said at last, the words reluctant, as though dragged out of her. "Ask. But if this is just another excuse to paint Chase as the homicidal villain, I'm done."

Hayley sat down across from her, perching on the edge of a wicker ottoman. "I wanted to ask about Doug Marsh's cocktail party."

"Oh." Kylie brightened slightly, as if the memory of wineglasses and gourmet canapés was a pleasant escape from her current reality. "That was fun. Well, until Hank made a scene."

"He did?"

Kylie sipped her drink. "He wasn't thrilled I'd gone without telling him. He showed up at the end, saw me sitting on some guy's lap, and stormed out again."

"Was it Chase's lap?"

"I don't think so. There were lots of handsome men at the party, as I recall."

Interesting, Hayley thought.

"I was having a good time. Sue me."

"So, who else was there?"

"Doug, obviously. Peter Baird. That grad student with the unibrow. Chase and me. Some others I didn't know."

Hayley leaned in. "So, Peter Baird was definitely there?"

Kylie nodded, twirling her straw. "He was weird. Kind of jittery."

"Was he there most of the night?"

Kylie nodded. "Yes. I mean, he did disappear for twenty minutes. Maybe more."

"You remember that specifically?"

"Uh-huh. I remember spilling red wine on Doug's rug. I looked around for club soda—Peter's usually the one who hovers and insists red wine binds to fabric the way barnacles cling to a hull. But he was just . . . gone."

"And the gun?" Hayley asked.

Kylie's brow creased. "What gun?"

"Doug's missing handgun. He kept it in a safe at the rental, right?"

Kylie shifted in her seat. "Yes. He hauled it out once—at that party. Wanted to show it off. Like some kind of cowboy."

"Who handled it?" Hayley pressed.

"Chase did. A couple of Doug's friends, too. He even passed the bullets around like they were party favors."

"And who was standing there when he opened the safe?"

Kylie hesitated. "I was. Chase. Some others. And Peter Baird." She gave a sharp exhale. "Doug didn't exactly shield the combination. Stood there spinning the dial in plain sight. Anyone watching closely could've caught it."

Hayley's eyes narrowed. "So whoever went back later didn't stumble onto that gun. They knew exactly where it was—and exactly how to get it. Which means Peter Baird walked out of that party with more than free cocktails."

Kylie flinched at the precision of the accusation but didn't argue.

From somewhere upstairs came the unmistakable sound of furniture being dragged across a hardwood floor. Then a *thud*.

Kylie rolled her eyes. "Chase is reorganizing the guest closet. He thinks we need more space for his golf clubs. Because he's the one living out of a suitcase, apparently."

Hayley didn't comment.

The only thing louder than Chase upstairs was the awkward silence hanging between them. She watched as Kylie topped off her drink from a crystal pitcher and added a sprig of rosemary.

"So. Does that help?"

"It does," Hayley said carefully, her mind already racing ahead.

She rose. "Thanks for making things clear."

Kylie gave her a polite, practiced smile. "Anytime." Then thought better of it. "Scratch that. You dropping by with more questions every other day is starting to feel like a bad habit."

As Hayley crossed back through the immaculate rooms, another muffled *thud* upstairs suggested Chase was still lurking in the background. She didn't slow.

Outside, she pulled the door shut behind her and drew in a steadying breath. Kylie hadn't told her anything she didn't already suspect—but she had confirmed it.

Peter Baird.

If the gray hair from the wet suit matched his, Hayley had him dead to rights. He'd taken the gun. He'd shot Hank. He'd silenced Tina. And now she was going to prove it.

Later that evening, Hayley stood at the stove, warming up the leftovers from her COA cooking demo while Leroy circled her feet like a shaggy, persistent shark.

Bruce sat at the kitchen table, scrolling on his laptop with one hand and sipping a bourbon with the other. His reading glasses were perched low on his nose, and he hadn't said more than five words since she walked in the door.

She plated the food, refilled his glass without asking, and sat across from him with a sigh. "You're awfully quiet."

"Just listening."

Hayley dove into her plate and launched into the day's events: the cooking demo, the student interrogation, the hijinks with Sage's grade distraction, the calendar note about Doug's cocktail party, Kylie's confirming answers—and then, lowering her voice for dramatic effect, her daring break-in at Peter Baird's office.

Bruce set down his fork. "Wait. What?"

Unfazed, she went on. "And that's where I found the brush in his desk drawer, plucked a couple strands—very carefully—and passed them to Earl."

He set down his fork. “You *what*?”

She blinked. “I mean, it wasn’t like I stole his passport.”

“You broke into his office, Hayley.”

“I entered an unlocked room. Briefly.”

“You could’ve been caught,” he said, voice low and tight.

“I wasn’t.”

“And what if you had been? You think Maddox would’ve bailed you out again after the stunt with the cave search? You think Baird doesn’t already suspect you’re still sniffing around?”

Hayley pushed a piece of congealed mac across her plate. “So, what? I’m supposed to sit on my hands while Zane gets railroaded for something he didn’t do?”

Bruce’s jaw tightened. “Maybe for once you should let the cops do their job.”

She looked at him across the table. “Tell me the truth. Do you think they will at this rate?”

He didn’t answer right away.

Finally, he said quietly, “No. I don’t.”

“Then you understand. I’m not going to sit by while Hank and Tina’s killer strolls around the COA campus like nothing happened.”

Bruce shook his head, frustrated. “I know, but you act like this is some cozy whodunit. It’s not a baking competition where the loser gets a pie in the face. This is real. This is dangerous.”

Before she could respond, knuckles tapped lightly against the back door.

Hayley crossed the kitchen and opened it to find Earl and Mona, holding empty take-out cups.

"We just came from dinner," Mona said, "and a double scoop of MDI Ice Cream. Don't judge us."

"You're safe here," Hayley said. "I had half a cheesecake for lunch."

Earl handed over a manila folder. "This is everything. Maddox took one look and said it was a waste of departmental resources. He's still pissed about the dive team being dragged to the sea cave and finding nothing but barnacles and one hair that, and I quote, 'wasn't even found near the body.' He said unless it was plucked from Baird's scalp with a signed confession attached, he's not interested."

Hayley exhaled, flipping the folder open and scanning the dismissive scribble of notes. "So we're back to square one."

"Pretty much," Earl said.

Mona put a hand on Hayley's shoulder. "You were right to try. But maybe it's time to let it go."

Hayley shook her head. "No. I'll bluff Baird. Make him think we've got something concrete. Spook him into slipping."

Bruce stood so fast his chair scraped back. "Absolutely not."

"It worked before."

"This isn't some ex-boyfriend with a gambling habit or a PTA bake sale scammer," he snapped. "This is a man who shot someone. Maybe drowned another. And you think a bluff is going to scare him into confessing? You're not bulletproof, Hayley."

"I'm not trying to be," she said. "I'm trying to stop someone else from getting hurt."

"You already almost drowned."

"That wasn't—"

"And what happens when Baird realizes you're bluffing? What happens when he stops seeing you as a pest and starts seeing you as a threat?"

Hayley didn't answer. She didn't need to. Bruce looked at her like he already knew she'd made up her mind.

Bruce picked up his glass. "I'm going to bed. Try not to get killed before breakfast."

He turned and marched up the stairs, the creak of the wooden staircase punctuating his frustration. The bedroom door closed with a quiet but pointed *click.*

Mona raised an eyebrow. "What's with him?"

Hayley let out a breath she hadn't realized she was holding. "He's been supportive—usually. All the other times I've gotten involved in things I probably shouldn't have? He might roll his eyes, but he's always had my back."

She toyed with the edge of the folder Earl had given her, smoothing a crease. "But this one's different. He's scared. I think he's really worried I'm in over my head."

Mona softened. "That's because he loves you. And because he's not wrong."

Hayley looked toward the dark hallway. "Maybe not. But I can't stop now."

Mona gave Hayley a long look. "If you do this, you'd better have a plan."

"I always do."

"Then make it better than usual," Mona said, and followed Earl out into the night.

Hayley stood in the quiet kitchen, heart hammering harder than she wanted to admit. She cleared the dishes, wiped the counter, then sat down at her laptop.

She opened a blank email and started typing.

To: Peter Baird

Subject: New Footage

We've recovered new video footage related to the Desmond case. Please advise if you'd like to discuss.

She hovered a moment, then hit SEND.

The reply came less than a minute later.

From: Peter Baird

Subject: Re: New Footage

We should talk.

Hayley stared at the screen, the words staring back like a dare.

Her pulse steadied.

Her path was clear.

Game on.

Chapter 36

Sunday mornings in Bar Harbor were normally made for blueberry pancakes and fuzzy slippers.

But not today.

Hayley pulled into Mona's driveway just after sunrise, the sky still a sleepy lavender-gray. Leroy whined from the passenger seat, pawing at the window. He hated early mornings almost as much as Hayley did, but he could sense the tension in her posture, her silence, her white-knuckled grip on the travel mug filled with her third cup of coffee.

Mona answered the door in pajama pants patterned with a cartoon moose and a plain gray sweatshirt. She was halfway through a bagel and had a smear of cream cheese on her cheek.

"Please tell me you're here to borrow sugar and not start another crime sting."

Hayley lifted her phone. "I need backup."

Earl was already in uniform, lacing his boots in the living room. He looked up, blinking. "You serious?"

"I've arranged a meeting with Peter Baird. Two p.m.

At the marine lab on COA's campus. It's Sunday—nobody's around."

"Bruce signed off on this?" Mona asked.

Hayley scoffed. "Bruce would chain me to the radiator if he knew. That's why you two are my team."

She explained the plan. Baird thought she had new evidence—video footage. In reality, she had the truth and a need to watch his face as she laid it bare. If things went south, she'd send a single text to both of them: *SOS*. If they didn't respond, she'd pull the fire alarm at the lab.

A last resort.

Earl frowned, pulling on his jacket. "Why not call Maddox now and bring him in?"

"With what? A hunch? Sure, we've got the murder weapon, but no prints—he must've worn those diver's gloves. No confession. And the one hair sample that could tie him to the wet suit? Maddox won't even test it. All I've got is me, putting the pieces together like a food columnist–turned–amateur sleuth—which, by the way, is exactly what I am."

Mona brushed the cream cheese off her cheek with the back of her hand. "And when he realizes you're bluffing?"

"Then you'd better not miss your cue."

The College of the Atlantic campus was deserted by early afternoon, the kind of sleepy, gull-covered stillness only a Sunday could bring. The ocean shimmered in the distance, quiet and endless. Most of the student cars were gone, the academic buildings locked and shuttered. But the marine lab sat open, the large windows overlooking the rocks, humming quietly with the sound of circulating pumps and bubbling tanks.

Hayley arrived five minutes early. She wandered the hallway slowly, pretending to look at the placards on the walls—photos of past research trips, tide pool studies, sonar scans.

She wasn't nervous, she told herself.

She was just . . . aware.

Hyperaware.

The air inside was chilly. She found the meeting room off the main lab: a long, narrow space with a steel table, dry-erase boards covered in notes, and a tall window overlooking the rear path and parking area. She pulled out her phone, double-checked her signal. Mona and Earl had texted a thumbs-up emoji twenty minutes ago. They were in position, parked in the admin lot nearby, waiting for her message.

She placed her phone on the table, screen up.

Baird entered two minutes later, punctual as always. He wore a fleece vest over a collared shirt, slacks, loafers polished to a sheen. His posture was perfect, his expression unreadable.

"Ms. Powell," he said smoothly. "You said you had something new you wanted to show me? A mysterious video recording?"

Hayley stood to face him. "There is a recording—one Tina Whitmore made the night Hank Desmond was killed. But that's not why I asked you here."

For the briefest moment, something flickered in Baird's eyes, then vanished behind a calm mask. "Of course. And what is it you want from me instead?"

She rested her hands on the back of a chair, grounding herself. "I want you to hear my theory. What I think really happened that night—and afterward."

Baird's smile thinned, equal parts curiosity and contempt. "By all means. Let's hear your grand solution."

Hayley drew in a breath, feeling the weight of the room settle around her like an expectant jury. If he wanted a performance, she was ready to give him one—chapter and verse, every twist, every turn.

Hayley took a breath, then launched in. "You sent Hank Desmond those photos. The ones of Kylie and Chase. You knew exactly what would happen—how he'd explode, how he'd confront them both and put the spotlight on Chase."

"Is that what I knew?" he asked, lightly amused.

"You timed everything perfectly. You knew the combination to Doug Marsh's safe at his rental and stole his gun sometime during the cocktail party. You swam out during the fireworks in your scuba gear, approached from the water, and shot Hank. Then, after that, you climbed aboard the *Slaughterhouse* and planted the gun in the cooler. Kylie had left in the dinghy. Chase was passed out below deck. No one saw you. You just disappeared into the water. The perfect plan. Until Tina saw you coming out. She recognized you."

Baird's face didn't change, but the temperature in the room seemed to drop.

"You drowned her to keep her quiet," Hayley continued, voice steady. "Then, once the investigation heated up, and suspicion started circling Zane, you leaned into it. Let him look guilty. Framed him with the dive gear, made him run. All the while, you played the grieving colleague."

He finally responded. "I was at Doug Marsh's cocktail party. I admit that."

"But you didn't take the gun?"

"I didn't need to. I already had one just like it. Same model."

Hayley stiffened. "Where is it now?"

"At the bottom of the sea," he said calmly. "Right where it belongs."

She stared at him. "So, someone else used Doug Marsh's gun? The one that turned up in Hank's cooler?"

"I wouldn't know," he replied. "You're the detective, aren't you?"

Hayley paced to the window, heart racing. "You're admitting to everything but the weapon?"

"I'm admitting to the facts as they are. Which, of course, means nothing without evidence."

She glanced out the window toward the admin building. Mona and Earl were there—she saw them. But they weren't watching the lab. They were standing with Chief Maddox, who had arrived in his police cruiser. He was pointing in the opposite direction, mid-rant. She guessed he was wondering what Earl was doing hanging around a college campus when he was supposed to be on duty. Mona looked exasperated. Earl opened his mouth to speak—but Maddox cut him off, stepping between them and gesturing furiously toward the lot.

Hayley reached for her phone and sent the text: *SOS. Now.*

No response.

She looked up again. Mona had her phone in hand—but Maddox stepped into her line of sight just as she looked down. Earl, too, was trying to disengage, but the chief was in full steamroll mode.

They didn't see it.

They didn't see her.

Hayley turned back to Baird—and realized the mask had dropped.

His expression had changed. No longer polite. No longer even curious. Just cold.

"I never expected it would be you," he said.

"Excuse me?"

"The woman who once wrote a column on cocktail garnishes using novelty toothpicks. You, of all people, putting this together? Following the breadcrumbs?" His voice was soft, dangerous. "I imagined someone . . sharper."

Hayley's voice was ice. "Sorry to disappoint."

"Oh, it's not disappointment," he said. "It's disbelief."

He moved closer, slow and deliberate.

"Do you know what it's like to be underestimated your whole life?" he asked. "To be overlooked, dismissed, passed over—for loudmouths and charmers and back-slapping frauds like Hank Desmond?"

"I do, actually," Hayley said. "That's why I've survived this long."

"You could walk away now," he said. "Forget what you think you know. Pretend you never connected the dots. Otherwise . . ."

Hayley didn't move. "Otherwise what?"

Baird's smile returned—but now it was reptilian.

"Otherwise, I'll have to silence you. Just like I did her."

Chapter 37

For one long, frozen second, Hayley couldn't move.

Peter Baird stood between her and the exit, a diving knife now in his hand—long, serrated, wickedly sharp. His face went still, the kind of stillness that comes right before something strikes.

"I could say I'm sorry," he said. "but I'm really not."

"What if I say I'll take you up on your offer? Walk away. Forget what I know?"

"I'd say I don't believe you."

Hayley glanced past him to the window. Outside, just beyond the admin building, Mona and Earl were still locked in a circular conversation with Chief Maddox, who appeared to be delivering a full-throated monologue, complete with finger-pointing and theatrical gestures. Mona tried to check her phone. Maddox cut her off. Earl looked visibly agitated, but neither of them turned toward the lab.

They didn't see her.

Didn't see the danger.

Didn't see Baird shifting the knife in his grip, like a chef testing its weight.

"I wasn't even going to kill her, you know," he said, tone conversational now, like he was delivering a lecture. "Tina. Not at first."

Hayley's eyes snapped back to him.

"She wasn't part of the plan," Baird said, almost reflective. "But after that night, I knew she'd seen me. She avoided me on campus. Wouldn't meet my eyes. Skipped our department meeting. I thought maybe—just maybe—she'd keep it to herself. Try to forget. People do that when they're scared."

Hayley clenched her jaw. "But she didn't."

"No," he said. "She emailed her sister. Said something had shaken her. That she saw someone coming out of the water that night. She was vague, but not vague enough."

Hayley blinked. "How would you even know that?"

"I had access to her office. To her computer," Baird said, tone clipped. "She never logged out of her email. After I saw her acting strange, I checked. I needed to know how much she'd seen . . . and who she told." He looked almost irritated by the memory. "She hadn't named me. But it was clear she was thinking about going to the police."

"And that's when you decided she had to die," Hayley said.

"I still hoped I could change her mind," he said. "I showed up at her door, but she pretended not to be home. I cornered her after class one day. Tried to reason with her. But I could see it in her eyes. She'd made her decision."

His voice hardened. "She was going to do the right thing."

He met Hayley's gaze.

"And that's when I knew. I had to do the same." His voice dropped lower, more intimate. "She was heading to Thunder Hole to monitor the algae bloom. Early, before sunrise. Alone. She always logged her plans. Very responsible, very scientific."

He smiled again, admiring the memory.

"So I got there first. In full gear. Waited offshore, just below the surface. When I saw her enter the water, I shadowed her. Let her think she was alone."

Hayley swallowed hard. "You pulled her mask?"

"I punctured her oxygen supply first," he said coolly. "Then pulled her mask. She panicked. Tried to surface. I let her get close. Then I grabbed her ankle."

His fingers curled around the air, miming it.

"She kicked, struggled, even clawed at me. But there's a moment, Hayley, when the body realizes it's not going to make it. That final gasp." He met her eyes. "It's quiet. Peaceful, even."

Hayley's whole body shuddered. "You're a monster."

Baird shrugged. "I'm a realist. She saw me. She would have ruined everything. And now so could you."

He took a slow, deliberate step closer, the knife still at his side like a promise.

"When the police started circling Zane, I knew I

had something better than silence—I had the perfect scapegoat. I didn't just let the narrative build—I reinforced it. Nudged it along. One piece of dive gear left in the right spot. One whisper in the right ear." He smiled faintly. "I didn't just let him fall, Hayley. I laid out the path."

"What about Doug? The gun?"

"I told you, I never took Doug Marsh's gun! I was never trying to set him up. I have no idea how his gun ended up in that ice chest with a bullet missing. Trust me, I wouldn't be so obvious."

She had a gut feeling he was telling the truth.

As he inched closer, Hayley felt her stomach turn, her skin prickling with a cold sweat. This wasn't just a killer confessing under pressure. This was a man proud of the game he'd played. He'd stood back and watched as Zane panicked, as Tina drowned, as an entire town looked the wrong way—because he told them to.

And now here she was.

The next one who knew too much.

The silence stretched between them, sharp as the blade in his hand.

Hayley's breath came shallower. Her eyes darted to the window again—no movement from outside. She was still alone.

Her voice dropped to a whisper. "What about me?"

Baird looked at her, truly looked at her.

"What's your plan for me?"

For a moment, he didn't answer. He just watched

her, as if studying a species he found interesting but not quite intelligent.

Then he said, almost gently, "You're too clever to let go."

He flexed the knife in his fingers. "And not clever enough to walk away."

Hayley took a step back, pulse thudding. "What are you planning to do?"

Baird's gaze flicked to the side of the room—to the wall of diving equipment. Tanks. Masks. Wet suits.

He smiled.

"You've been taking lessons from Zane, haven't you? Everyone knows that. Talking about it. You've probably got gear in your trunk, a wet suit you barely know how to use. A beginner, trying to prove herself."

He took another slow step forward, knife gleaming in his grip.

"You go out on a solo dive. You shouldn't—everyone says it's too soon—but you're stubborn. Determined. You lose track of your depth. Maybe your air runs low. Maybe something goes wrong with your equipment. Word around town is it's already happened to you once. I may have played a small part in that faulty equipment that nearly did you in."

He had been following her from the start.

He tilted his head.

"A tragic accident. A careless mistake. Happens all the time. Zane will undoubtedly back me up to save his own skin."

Hayley felt the chill of the words settle into her bones. The calm in his voice was worse than shouting—like he'd rehearsed this, played it out in his mind until it felt real.

"You'll be mourned," he added. "But no one will be surprised."

She shook her head. "No one's going to believe that."

"Oh, I think they will," he said. "You've already admitted to poking around. You're reckless. You trespass, you confront people alone. I'll tell them you were investigating that sea cave again—against everyone's advice. You slipped. Sank. Rookie mistake."

He held the knife at his side. "You're not special, Hayley. Just another cautionary tale."

Hayley took one small step back, her foot bumping something solid behind her—the fiberglass model of a humpback whale calf that had been part of an outreach display. It was bolted to a rolling stand, waist-high, life-sized, its wide, rubbery flippers spread.

She was out of options.

"I won't be your next victim," she whispered.

His expression hardened.

Then he lunged.

Hayley grabbed the whale with both hands and shoved it forward—hard. It hit Baird square in the chest, knocking the wind out of him with a gasp and sending him stumbling back into a metal stool, which clattered and fell.

She didn't wait.

She ran.

Bolted out of the lab, heart in her throat, shoes pounding against the tile floor. Her breath came fast, sharp. She didn't know where she was going—just away from the man who had just detailed, without remorse, how he had drowned Tina and planned to do the same to her.

She tore down the corridor past the specimen prep room, past the offices with their lights off and blinds drawn, the marine lab stretching out like a haunted maze. Glass tanks lined the walls in places—some filled with murky water, some dark and seemingly empty. One held a limp sea cucumber that jiggled slightly as she sprinted past it.

Behind her, she heard him curse.

Then the footsteps.

He's coming.

He's fast.

She pushed through a swinging door and stumbled into a room she didn't recognize. Dim light filtered in from a red overhead bulb—probably something to do with preserving circadian rhythms in fish, though she couldn't recall why she knew that.

Rows of aquariums lined the walls, bubbling softly, full of movement. Fish swam lazily through reeds and artificial coral, indifferent to the human panic in the room.

She ducked behind one of the larger tanks, heart pounding, lungs aching.

As she crouched there, trying to quiet her breathing,

she turned her head—and came face-to-face with a puffer fish.

It had drifted silently to the edge of the glass, staring at her with its giant, unblinking eyes and pursed little mouth. It looked both judgmental and deeply unimpressed.

Hayley clamped a hand over her mouth to stifle a gasp.

"Well, you're not helping," she mouthed.

Somewhere outside the room, the footsteps grew louder.

Then paused.

Her ears strained, every nerve tuned like piano wire.

The handle turned.

She flattened herself beside the tank, hiding between it and a metal cart stacked with sample jars and tubing. The door creaked open.

She could hear his breathing now. Slow. Controlled. Like a diver before a descent.

"Hayley," he called out, singsong. "You're only making this worse."

She didn't move.

The tank next to her let out a mechanical bubble blurp, and she nearly jumped out of her skin.

"I'm actually impressed," he said, voice closer now. "That whale move? Inspired. If only you put that kind of energy into your cocktail recipes."

She heard the sound of something scrape—his knife dragging along the glass of one of the aquariums, slow and deliberate.

He was close.

Hayley crept along the back wall and slipped out the opposite door, emerging into another hallway—this one darker, lit only by exit signs.

Her shoes squeaked.

She winced.

Then she ran again.

He gave chase.

She hit the main lab. The fire alarm was across the room.

Forty feet away.

Open, exposed space.

No furniture to duck behind.

She sprinted for it.

Baird rounded the corner behind her. "Don't!"

She reached out, slammed her palm against the pull lever—

BWWAAAAAAAH.

The alarm shrieked to life, a mechanical scream echoing through the building. Red strobes flashed from the walls. Sprinklers hissed slightly overhead, teasing at activation.

Outside, she saw movement—Mona turning, Earl sprinting toward the door, Maddox still shouting about something but now following.

Baird stood at the edge of the room, breathing hard, knife still in hand.

"You just signed your own death warrant," he growled.

Hayley met his gaze, shaking but standing tall.

"No," she said. "I just made sure someone else would finally stop you."

The doors burst open behind her, and in seconds Earl was between them, gun drawn. Mona followed, shouting her name.

Chief Maddox pushed in last, taking in the scene with his mouth half-open and his usual bluster suddenly gone.

"Drop the knife!" Earl barked.

Baird hesitated—then slowly let the blade fall to the floor with a clatter.

Hayley finally let herself breathe.

She turned to Mona and whispered, "Told you I had a plan."

Chapter 38

It was a clear, bright late-September afternoon—crisp but calm. The College of the Atlantic had chosen the perfect spot for Tina Whitmore's memorial. The folding chairs formed gentle arcs on a grassy bluff overlooking the bay, with the afternoon sun glinting off the water like scattered coins. Beyond the driftwood arch stood the ocean—vast, silent, eternal. It was the place Tina had loved best, and the one that had taken her.

Hayley stood in the back row, one of Liddy's shawls wrapped around her shoulders, borrowed last-minute because Hayley claimed she didn't have anything "respectful" that wasn't covered in flour or lemon zest. Beside her, Bruce stood with his hands in his coat pockets, eyes fixed on the horizon.

Students filed in quietly, many wearing sea greens and soft blues. Professors arrived in somber clumps, some in academic robes, others in Bar Harbor–appropriate fleece and jeans. Townspeople showed up, too—people who'd seen her organizing beach cleanups or teaching kids about tide pool life, others who knew Tina through volunteer work or marine conservation talks at the public library.

The service was simple and sincere. A professor from the marine biology department spoke first, describing Tina's fierce intellect and unfailing kindness. A few students shared memories—a funny one about Tina diving into the harbor to untangle a lobster trapline from a motorboat, another about her correcting a guest speaker's misstatement about cephalopods with both tact and glee.

Then came a haunting string quartet performance of "The Water Is Wide," and when the last note faded into the wind, no one spoke for several minutes. The surf said enough.

Hayley didn't cry, but her throat ached with the effort of holding everything back—the guilt, the relief, the rage, the sense of something unfinished.

When the service ended, the crowd began to disperse.

Hayley and Bruce lingered.

"Look, it's the Baked Goods Bloodhound!" someone shouted.

Hayley turned to find three familiar faces from her recent cooking class: Sage with her usual sardonic look, Whisk Taker Guy now in a sports coat and fish-printed tie, and the earnest student who'd lobbied for Natasha Lyonne to play Hayley in the inevitable streaming series.

"You're kind of a campus legend now," Sage said. "You should teach a class in crime-solving with leftover kitchen tools."

"I hear the whale swing is now part of COA folklore," said the guy in the tie.

"I'm just glad it wasn't bolted down," Hayley said, managing a smile.

"So, what's next?" the *Poker Face* fan asked. "Cold case? Political scandal? Missing mascot?"

"I think my sleuthing days are officially behind me," Hayley replied.

None of them believed her.

She could tell.

"Sure. And I'm switching to a business major."

They moved on, calling her Professor Powell as they went.

Bruce, still standing beside her, arched an eyebrow. "'Professor'?"

"I'll explain later," Hayley muttered.

They moved to the far edge of the bluff, where the crowd was thinner and the air quieter.

"You still mad at me?" she asked.

Bruce looked out at the waves. "No. I'm just . . . relieved. And a little shaken. This time was different, Hayley. You almost didn't come back."

Hayley nodded. "I know. I didn't plan for it to get that close."

"You were nearly drowned. Then nearly stabbed. You really want to make that a habit?"

She gave a small laugh. "You're right. I promise to stick to food and drink from now on. And maybe some light gossip." She reached for his hand. "I'll rein it in. I promise."

Bruce didn't speak, but he gave her hand a gentle squeeze.

That was something.

Across the lawn, Tina's sister stood quietly near the now-empty arch, shoulders hunched, eyes red.

Hayley approached her slowly. "Lacy?"

The woman turned. "Oh—Hayley."

"I just wanted to say how sorry I am. For everything. I wish I'd figured it out sooner."

"You figured it out," Lacy said, voice thick. "That's what matters."

"I just keep thinking . . . if I'd put the pieces together quicker, maybe Tina might not have—"

"You were brave," Lacy said. "You brought my sister's killer to justice. That's more than a lot of people ever get."

Hayley nodded. "She was brave, too."

They embraced briefly. Then Lacy stepped away and joined a group of faculty near the chairs.

Hayley turned—and came face-to-face with a man she didn't recognize. Late twenties, early thirties. Stocky, with thick arms that suggested manual labor—or a past life in it. He wore a black windbreaker zipped halfway up, jeans that had seen airports and dust, and hiking boots with bits of dried red clay stuck in the soles. His short, dark hair was wind-tossed, and a duffel bag sat at his feet.

"You're Hayley Powell?" he asked.

"I am," Hayley said cautiously.

He stuck out his hand. "Buddy Desmond. Hank's son."

She blinked, genuinely surprised. "Oh. Wow. I wasn't sure if you were coming."

"I wasn't, either." His handshake was firm, dry, businesslike. "Didn't find out he was dead until a few days ago. I've been off the grid—literally. Backpacking in South America. No cell service, no news alerts. Had to get back into a town with a post office just to check my email."

"Wow," Hayley said again.

"Yeah. Been bouncing around. Kilimanjaro last winter. Parts of Patagonia this spring. I like to keep moving."

She glanced at his mud-spattered boots. "I can tell."

"My dad used to say I was a layabout," Buddy said with a tight smile. "Thought I didn't want responsibility. Said I'd rather climb rocks than corporate ladders. He wasn't wrong—for a while. I had no interest in the business. Barbecue was his thing. Not mine."

"But that's changed?"

Buddy nodded. "It has. I got the news and came straight here. Took the first flight I could book. Turns out, the business is still in my name. Kylie never had a legal claim, and they never got around to actually marrying. They just told everybody they were. She's been acting like she's queen of the castle, but she's not getting the throne."

Hayley looked past him toward the edge of the bluff, where Kylie and Chase were practically glued to each other, charming their way through a group of local donors. Chase laughed and rubbed her back with an intimacy that looked routine.

"Kylie thought she could offer me a check and send me on my merry way," Buddy added. "Like I was some low-rent obstacle to be cleared with a payoff and a pat on the head."

Hayley raised an eyebrow. "That didn't go well?"

"Oh, it was cute. She tried to wrap it in sympathy, but the math was clear. She doesn't just want the restaurant," Buddy said, his voice tightening. "She wants the whole package—Dad's name, the sauces, the rubs, the branded merchandise, the wholesale contracts, the retail shelves. She and Chase have it all worked out. Keep the legacy alive, rebrand it just enough to make it theirs. She wants to slap a fresh label on everything my father built and call it love. But the paperwork doesn't lie. I've got controlling interest in everything Dad built."

There was a flash of something darker behind his eyes.

Frustration, maybe.

Or something sharper.

"When I first heard about the shooting," Buddy said quietly, "I figured it had to be Kylie. I always thought she was playing at being my dad—saying the right things, playing the role he wanted. She wore the act like a designer label. Sweet little trophy wife of smoke and sauce."

"But she wasn't the one who killed him," Hayley said.

"No," Buddy said. "She wasn't."

He looked annoyed by that. Not relieved. Just . . .

annoyed. "I mean, the guy who did it? Some marine biology nut with a grudge and a wet suit? What is this, a James Bond movie?"

Hayley shrugged. "Bar Harbor's been weirder."

Buddy let out a dry chuckle. "Still feels wrong. Like the cast list doesn't match the plot."

Hayley didn't disagree.

That's when she noticed Kylie and Chase again, holding hands in a way that felt more like a performance than affection. They looked content.

Too content.

"Anyway," Buddy said. "just wanted to say thanks. Heard you had something to do with catching the guy."

"I helped," Hayley said.

He nodded. "Good. Whatever else happens, I'm glad my dad's killer is off the street."

Eventually, the chairs were folded back up. The snack tables were cleared. The crowd thinned.

Hayley stood alone for a moment, watching the sea.

Peter Baird had confessed to everything.

Almost everything.

But he was adamant that he hadn't taken Doug Marsh's gun. Said he'd used his own. Said the murder weapon—the real one—was at the bottom of the sea.

But if he was telling the truth, who planted the gun in the cooler? And why was a bullet matching the one found in Hank's chest missing?

She didn't like loose ends.

They kept her up at night.

Bruce returned to her side.

"What's got you so distracted?"

She turned quickly. "Nothing. Just . . . thinking about Tina."

He gave her a look. She gave him a smile.

He didn't buy it.

But he didn't press.

She slipped her arm through his and walked with him toward the path that led back to the parking lot. The waves behind them continued to lap at the shore, as if it knew there was more to bring ashore.

The case was closed.

But Hayley knew better than anyone—

Sometimes the past has a way of washing back in.

Chapter 39

Hayley took a deep breath as she stood in the narrow hallway of the Bar Harbor Police Department. Everything about the place suggested someone was about to get scolded, and Hayley had a sneaking suspicion it was her. She'd been summoned by Chief Caleb Maddox first thing that morning, the tone of his voicemail flat and humorless.

Never a good sign.

As she waited outside his office, she could already imagine the lecture brewing behind that closed door. She considered turning around, faking a sudden need to bake muffins or write a column about clam juice cocktails. But no, she owed him this.

She knocked once, pushed open the door, and stepped in before he could call out. Maddox sat behind his desk, arms crossed, his eyes sharp and unreadable beneath furrowed brows.

"Before you say anything," Hayley blurted, raising

both hands like a burglar caught with the missing jewelry, "let me just start with an apology."

His lips tightened, but he didn't interrupt.

"I know what I did was reckless. I shouldn't have confronted Peter Baird alone. Well—I wasn't *alone*. I brought Mona. But she's tougher than most people, and I figured if things went sideways, she could hold her own. And Earl had nothing to do with it. He didn't even know what I was planning. I tricked him. I said we were going for donuts."

Maddox blinked. Slowly.

"I know, I know," she said quickly. "It was a stupid move. I just—when I realized Baird was behind it all, that he killed Hank and Tina—I had to act fast. I didn't want him to slip away. And it worked, didn't it? He's in custody. That's a good thing, right?"

Still, no reaction.

Hayley's mouth twitched. "Okay. You're doing the silent scolding. Got it."

She paced a few steps, then turned back to him, arms crossed now herself. "Do you know why I do this? Why I get involved in these things?" She gave a weak chuckle. "It goes back to 2012. I'd just become the food and cocktails columnist for the *Island Times*—after years of being the paper's office manager, mind you. Single mom, trying to keep things together. I was thrilled. It felt like a fresh start."

Maddox's gaze didn't waver.

"But then this rival cooking columnist from the

Bar Harbor Herald—Karen Applebaum, not the nicest person FYI—she accused me of stealing her clam chowder recipe. Total nonsense. But a week later, she was found dead. Right there in her kitchen, face-down in a bowl of her own chowder. Poisoned."

Hayley paused, waiting for a flicker of interest.

Nothing.

"That kind of thing gets under your skin. I couldn't let it go. I had to figure it out. And when I did—I realized I was good at it. Or at least stubborn enough to keep digging." She smiled faintly. "I assume you don't want to hear the rest. There were a lot of murders after that. Like, a lot."

Maddox finally leaned forward, elbows on his desk, voice cold and clipped. "You're reckless. Invasive. And lucky. Try this again, and I'll make sure your luck finally runs out."

Hayley gave a weak smile. "So . . . I guess I'll see you at the next murder?"

He didn't smile.

Not even a twitch.

She stood there a beat longer, the air thick with disapproval, then gave a small nod and turned to leave. Her hand touched the door, but she paused.

There was something she couldn't shake.

The gun.

Doug Marsh's gun.

Everyone seemed satisfied with the theory that Peter Baird had climbed aboard the *Slaughterhouse* after shooting Hank from the water and tucked the revolver neatly in the ice chest to frame Chase Wingate.

Case closed.

Except Baird had told her something else.

He claimed he didn't steal the gun.

The cops dismissed that as self-serving nonsense, of course. The bullet in Hank matched Doug's revolver. One round was missing. But that didn't mean Baird used that gun.

The bullet could've been fired at any time.

The cops just assumed Baird's prints weren't on the gun because he had been wearing rubber gloves, part of his wet suit.

Hayley turned slowly. Maddox looked up from a manila folder.

"I need to see Peter Baird," she said.

Maddox frowned. "Why?"

"Because there's something I don't understand. And I think he might be the only one who can clear it up."

He leaned back in his chair. "He's awaiting transfer to county lockup. He's not exactly taking visitors."

"I won't be long. I promise."

He glared at her.

"Please."

A long pause. Finally, with a huff, he stood. "Fine. Don't touch anything. And don't say anything that'll screw up my arraignment."

"Would I ever?"

He glared again.

The holding cell had the ambience of a discount motel bathroom—minus the complimentary soap. Peter

Baird sat on the bench, wearing county orange now instead of his usual starched khakis and smug marine biologist button-downs. He looked tired. Not defeated—but diminished.

When Hayley stepped in, flanked by Maddox just behind, Baird glanced up. His eyes narrowed.

"Come to gloat?"

"No," she said evenly. "I came because you said something to me. About the gun."

His lips thinned.

"You said you didn't steal it. That you used a different revolver. That after shooting Hank with it, you tossed yours into the ocean."

Baird said nothing.

Maddox stepped closer. "Is that true?"

Baird shrugged. "I'm not answering anything without my attorney."

"Come on," Hayley pressed. "Tell him what you told me. You said the gun in the ice chest wasn't the one you fired. That you didn't plant it."

He glanced at her, then at Maddox, and turned away. "I'm not saying another word."

Maddox exhaled sharply, looked at Hayley. "He's playing games."

"I'm not playing anything," Baird muttered. "I'm protecting myself. You've already made up your mind."

Hayley took a step forward. "If Chase or Kylie were involved, if they stole that gun from Doug Marsh, or if something else happened that night—don't let them walk free. You killed Tina because she saw you that night—because she knew. But now it's over. So stop pretending you're protecting anyone. Tell the truth. Don't let this get buried."

But Baird was stone.

"Time's up," Maddox said, then ushered her out.

Back in the lobby, Hayley dropped down on a wooden bench, arms folded tight, her mind a tangle of doubts.

If Baird had a second revolver, and that was the one that had killed Hank, then the matches to Doug's gun weren't relevant. Chase's print on the bullets, Doug's on the gun itself. None of that mattered if it wasn't the murder weapon. The only indisputable fact was that it had been fired once. That didn't mean the bullet ended up lodged in Hank Desmond's chest.

Could Kylie have planned to kill Hank and talked Chase into helping, only for Chase to get blackout drunk and ruin it? Maybe Kylie took the gun from Doug's party and planned to use it later—but never got the chance. Maybe Chase had it and panicked. Maybe the gun went off accidentally. Either way, it ended up in the ice chest. But not because Baird put it there.

She stood slowly, heart racing.

There was still a thread dangling. And it led straight back to that ice chest—and to the truth Baird refused to tell.

Outside, the air was crisp, the sky pale blue with a bite of fall on the wind. Leroy would need his sweater soon.

Hayley pulled out her phone and dialed Mona.

"I think we've still got one more mystery to solve."

Island Food & Spirits
By
Hayley Powell

When I first started my job as office manager at the *Island Times*, I thought it would be a lovely idea to invite my boss, Sal, and his wife, Rosana, over for a get-to-know-you barbecue.

I was a little nervous about the whole thing, so for moral support (and strategic flattery), I also invited my BFFs, Mona and Liddy. Their job was simple: casually drop a few compliments about my cooking so Sal wouldn't regret giving me the Food & Cocktails column.

After some light detective work, I learned that Sal was a huge fan of grilled steak kabobs. Perfect. I spent the afternoon chopping, slicing, dicing, cubing, and marinating like a woman auditioning for *Top Chef: Bar Harbor Edition*.

By the time everyone arrived, the yard smelled amazing, the cocktails were flowing, and I was feeling cautiously optimistic. I mixed up a round of Sea Breezes, handed them out, and while we were nibbling on prosciutto-stuffed figs, Mona decided it was time for her performance review of my cooking.

She took one bite, shouted my name loud enough to startle the seagulls, then turned to Sal with a mouthful of fig and announced it was the best thing she'd ever eaten. I nearly died. But Sal laughed, said he agreed, and added that if my main course was even half as good, he had no regrets about me writing the column. I could finally breathe again.

While everyone sipped their drinks and listened to Rosana tell a hilarious story about their first camping trip ("Never trust a raccoon with your cooler," she warned), I pulled the kabobs off the grill, covered them with foil, and set them proudly in the center of the picnic table to rest.

When it was time to eat, I told Sal I'd heard a little rumor that steak kabobs were his favorite. His eyes lit up. I made a dramatic show of whisking away the foil—and then froze.

The platter was empty.

For a moment, nobody moved. Then, from the bushes, my dog, Leroy, emerged, looking blissfully content, with not one but two kabob skewers dangling from his mouth. He trotted right up to Sal, tail wagging, and dropped them at his feet like a proud hunter presenting his kill.

I was mortified. Everyone else burst out laughing. Sal, wiping tears from his eyes, said. "How about that? Headline: Employee's Dog Steals Show—and Dinner—at Barbecue!"

I chased Leroy around the yard trying to

salvage what was left of dinner, while Sal good-naturedly assured me he was perfectly happy with a couple of hot dogs instead. Thankfully, he meant it—and to this day, whenever Sal stops by the office, he brings Leroy a beefy treat. They've been best buds ever since.

I definitely earned a Sea Breeze that day.

SEA BREEZE

INGREDIENTS

1½ ounces vodka
2 ounces pink grapefruit juice
1 ounce cranberry juice
Lime wedge (optional)

Add the vodka and grapefruit juice to a cocktail glass over ice. Top with the cranberry juice, and garnish with the lime wedge if you're feeling fancy.

Stir, sip, and enjoy.

LEROY'S FAVORITE GRILLED STEAK KABOBS

INGREDIENTS

2 pounds sirloin steak, cut into 1-inch cubes
1 bottle Italian dressing (your favorite brand)
Assorted veggies: bell peppers, red onions, mushrooms, cut into 1-inch pieces
Metal or wooden skewers

Marinate the steak in the Italian dressing for at least 2 hours (up to 8 if you plan ahead).

Thread the meat and veggies onto skewers, alternating for color.

Preheat the grill to medium-high. Cook kabobs for 8–10 minutes, turning occasionally. For medium-rare, aim for 145°F. Let rest for 5 minutes before serving to keep them juicy.

Serve with your favorite side dish—and keep an eye on the dog.

Chapter 40

Hayley had no intention of going back to the police station. And yet, ten minutes after she'd left it, there she was again—turning into the gravel lot behind the Bar Harbor Police Department with a tight jaw and a firmer resolve.

She wasn't doing Caleb Maddox's job.

She wasn't interfering.

She was . . . nudging.

Inside, the station buzzed with low-level chatter and the hum of fluorescent lights. Maddox was hunched over his desk, jacket off, sleeves rolled up, and surrounded by an explosion of paperwork. He didn't even look up when Hayley stepped in.

"I swear, Powell," he muttered, "if you're here to tell me you've changed your mind and Peter Baird's suddenly a misunderstood sweetheart who rescues kittens and composts—"

"He's a sociopath with a God complex," Hayley cut in. "But if he's so proud of killing Hank and drowning Tina, why deny planting the gun in the cooler?"

Maddox finally looked up. "Because it muddies motive. It makes it look like premeditation. If he sticks to passion and revenge, a jury might see him as temporarily unhinged."

Hayley crossed her arms. "Maybe. Or maybe he's telling the truth. Maybe someone else put that gun in the cooler. Someone who wanted to frame Doug Marsh."

Maddox stared at her for a long beat. "Unless you're holding proof, we're done here."

She didn't flinch. "Not yet."

He pointed a pen at her. "No field trips."

She smiled sweetly. "I'm going home."

Which was technically true—if home had a pit stop first.

Liddy was slumped in her rolling chair, one bare foot tucked beneath her as she nursed a bottle of vitamin-enhanced water like it was her final lifeline. Her hair was in a lopsided ponytail, sunglasses perched on her head.

Hayley stepped into her office and gave her a once-over. "Rough night?"

Liddy raised the bottle. "Celebrated a closing with a client. A full cash offer on a property with original linoleum, can you believe it? We hit Side Street Café like it was Mardi Gras, and I woke up with glitter in my bra and a text from someone named 'Todd (Boat Guy)'."

Hayley dropped into the chair across from her. "Let me guess—you were also at Doug Marsh's cocktail party a few weeks back?"

Liddy froze. "Um, no. I mean, why would you think that?"

"Because you haven't missed a single social gathering in Bar Harbor since the Obama administration. And because I asked around and your name wasn't on the guest list."

Liddy shrank a little behind her desk. "Technically . . . I wasn't invited."

Hayley's eyes narrowed. "Liddy . . ."

"I crashed it, okay? This was long before Doug and I started seeing each other. Before he knew who I was. I'd seen him around, thought he was cute in that 'divorced dad who collects barware' kind of way. I figured if I showed up with a nice bottle of wine and a plunging neckline, no one would kick me out."

Hayley blinked. "And?"

"And I got trashed. Like, sangria-in-a-sippy-cup trashed."

"You remember anything useful?"

Liddy rolled her eyes toward the ceiling. "Let's see . . . the shrimp was warm, the punch was flat, and I think someone stole my lipstick. Possibly me. Honestly, it was chaos. As you know, Doug didn't even remember me being there. We officially met at Betty and Kelton's wedding reception in your backyard."

"What else do you remember?"

She closed her eyes and began to reconstruct the night like a psychic channeling foggy spirits.

Hayley kept her voice light. "Did you see Kylie there with Hank?"

Liddy nodded slowly, remembering. "Yeah. They arrived separately, though. I remember Hank showing up late and slapping a lot of backs and introducing himself like nobody knew who he was."

"And Chase Wingate?"

"Oh, lurking. Definitely lurking. He was pretending to talk to everyone but kept floating near Kylie like a frat boy playing musical chairs. She was trying to keep a safe distance from him whenever Hank was around."

"Anything else?"

Liddy closed her eyes, thinking hard. "Roger Larkin did karaoke in the living room with an unplugged mic, which was excruciating. Betsy Klein tried to body-block Nancy Everett away from the deviled eggs, which devolved into what I'd call a passive-aggressive standoff over hors d'oeuvres. And Chuck Alley told everyone he was on a juice cleanse but kept sneaking whiskey from the bar area."

Hayley gave her a look.

Liddy shrugged. "People get weird when there's free booze and bad cheese. I do remember Kylie brought these amazing maple-glazed tri-tips—people were raving. Said it was Hank's mother's recipe."

Hayley perked up.

"Anyway," Liddy went on, "she disappeared down the hall at one point. Said she needed the bathroom, but Doug only has one and it's by the kitchen. I think she was snooping. Or crying. Who knows? I can't count the number of times I've wept at a party."

Hayley leaned forward. “Do you remember Doug showing off his gun?”

Liddy blinked, then slowly nodded. “Yeah. He opened a safe at one point and did this ‘oh, what’s this?’ routine. Doug was bragging about how manly he was for owning it. I think the exact phrase was ‘burglar deterrent and conversation starter.’ Of course, in my condition, I found it all incredibly sexy.”

“Was Chase hanging around him when he had the gun out?”

Liddy struggled to remember. “Yes, I think so. I remember because he spilled sangria on Doug’s ‘Persian’ rug, which I’m pretty sure is from IKEA. But I’m fuzzy on the details of what happened next.”

Hayley stood. “That’s all I needed. Oh—and thank you for remembering the tri-tips.”

Liddy pointed at her bottle. “This stuff works wonders. Memory, skin, metabolism. Probably makes you less judgmental, too, but I can’t be sure.”

Hayley rang the Desmonds’ doorbell with a mason jar of homemade BBQ sauce in hand and her phone recording in her purse.

Kylie answered the door wearing linen culottes and a gauzy top that smelled faintly of vanilla lotion.

She sighed, deadpanning, “Hayley. What a surprise.”

“I hope I’m not intruding,” Hayley said with a practiced smile. “I’m doing a little tribute piece for my food column—Hank’s favorite BBQ recipes. Liddy mentioned the maple-glazed tri-tips you brought to Doug's party were his mom's."

Kylie blinked, flattered and hesitant. "Oh . . . yes. They were her specialty."

"Mind if I ask a few questions? You could be the emotional heart of the article."

Kylie opened the door wider. "Uh, sure. Come in."

Kylie led her to the kitchen, where Hayley sat with her notebook out, doing a convincing impression of a food writer not on the scent of a criminal conspiracy.

She asked about the tri-tips, Hank's preferences—did he like spicy? Smoky? Kylie warmed to the topic, reminiscing about backyard cookouts and Fourth of July sauces that burned your eyebrows off.

Then Hayley pivoted.

"Doug's cocktail party—you mentioned before that Doug showed off his gun. Just so I'm clear, who was right there when he opened the safe?"

Kylie's expression hardened. "We've been over this. Chase was nearby. So was I. And Peter Baird. And now that everyone in town knows Peter pulled the trigger, why are you still circling me?"

Hayley held her gaze. "Because confirmation matters. And because someone had to see that safe combination before the gun disappeared."

Kylie let out an exasperated breath. "Well, it wasn't me. If you're still chasing ghosts after Baird's confession, that's your problem."

Hayley stayed quiet, letting the irritation hang in the air until a new voice broke in—

"What's going on?"

Chase.

He appeared in the doorway, rumpled and pale. His eyes darted to Hayley, then to Kylie. "What is this?"

"Just a quick interview for the *Island Times*," Hayley said smoothly. "Reminiscing about Hank."

Chase's eyes narrowed. "Maybe now's not a good time."

Hayley stood, gathering her things. "Understood. I'll get out of your hair."

She made it to the foyer before turning back.

"You know," she said lightly, "it's funny how things work out. Someone takes Doug's gun. Someone brings it aboard the boat the night of the fireworks. Maybe they meant to scare Hank. Or worse. But maybe they lost their nerve. But then someone else got there first."

Kylie's lip trembled.

Chase went stone-still.

"Maybe someone panicked. Maybe someone passed out drunk. Maybe someone else swam up in a wet suit with murder on his mind."

Kylie opened her mouth—but no sound came out.

"And maybe," Hayley added softly, "if things had gone according to plan, Peter Baird wouldn't have beaten you to it."

The room was silent except for the faint hum of the refrigerator in the kitchen.

Hayley let it hang a moment longer.

"The prints were interesting," she said. "Doug's were on the gun. Of course—he owned it. But the bullets?

Only Chase's prints were there. Not Peter's. Not yours. Everyone at the party knew Chase had handled the bullets, so that would explain why your prints were on them, right, Chase?"

He nodded warily.

Hayley tilted her head, eyes fixed on Kylie. "So if someone else on that boat handled the gun or the bullets, where were their prints? It was a chilly night. Gloves would explain a lot. Especially if someone only fired once."

Kylie's lips parted, then closed again. She drew a shaky breath, her gaze darting toward Chase, then back to Hayley. "You're twisting things," she said weakly. "You don't know what happened that night."

Hayley didn't answer. She just waited.

Kylie's composure wavered—the brittle calm giving way to panic. "You weren't there," she said, louder now. "You don't know—"

She broke off, voice splintering. "I didn't even hit him!"

Chase spun on her. "What the hell are you doing?"

Hayley's pulse thundered. She stepped back toward the door.

Then Chase's eyes flicked to Hayley's purse—where a faint red recording light glowed through the cracked zipper.

"She recorded that!" he shouted. "Give me the phone!"

"Don't come near me," Hayley snapped, stepping back.

Chase lunged. "We're not letting you ruin everything!"

Hayley braced for a struggle as Chase turned on her, eyes wild.

"You're not leaving with that recording," he said, stepping between her and the door.

Hayley's hand tightened around the strap of her purse. "Don't be stupid, Chase."

He took a step closer. "Give me the phone."

"No."

His jaw flexed, fury rising. "Then I'll take it."

Hayley didn't flinch. "You think I'd walk into this alone? I made that mistake with Peter Baird."

She met his gaze, steel in her voice.

"This time, I brought professional backup."

The front door burst open with a crash.

"Bar Harbor PD!" Maddox bellowed. "Hands where I can see them!"

Sergeant Earl charged in behind him, weapon drawn and eyes scanning.

Chase froze mid-lunge. Kylie collapsed onto the couch, sobbing uncontrollably.

"You're both under arrest," Maddox said, voice cold and commanding. "For conspiracy to commit murder."

"We didn't kill him," Chase said weakly.

"No," Maddox agreed. "Peter Baird did. With a completely different gun."

He nodded to Earl. "But you planned it. You brought your own weapon. You set it all in motion."

Cuffs clicked.

The room emptied.

Outside, the sky was deepening to twilight, the edges of Frenchman's Bay gilded in gold.

Hayley stood beside Maddox, both of them watching the cruiser disappear down the drive.

"Two people dead," Maddox said quietly. "All because Peter Baird wanted revenge."

Hayley rubbed her arms against the chill. "And because Kylie and Chase were too selfish and sloppy to pull off a murder of their own."

Maddox gave a small shake of his head. "Lucky for them—and unlucky for Hank—Baird got there to finish the job for them."

Maddox turned to her. "You done sleuthing?"

"After I finish this column. Barbecue season waits for no woman."

Maddox shook his head and walked away.

Hayley stayed a moment longer, the sea breeze tugging at her hair.

Peter Baird was in jail. Kylie and Chase were headed there, too. And somewhere in the bottom of her purse, the mason jar of sauce was wedged sideways, the lid barely holding.

She'd deal with the mess later.

Right now, it was time to wrap things up.

For good.

Chapter 41

Drinks Like A Fish had never been louder, or lovelier. Paper lanterns floated from the rafters in red, gold, and green—a nod to Brazil's vibrant palette—while someone had strung tiny flags from the dartboard to the mounted swordfish like festive bunting. The jukebox alternated between Sergio's favorite bossa nova playlist and Randy's country line-dancing favorites—heavy on Reba, with the occasional disco remix thrown in just to mess with the rhythm.

Hayley stood near the bar and sipped Sergio's homemade caipirinha—a limey, boozy tribute to their new life in Brazil. She was barely five steps in the door and had been hugged six times. The whole town had turned out for her brother and his husband's farewell bash, and the send-off was exactly what you'd expect for two of Bar Harbor's biggest personalities: sentimental, loud, and soaked in liquor.

She'd baked two of her signature rum cakes—one for slicing, one for "emotional emergencies"—and both were disappearing quickly under the eager forks of regulars. Randy, his cheeks flushed with drink and love, held court near the pool table, squeezing shoulders and kissing cheeks like a benevolent, tipsy monarch.

"I'm gonna miss this guy," murmured Chelsea Mahoney, now comfortably behind the bar and glowing with a mix of nerves and pride as she poured pints and accepted tips with her usual flair. She reached into her apron and pulled out a key ring. "They gave me the keys today. Officially mine."

Hayley smiled. "You're gonna crush it."

Just then, Mona clanged a spoon against a beer glass with the subtlety of a cymbal crash. "Can I get everyone's attention?" she called, standing on one of the sturdy bar stools and wobbling only slightly. "Don't worry, I'm not here to sing, strip, or sell you lobster rolls. I'm here to roast the guests of honor."

The crowd erupted with laughter as Earl grinned from his stool beside her and raised his beer in salute. "And that's why I love her," he said. "Never boring."

Mona beamed. "We're here to say goodbye to two of the finest men Bar Harbor ever had the luck to call their own. Randy, our snarky little firecracker, and Sergio, who somehow ran the police department for twelve years without ever figuring out the difference between 'undercover' and 'off-duty'."

The crowd laughed, and Sergio—dressed in his finest linen shirt and shell necklace—raised his beer.

"It wasn't easy in the beginning," Sergio said. "When

I first started, someone told me to 'take him downtown.' So I drove him to the actual downtown. We had chowder."

Everyone laughed again.

Mona went on. "Sergio once told me I was 'as strong as an ox and just as contagious.' I think he meant courageous. I hope."

"I did!" Sergio called.

"And Randy?" Mona smirked. "Randy once talked me into riding on the Bar Harbor Pride float dressed as a giant glitter lobster. I got heat rash in places I won't name. But he was right—it was fun."

The room dissolved into cheers. Randy pretended to curtsy and then flung his arms around Mona in a dramatic hug.

Sergio stepped forward, glass in hand, and silence settled gently over the room. "When I came to this town," he began, his accent thickening with feeling, "I was only planning to be here for one summer. A temporary job. But then I met the man who told me Bar Harbor could be home. And . . . it became one."

A beat passed, and his voice trembled. "Thank you all for your kindness. Your weirdness. Your potlucks and patience and your habit of yelling, 'Hey, Chief!' even after I was off-duty." He paused, then added, "I do not know if Brazil has Whoopie Pies, but I will write letters. Or emails. Emails are faster." He raised his glass. "To family. Of the heart."

Glasses clinked across the bar as Hayley wiped her cheek with the back of her hand. Sergio had always had a way of mangling the language and nailing the emotion.

Later, as the party wound down and the music softened, Hayley found Randy near the dartboard, hugging a weepy Mrs. Penrose from the Jessup Library's reference desk.

When Mrs. Penrose finally drifted off in search of tissues, Hayley slipped in beside her brother. "You good?"

Randy nodded, eyes a little glassy. "I'm good. A little buzzed. A lot grateful."

They clinked plastic cups.

"Place won't be the same without you," she said.

"Place hasn't been the same since you stopped singing karaoke in cowboy boots."

Hayley smiled. "That was a phase."

"Everything's a phase until you pack it up in a box and ship it to Brazil."

A pause.

Randy leaned against the wall, swirling the last inch of something dangerously pink in his plastic cup. His cheeks were flushed, eyes bright, but there was a wistfulness creeping in around the edges now. The kind that comes when you realize you're really leaving.

"You know," he said, nudging her arm. "you and Bruce could do worse than ending up in that house."

Hayley blinked. "What house?"

Randy looked at her like she'd just confessed she didn't believe in brunch. "Mine. The house. On the Shore Path."

She laughed. "Randy, that place is huge. And gorgeous. And has a view of the ocean I don't deserve."

"You'd take care of it," he said. "You'd fill it with food and people and gossip. You know that house loves gossip."

Hayley opened her mouth to protest again, but something fluttered in her chest—an idea catching a draft.

She turned to him more slowly now. "Wait. Are you serious? What are you doing with the house?"

Randy's grin turned sly. "Make me an offer."

"I could never—" Hayley began, but stopped. Because now she was picturing it. Morning coffee with the waves rolling in just beyond the window. A quiet office space for Bruce. A garden. A bigger kitchen. A fresh start.

"Did I just walk into a real estate negotiation?" Bruce's voice broke in behind her, low and amused.

Hayley turned to find her husband slipping in beside them. He kissed her temple, then raised an eyebrow at Randy. "You offering up the palace on the Path?"

"Maybe," Randy said, "if the right buyers walk through the door."

Bruce looked at Hayley, that thoughtful glint in his eyes she'd come to recognize. The writer glint. The one that meant he was already rewriting the next chapter of their lives in his head.

"I could live with that view," he said. "As long as I still get coffee in bed."

Hayley didn't say anything just yet. But her pulse had already quickened.

And her heart had already moved a few inches closer to that window.

Toward something new.

They raised their glasses again, to Bar Harbor, to beginnings and endings.

The next morning, Hayley unlocked the front door to Hayley's Kitchen and stepped inside alone.

It was before opening hours, the golden hush of sunrise slanting across the floor. Chairs were still turned upside down on the tables. The counter gleamed. The kitchen waited behind its swinging doors like a loyal old friend.

She walked through the space, running her hand along the edge of the prep station, past the espresso machine, around the corner where Kelton used to sneak snacks. So many service rushes. So many last-minute specials, shouted orders, slammed walk-in doors, and bursts of laughter over burned garlic bread.

Footsteps echoed behind her.

Liddy appeared, heels clicking, blazer immaculate, hair in place. "Well," she said, unfolding the final folder. "Time to make it official."

Kelton and Betty were already seated at the bar, papers spread out before them. Betty, calm and collected in a crisp collared shirt, smiled warmly. Kelton looked like he was mentally reviewing the kitchen's inventory, the wine list, and his entire life's decisions—all at once.

Hayley slid onto a high-backed bar chair beside them, and Liddy guided them through the paperwork with the confidence of a woman who had finally passed the licensing exam on her fourth try and would never let anyone forget it.

When Kelton's hand knocked over a saltshaker on top of the bar, he flinched and scrambled to mop it up with a napkin, mortified.

Betty rolled her eyes fondly, pinched a bit of salt, and tossed it over her shoulder. "Good luck. Old family tradition."

Liddy nodded. "Also good for absorbing nervous sweat."

The final signature was signed, although Kelton was so nervous he almost tried writing his name with a spoon, and a quiet hush fell over the table.

Kelton sniffed.

Betty blinked quickly.

Hayley swallowed hard.

She'd told herself it was just business—a clean hand-off, nothing more—but watching Betty and Kelton beam across the table made her realize what she was really letting go of. Hayley's Kitchen had been her fresh start, proof she could build something of her own. But lately she'd been walking through those doors and feeling . . . done. Maybe it was the near-drowning, or seeing Hank's body pulled from the water—a reminder that life doesn't wait for you to catch up. She didn't want to cling to a routine just because it felt safe. Betty and Kelton still had that spark she'd lost somewhere along the way.

Maybe it was time to let them run with it—and finally give herself permission to figure out what came next.

When they stood to leave, Hayley hugged Kelton longer than she meant to. He hugged her back just as tightly, his arms shaking a little.

"Don't mess it up," she whispered into his ear.

"We won't," he whispered.

Hayley stepped out into the sunlight with Betty and Kelton close behind, the final paperwork tucked under Liddy's arm like a sealed goodbye.

The old, hand-painted sign creaked gently in the sea breeze above the door: HAYLEY'S KITCHEN.

Hayley paused, looking up at it. The brushstrokes were a little faded, the red in her name pinker now, but it still made her heart squeeze.

She turned to Betty and Kelton, trying to keep it light. "You two thought of a new name yet?" she asked. "I always liked 'The Dinner Bell.' Or maybe 'Bet and Kel's'—very Maine diner meets mom-and-pop empire."

Kelton looked panicked at the idea.

Betty just smiled.

"We're not changing it," she said.

Hayley blinked. "You're not?"

Betty shook her head. "It's always going to be Hayley's Kitchen. Doesn't matter who's in the back or out front. This place has heart. And the name's part of that."

For a second, Hayley couldn't speak. Her throat tightened too fast, too full.

Kelton reached over and gave her hand a quick, clumsy squeeze. "Hope that's okay," he added, eyes wide with earnestness.

Hayley looked back up at the sign.

Then at them.

"It's more than okay," she said. "It's everything."

And then, without looking back, she walked down the sidewalk into the Bar Harbor morning.

Chapter 42

Sunday brunch at Mona Barnes's house was usually loud, heavy on salt and sarcasm, and made entirely from things she'd hauled out of the sea or picked up from the Bar Harbor Farmers Market that morning. But today had a strange undercurrent—like something was just about to happen.

The windows were cracked open to let in the September breeze. A pot of coffee burbled on the counter. The table, a big, weathered thing scarred by decades of elbows and spilled chowder, not to mention nine kids of various ages growing up around it, was packed with plates: flaky corn bread, roasted potatoes, a cast-iron skillet full of lobster quiche, and a bowl of fruit salad that was trying its best to be ignored.

Hayley reached for the basket of blueberry muffins just as Bruce stabbed his fork toward a piece of cantaloupe.

"Why do we keep pretending melon is food?" he muttered. "It's just water with a rind."

"You're only mad it's not covered in a chocolate glaze."

Mona sat across the table, arms crossed, watching with a grin. "You could've just had a second muffin, Linney. I made them with triple brown sugar and a dangerous amount of butter."

Bruce perked up instantly. "Well, that changes everything."

Earl, seated beside her in a red-and-black flannel that looked like he'd ironed just for the occasion, had barely touched his quiche. He was uncharacteristically quiet, eyes darting from Mona to his coffee to something in his shirt pocket.

Hayley noticed the way he kept fidgeting. "You okay there, Earl? You've stabbed that crust four times."

Bruce leaned in. "Either he's having a nervous breakdown or he's about to propose."

Earl immediately dropped his fork with a loud *clang*.

Mona squinted at him. "You've been weird all morning. You're not trying to tell me you clogged the septic tank again, are you? Because I swear to God, Earl—"

But Earl was already pushing his chair back and standing—no, not standing. Dropping.

To one knee.

Hayley's mouth opened. Bruce froze, fork midair.

Mona stared like she wasn't sure if she was being pranked.

From his shirt pocket, Earl pulled a small, smooth white clamshell, its two halves held together with a loop of faded blue ribbon. He opened it carefully, revealing an antique ring—simple, modest, and glowing faintly in the morning light.

"I love you," he said, voice low and trembling. "I want to spend the rest of my life with you. If you'll have me."

Mona stared at him.

Then at the clamshell.

Then back at Earl.

And laughed.

Not a cruel laugh.

Not dismissive.

But full-bodied, bright, and startled—like she couldn't quite believe the moment was real.

"Oh, Earl," she said, reaching out to cup his face. "I've had the wedding cake. Let's just keep the frosting."

There was a collective exhale around the table—half-laughing, half-crying. Hayley let out a sound that was suspiciously close to a sob. Bruce reached over and handed her a napkin without looking.

Earl stayed kneeling, blinking up at her, still clutching the clamshell.

Mona shook her head, eyes shining. "My first husband, Dennis, set the tone early. He spent our honeymoon re-grouting the shower and eating cold beans from a can. I should've poisoned the cake and saved myself twenty-five years married to a man who thought romance was letting me pick the TV channel during hunting season."

Bruce choked on his coffee.

Hayley laughed through her tears.

Earl cleared his throat. "So . . . is that a 'no'?"

"It's a 'not yet,'" Mona said, brushing his cheek with her thumb. "But it's a 'yes' to more of this." She gestured around the table. "The food. The Sundays. The us."

Earl chuckled and pocketed the ring without offense. "Does this mean I still get to love you out loud?"

Mona grinned. "Long as you keep doing the dishes."

Hayley raised her glass. "To unconventional love—"

Bruce added, "And very good frosting."

Later, with the men on the porch nursing second coffees and talking about outboard motors, Hayley found Mona in the kitchen with the fridge door open, spoon-deep in the remains of a blueberry cobbler.

"Forks are clean," Mona said, "but spoons have more surface area."

Hayley grabbed one from the drawer without asking and leaned her hip against the counter. They stood there in companionable silence, eating straight from the dish like they'd done a hundred times before.

"You think you'll ever bite the bullet?" Hayley asked casually.

Mona blinked. "You mean, try marriage again?"

Hayley nodded. "Your kids are all grown. Out in the world doing their own thing. You've got the house, the boat, the guy. Why not the ring?"

Mona let out a slow breath and scraped at a stubborn bit of crust. "I was never in love with Dennis," she said, not looking up. "I liked him. At first. He was safe. Reliable. Built like a La-Z-Boy and had about as much personality. But I wasn't in love."

Hayley stayed quiet.

Mona finally met her eyes. "With Earl, it's different. It's the first time I feel like I'm . . . in it. Like I'm being loved for who I am, not just tolerated."

Hayley felt her eyes sting. "Well, that's kind of beautiful. And incredibly disturbing, coming from you."

Mona snorted. "Don't get used to it. It's probably the sugar talking."

There was a beat.

"Does that mean there's still hope for Earl?" Hayley asked gently. "That someday, in the not-too-distant future, he might get to call you his bride?"

Mona laughed. "I mean, don't go buying flower arrangements just yet. But I'm not ruling it out."

She grinned, then added. "Though, if I do walk down the aisle again, I'm not doing the traditional thing. I'll wear white, sure—but it'll be a sweatshirt that says I'M NOT A TROPHY WIFE, I'M THE WHOLE DAMN SHELF."

Hayley burst out laughing.

Mona scraped up another bite. "I think this time . . . I might actually get it right."

Hayley smiled. "Seafood and love. Best when they're fresh."

Mona nodded. "And not overcooked."

They clinked spoons like wineglasses and went back to eating.

Chapter 43

The knock on Hayley's door was hesitant, but persistent—like someone both eager and terrified to be there. Leroy bounded to the entryway, yipping like a creature convinced the world was full of postal workers and burglars.

When she opened the door, Doug Marsh stood on her porch with the strangest bouquet she'd ever seen. No roses, no lilies——instead, long stalks of fennel fanned out like green fireworks, bound together with cinnamon sticks and dried red chilies. The scent was half farmers market, half Christmas.

Hayley raised an eyebrow. "Either you're launching a spice company, or you've gotten into some very strange foreplay."

Doug grinned, a little sheepish. "Actually . . . both. Kind of."

He stepped inside, glancing around like he wanted to make sure no one else was listening. "I'm here because I need your opinion before I talk to Liddy. You know her better than anyone."

"Why not just go straight to her?" Hayley asked, closing the door.

"Because if it's a bad idea, I don't want her to turn me into one of her dramatic cautionary tales," Doug said. "And because . . . the timing's important. I've been cleared of everything. No more suspicion. No more whispers about that gun or Hank. I can finally start something new without half the town looking sideways at me."

Hayley tilted her head. "And?"

"And," Doug said. "I want Liddy to come with me. Not just for the business, but for . . . me."

Her eyebrows shot up. "Are you asking me to bless your . . . whatever this is?"

"Your blessing, your advice, and maybe a pep talk," Doug said. "You've been friends forever. You'll know if I'm crazy."

"Oh, you're crazy," Hayley said. "But that's never stopped Liddy before."

Doug paced while Hayley texted Liddy an urgent *come over right now* message. Ten minutes later, Liddy breezed in, wearing oversized sunglasses and a scarf like she'd just stepped off a yacht, even though the only boat she'd been on lately was Mona's lobster boat.

She froze at the sight of Doug holding the spice bouquet.

"What is this?" she asked.

Doug launched in before his nerve failed. He told her about the plan—hanging up accounting and opening a spice company in Santa Fe. The test recipes. The branding ideas. The market for Maine-meets-Southwest flavors.

And then he got to the real pitch.

"I want you to come with me, Liddy. Not just as a partner in the kitchen. As . . . my partner."

Liddy's mouth opened and closed twice. "You mean—leave Bar Harbor?"

"Come to Santa Fe," Doug said, holding out the bouquet. "Help me build something—spice blends, a brand, a whole life in the sun."

Liddy's smile wavered. "I've built my own company here, Doug. My clients, my listings—it's taken years."

Doug's grin didn't falter. "And you can do it again there. Different-style adobe instead of clapboard, courtyards instead of wraparound porches. Still the same hustle, still the same Liddy Crawford charm. You'd just swap out the ocean view for a mountain one."

Liddy tilted her head, the corners of her mouth twitching as the idea started to land. "Adobe," she murmured, tasting the word like a new cocktail. "Kiva fireplaces. Big wooden doors. Clients in turquoise jewelry instead of fleece jackets. And I wouldn't have to scrape ice off my windshield six months out of the year."

Hayley could practically see the mental real estate listings forming behind Liddy's eyes—her name printed in bold over sun-washed stucco and hand-painted tiles.

Liddy was already pacing the kitchen, rattling off half-formed to-do lists: "I'll have to tell my clients, list the house, book a flight—oh my God, what do people even wear in Santa Fe? And when are we leaving?"

Doug shrugged. "Soon. Next week?"

"Next week?!" Hayley sputtered.

That's when Bruce wandered in with Leroy at his heels, stopping short when he clocked the scene—the bouquet of dried chilies on the counter, Doug looking smug, Liddy looking like she'd just been handed a crown and a subpoena.

"What did I miss?" Bruce asked.

"Apparently," Hayley said, "we're helping Liddy uproot her entire life and move halfway across the country by next Thursday."

Bruce glanced at Doug, then at Liddy. "Well," he said slowly, "at least she won't need to pack her snow shovel."

The room burst into overlapping chatter—Liddy peppering Doug with questions about flights and housing, Hayley trying to get a word in about how you can't just spring a life-changing move on people in Bar Harbor—news like that needs to make the rounds before the coffee's cold, preferably with half the town invited to gawk—and Bruce quietly feeding Leroy a piece of toast like this was any other Sunday morning.

By the time the initial chaos settled, Hayley had been roped into organizing an impromptu gathering before Liddy's "big leap."

* * *

By that afternoon, Hayley and Mona had decided a proper send-off was nonnegotiable. It wasn't to be a sit-down brunch like the last two gatherings—this was a pop-up backyard farewell, thrown together in record time. They set the dining table with mimosas in mismatched champagne flutes, a platter of lobster sliders, deviled eggs dusted with paprika, and a mountain of golden hash browns—because in Bar Harbor, breakfast food refuses to respect the clock. Mona added a bubbling dish of baked mac and cheese "for ballast," claiming she didn't trust anyone to make life-changing decisions on an empty stomach. Hayley had strung mini Maine flags between the posts of her back deck, and Bruce had threaded chili peppers through the lines for a Santa Fe touch.

Neighbors dropped by in shifts. Randy and Sergio arrived halfway through, sunglasses on and already holding drinks.

Randy took one look at the scene and smirked. "Well, well, well. Liddy couldn't let us have the last big send-off, could she? Had to make it about her and move away, too."

"Always the center of attention," Sergio said, deadpan.

"Yeah, when it comes to stealing focus, she's a master criminal."

Sergio nodded gravely. "Yes . . . the most notary criminal I ever met."

Randy laughed. "You mean notorious."

Sergio grinned. "That, too."

Mona clinked her mimosa glass with a serving spoon until the chatter quieted. "I just want to say," she began, "sending Liddy off is like sending a crate of lobsters to New York—you know she'll make a splash there, but we're gonna miss the claws around here. And Doug—well, bless you for taking her on. May your spice business thrive, your love life sizzle, and your patience never boil over. And if you two ever break up, you're keeping her. We're not taking returns—especially ones that can outtalk the weatherman during a nor'easter."

The crowd laughed and raised their glasses.

Mona, as usual, had nailed her second goodbye toast in less than a week.

The following Thursday, Hayley was pulling up to Bangor International Airport with Liddy in the passenger seat and Doug riding in Bruce's truck behind them, the bed loaded with her oversized suitcases. Liddy had packed enough for a yearlong fashion shoot: two oversized suitcases, a matching carry-on, and a tote bag stuffed with glossy magazines.

Hayley eased her car up to the curb, eyeing the mountain of suitcases Doug had somehow crammed into the back of Bruce's truck. "Good grief, Liddy—are you moving to Santa Fe or opening a department store?"

Liddy waved a dismissive hand. "Sweetheart, this is merely my starter set. You and Mona can ship the rest when you have a moment—picture Elizabeth Taylor in

Cleopatra, but with a better luggage collection. And maybe a little less eyeliner."

Inside the small terminal, the four of them stood in an awkward bubble of last-minute advice and quick hugs. When the boarding call came, Liddy clutched Hayley tightly.

"I can't believe I'm doing this," she murmured. "I'm terrified."

"You'll be fine," Hayley said. "Santa Fe's about to get a whole lot more Liddy."

Liddy gave a watery laugh. "They have no idea what's coming." She blinked fast, fanning her eyes. "Oh, for heaven's sake, I promised myself I wouldn't cry."

"Too late," Hayley said, her own throat tightening. "Don't you dare make me start."

They were about to hug when a commotion broke out near the doors.

"Hey! You can't park there!" an airport employee shouted.

Both women turned just as Mona came barreling through the automatic doors, windblown and red-faced, keys in one hand, her lobster boots squeaking across the tile. "Like I was gonna let you two have a tearful goodbye without me!" she yelled.

"Mona!" Liddy gasped. "You said you were too busy!"

"I lied," Mona said, voice breaking as she threw her arms around them both. "You're not leaving this town without one last group hug."

All three clung together—laughing, sniffling, muttering about mascara and bad parking decisions. Even Bruce looked misty-eyed, though he tried to hide it.

When they finally pulled apart, Hayley managed a wobbly smile. "Go sell half of Santa Fe a house they can't afford—and make sure Doug sprinkles his spice empire on everything they eat." She hesitated, her voice softening. "Just promise you'll remember where home really is."

Liddy's eyes shimmered again. "Always," she said. "You and Mona are stuck with me—no matter how far I go."

Hayley laughed, blinking fast. "Good. Because Bar Harbor won't be the same without you."

Liddy squeezed her hand one last time before turning toward the gate, Doug close behind.

Hayley, Bruce, and Mona (who was already complaining about the cost of her parking ticket) stood together at the big window watching as the plane taxied, lifted, and then climbed into the soft evening sky.

And for the first time that day, Hayley realized she didn't feel loss at all.

What she felt was joy.

Chapter 44

The September afternoon looked like it had been staged by a postcard photographer—sky the color of a robin's egg, clouds so high and thin they seemed sketched in pencil, and sunlight that made the ocean glint like polished glass. The breeze was gentle, carrying the briny tang of Frenchman's Bay, along with the faint, salt-softened chatter of gulls.

Moving boxes lined the front walk like a cardboard parade. Each trip from the car into the house felt like a small victory, even if Bruce insisted on making exaggerated groaning noises with every load.

Hayley stepped into the foyer, her sneakers whispering across the wide-plank floors worn smooth by decades of sandy feet and lobster-boot scuffs. The house had the kind of calm presence she'd always admired—painted in soft coastal tones that caught the shifting light, filled with big windows framing the water like a work of art.

The view made her pause every time she turned her head. Lobster boats dotted the bay, each pulling a line of gulls behind it like kids chasing an ice cream truck. Beyond them, the Porcupine Islands floated on the horizon in a haze of blue-gray. Along the porch, a bank of hydrangeas nodded in the breeze, their vibrant summer purples now fading into antique mauves.

Bruce was already fussing over a corner of the living room, arranging his desk at the perfect angle to the water. "You realize," Hayley said, passing by with a box labeled COOKBOOKS & COCKTAILS, "if you stare at that view all day, you're never going to write a single word."

"I'll write," he said, setting down his laptop with a satisfied sigh. "Eventually. After a reasonable amount of staring."

Hayley lugged her box into the kitchen and began unpacking her cookbooks in the only organizational system that made sense to her—arranging them by cocktail pairing. Tequila to the left, whiskey to the right, rum dead center. Bruce liked to claim this method was "chaotic neutral," but she knew it was genius.

They kept passing each other in the hallway, each carrying something, each stopping to glance out a window as if they still couldn't quite believe this house was theirs. Leroy, meanwhile, was trotting from room to room like a Realtor on commission, sniffing every corner and claiming each sunny patch of floor as his own.

At one point, Hayley stood with a spice rack in her hands, looking out at the glimmering water, and said,

"Feels like we're house-sitting for someone far more responsible."

By the time the sun began its slow descent toward the horizon, the boxes were mostly unpacked, or at least stacked artfully in corners so they looked like décor. Bruce appeared in the kitchen holding two glasses of wine and a stack of freshly printed pages.

"Dangerous to hand me a manuscript when I've been unpacking heavy objects all day," she warned, following him out to the porch.

They settled into a pair of Adirondack chairs, the wood warm from the afternoon sun. The air was cooler now, touched with the scent of seaweed and the faint, smoky sweetness of a distant chimney fire. Hayley took the pages, curling her legs under her.

She began to read aloud. The heroine was whip-smart, stubborn, and had a habit of being absolutely convinced she was right at all times. By page three, Hayley's eyebrows were creeping higher. By page five, she stopped and squinted over the stack at him.

"This heroine is insufferable," she announced.

Bruce grinned. "So's the muse."

She swatted him with the pages, but her mouth betrayed her with a smile. They sat for a while without speaking, the laughter lingering between them. Somewhere down the Shore Path, a dog barked.

The tide was inching in, lapping at the rocks below. Bruce reached for her hand without looking, and she let him take it, their fingers fitting together in the easy, well-worn way of people who'd weathered a few storms and come out stronger.

For the first time in months, Hayley felt it—a quiet certainty in her bones. They had survived the chaos, the danger, the heartbreak. And now, here on this porch, with the sea stretching out before them and the boxes of their life unpacked behind them, they were exactly where they were meant to be.

Island Food & Spirits

By

Hayley Powell

After a lovely grilled fish dinner prepared by my very own barbecue master, Chef Bruce, I found myself sitting out by the firepit, watching the last flickers of flame dance against the night sky. In my hand—a Lemon Drop Martini. One of Liddy's favorites. An oldie but a goodie.

It's been a couple of months since Bruce and I moved into our new home, and I can honestly say we love it here. The view, the quiet, the easy walk to town—it all feels just right. Well, almost. I've caught Bruce sneaking peeks at cruise brochures lately, pretending he's "just curious." I'm not worried yet. As long as he's browsing and not booking, I'm safe.

Maybe it was that call from Liddy earlier that made me feel sentimental enough to reach for a Lemon Drop tonight. She and Doug are apparently taking Santa Fe by storm—I can picture her now, sun-kissed and fabulous, cocktail in hand, making friends wherever she goes. Randy and Sergio are living their best lives down in Brazil, sending us photos of beaches so gorgeous I briefly considered deleting my social media out of jealousy.

Even my mother called today. She wanted to know if Bruce and I plan to host Christmas now that we "finally have the space," before adding, "Nothing says holiday spirit like a houseful of relatives!" I told her I'd think about it. Privately, I'm thinking a cruise might be a safer bet. Although, knowing my mother, if she found out we were boarding a ship in Florida, she and her boyfriend, Carl, would somehow appear on the deck just as we were pulling out to sea—with no chance of escape.

As for Hayley's Kitchen, I thought I'd feel a pang of loss once it was in new hands, but instead I find myself . . . happy. It's still busy, still beloved, and it warms my heart to sit there with Bruce, eating dinner like any other couple in Bar Harbor. For once, I'm not worrying about reservations, payroll, or whether the fryer's on the fritz. It's someone else's adventure now—and that's okay.

Bruce, of course, got tired of me grilling him (pun intended) for police gossip every night after work. These days, he just gives me a quick "Bar Harbor Crime Report" summary before dinner. And lately, there hasn't been much to report. The new chief probably thinks he's landed himself a job in Mayberry R.F.D.

Still . . . you know that feeling? When everything's perfect—almost too perfect—and you can't shake the sense that something might be waiting just around the corner? Maybe it's just the martini talking. Or maybe the universe is reminding me that quiet moments never last forever around here.

But for now, I'm content to sit by the fire, sip my Lemon Drop Martini, and gaze at the stars. What else could possibly happen in Bar Harbor that hasn't already happened?

LEMON DROP MARTINI

INGREDIENTS

3 ounces vodka
2 ounces fresh lemon juice
1 ounce simple syrup
Lemon slice, for garnish

Add ice to a cocktail shaker, then pour in the vodka, lemon juice, and simple syrup.

Shake well for about two minutes, strain into a chilled martini glass, and garnish with the lemon slice.

Sip slowly, savor, and remember the good times.

GRILLED HADDOCK FILLETS

INGREDIENTS

4 (6-ounce) haddock fillets
4 teaspoons olive oil
1 teaspoon Old Bay seasoning
½ teaspoon paprika
½ teaspoon salt
½ teaspoon black pepper
½ lemon

Preheat the grill to medium-high and set a grill pan over the heat.

Brush one side of each fillet with olive oil, season, and place seasoned sides down on the grill. Brush the top sides, as well.

Grill about 3 minutes per side, or until the fish flakes easily.

Remove to a platter, squeeze the lemon over the top, and serve immediately.

Until next time—keep your grill hot, your cocktails cold, and your heart open to whatever's next.

Recipe Index

A Letter to Our Readers

As we type these words, it's hard to believe this is the final chapter in the Hayley Powell Food & Cocktails Mysteries. What began as a lighthearted idea about a food columnist who always found herself in the middle of murder investigations turned into nineteen books, countless cocktails, and a whole lot of laughter, friendship, and lobster rolls along the way.

Writing Hayley has been one of the greatest joys of our careers. She's grown from a single mom juggling deadlines and dinner to a woman who's learned that sometimes the best recipes in life are the messy ones—the ones that surprise you. But don't worry—this isn't goodbye. Hayley isn't going anywhere. She'll be back soon in a brand-new series, teaming up with her daughter, Gemma, for a fresh round of culinary adventures (and, of course, more murder) right here in Bar Harbor.

And if you're looking for more mysteries set along the rocky coast of Maine, I hope you'll check out our Downeast Maine Mysteries series, featuring three generations of strong Maine women—Maggie Holbrook, her daughter Jill, and granddaughter Audrey—as they solve crimes in the charming seaside town of Halibut Cove. The first book, *The Chowder House Murder*, is available now, with more to come.

Thank you, from the bottom of our hearts, for reading Hayley's stories all these years—for inviting her into your kitchens and your bookshelves, and for sharing your love of food, friendship, and a good whodunit.

With gratitude and affection,
Lee Hollis